ACCLAIM FOR GAIL BOWEN AND
THE JOANNE KILBOURN MYSTERIES

"Bowen is one of those rare, magical mystery writers readers
love not only for her suspense skills but for her stories' elegance, sense of place and true-to-life form. . . . A master of
ramping up suspense"   – *Ottawa Citizen*

"Bowen can confidently place her series beside any other
being produced in North America."
                                 – Halifax *Chronicle-Herald*

"Gail Bowen's Joanne Kilbourn mysteries are small works
of elegance that assume the reader of suspense is after more
than blood and guts, that she is looking for the meaning
behind a life lived and a life taken."   – *Calgary Herald*

"Bowen has a hard eye for the way human ambition can take
advantage of human gullibility."   – *Publishers Weekly*

"Gail Bowen got the recipe right with her series on Joanne
Kilbourn."   – *Vancouver Sun*

"What works so well [is Bowen's] sense of place – Regina
comes to life – and her ability to inhabit the everyday life of
an interesting family with wit and vigour. . . . Gail Bowen
continues to be a fine mystery writer, with a protagonist
readers can invest in for the long run."
                                                – *National Post*

"Gail Bowen is one of Canada's literary treasures."
                                               – *Ottawa Citizen*

DEADLY APPEARANCES

A Joanne Kilbourn Mystery

GAIL BOWEN

McClelland & Stewart

Copyright © 1990 by Gail Bowen
First published by Douglas & McIntyre Ltd., 1990

First M&S paperback edition published 1996
This edition published 2011

Library and Archives Canada Cataloguing in Publication

Bowen, Gail, 1942-
Deadly appearances : a Joanne Kilbourn mystery / Gail Bowen.

ISBN 978-0-7710-1324-9

I. Title.

PS8553.O8995D43 2011   C813'.54   C2011-900299-X

We acknowledge the financial support of the Government of Canada
through the Book Publishing Industry Development Program and that
of the Government of Ontario through the Ontario Media Development
Corporation's Ontario Book Initiative. We further acknowledge the
support of the Canada Council for the Arts and the Ontario Arts
Council for our publishing program.

Published simultaneously in the United States of America by
McClelland & Stewart Ltd., P.O. Box 1030, Plattsburgh, New York 12901

Library of Congress Control Number: 2011925596

This book was produced using ancient-forest friendly papers.
Typeset in Trump Mediaeval by M&S, Toronto
Printed and bound in Canada

McClelland & Stewart Ltd.
75 Sherbourne Street
Toronto, Ontario
M5A 2P9
www.mcclelland.com

1 2 3 4 5   15 14 13 12 11

To my mother-in-law,
Hazel Wren Bowen,
with love and gratitude

DEADLY
APPEARANCES

CHAPTER

1

For the first seconds after Andy's body slumped onto the searing metal of the truck bed, it seemed as if we were all encircled by a spell that froze us in the terrible moment of his fall. Suspended in time, the political people standing behind the stage, hands wrapped around plastic glasses of warm beer, kept talking politics. Craig and Julie Evanson, the perfect political couple, safely out of public view, were drinking wine coolers from bottles. Andy's family and friends, awkward at finding themselves so publicly in the place of honour, kept sitting, small smiles in place, on the folding chairs that lined the back of the stage. The people out front kept looking expectantly at the empty space behind the podium. Waiting. Waiting.

And then chaos. Everyone wanted to get to Andy.

Including me. The stage was about four and a half feet off the ground. Accessible. I stepped back a few steps, took a little run and threw myself onto the stage floor. It was when I was lying on that scorching metal, shins stinging, wind knocked out of me, chin bruised from the hit I had taken, that I saw Rick Spenser.

There was, and still is, something surreal about that moment: the famous face looming up out of nowhere. He was pulling himself up the portable metal staircase that was propped against the back of the truck bed. His body appeared in stages over the metal floor: head, shoulders and arms, torso, belly, legs, feet. He seemed huge. He was climbing those steps as if his life depended on it, and his face was shiny and red with exertion. The heat on the floor of the stage was unbearable. I could smell it. I remember thinking, very clearly, a big man like that could die in this heat, then I turned and scrambled toward Andy. The metal floor was so hot it burned the palms of my hands.

Over the loudspeaker a woman was saying, "Could a doctor please come up here?" over and over. Her voice was terrible, forlorn and empty of hope. As soon as I saw Andy, I knew there wasn't any point in a doctor.

Andy was in front of me, and I knew he was dead. He looked crumpled – all the sinew and spirit was gone. For the only time since I'd known him, he looked – no other word – insignificant.

The winter after my husband died I had taken a course in emergency cardiac care – something to make me feel less exposed to danger, less at the mercy of the things that could kill you if you weren't ready for them. As I turned Andy over on his back, I could hear the voice of our instructor, very young, very confident – nothing would ever hurt her. "I hope none of you ladies ever have to use this, but if you do, just remember ABC." I was beginning to tremble. *Airway.* I took Andy's chin between my thumb and forefinger and tilted his head back. His flesh felt clammy and flaccid, but the airway was clear. *Breathing.* I put my ear on his mouth, listened, and watched his chest for a sign of breathing. There was nothing. I was talking to myself. I could hear my voice, but it didn't sound like me. "Four quick rescue breaths and then C. *Check circulation.*" I bent over Andy and pinched his nostrils shut. "Oh, I'm sorry, Andy. I'm sorry," and I bent my mouth to cover his. ABC – but I never got to C.

There was a smell on his lips and around his mouth. It was familiar, but I couldn't place it. Something ordinary and domestic, but there was an acrid edge to it that made me stop. Without forming the thought, I knew I had smelled danger.

Then I looked toward the podium and saw Rick Spenser filling the glass from the black Thermos. I didn't hesitate. His hands were shaking so badly he could barely hold the glass. Water was splashing down his arms and on his belly, but he must have filled his glass because he raised it to his lips.

Suddenly the world became narrow and focused. All that mattered now was to keep him from drinking that water. I opened my arms and threw myself at Rick Spenser's knees. It was a surprisingly solid hit. He fell hard, face down. He must have stunned himself because for a few moments he was very still.

The next few minutes are a jumble. The ambulance came. Spenser regained consciousness. As the attendants loaded Andy on the stretcher, Spenser sat with his legs stretched in front of him like the fat boy in the Snakes and Ladders game. When I walked over to the podium to pick up Andy's speech portfolio, my foot brushed against his.

In the distance I could hear sirens.

That last day of Andy Boychuk's life had started out to be one of the best. In June he had been selected leader of our provincial party, and we had planned an end-of-summer picnic so that people could eat, play a little ball and shake hands with the new leader of the Official Opposition. Simple, wholesome pleasures. But in politics there is always subtext, even at an old-fashioned picnic, and that brilliant August day had enough subtext for a Bergman movie.

Nomination fights can be intense, and Andy's had been particularly fierce because odds were good that we would form the next government. The prize had been worth having. And for more than a few people in the park that day, watching the leadership slip into someone else's hands had been a cruel blow. Soothing those people, making it possible for them to forgive him for winning, was Andy's first priority at the picnic, but there was another matter too, and this one was going to need skills that weren't taught in Political Science 100.

For years, there had been unanswered questions about Andy Boychuk's domestic life. His wife, Eve, was odd and reclusive. There had been a dozen rumours about her strange behaviour, and now that Andy was leader we had to put those stories to rest.

So behind the homespun pleasures of concession stands selling fresh-baked pies and corn on the cob or chances on quilts and amateur oil paintings, there was a deadly serious purpose. That day we had to begin to lay to rest Andy Boychuk's ghosts. It wasn't going to be easy. I had driven into the park earlier that morning to check things out. Two hard-muscled young women had been stringing a sign across the base of the truck bed we were using as a stage. It said, "Andy Boychuk Appreciation Day," and when I saw it, I crossed my fingers and said, "Let it work. Oh, please, let it be perfect."

For a while it was. The day was flawless: still, blue-skied, hot, and by noon, the fields of summer fallow we were using for parking areas were filled, and we had to ask the farmer who owned them to let us use more. All afternoon the line of cars coming down the hill continued without a break. In the picnic area, the food was hot, the drinks were cold, and the music drifted, pleasant and forgettable, from speakers hung on the trees. Everybody was in a good mood.

Especially Andy. On that August day so full of politics

and sunshine and baseball, he was as happy as I had ever seen him.

I'd watched him play a couple of innings in the slo-pitch tournament, and he'd been sensational. He'd come off the field sweating and dirty and triumphant.

"The man can do no wrong today," he'd said, beaming. "It's never too late, Jo. I could still be a major-leaguer."

And I had laughed, too. "Absolutely," I said, "but there are five thousand people here today who want to hear this terrific speech I wrote for you, and –"

"And I have to sacrifice a career with the Jays to your vanity." He grinned and wiped the sweat from his forehead with the back of his hand.

"That's about the way I see it," I said. "Remember that line from your acceptance speech about how it's time to put the common good above individual ambition? Well, your chance is here. There's one bathroom in this entire park that has a functioning hot-water tap, and Dave Micklejohn said that at three-thirty he'll be lurking there with a fresh shirt for you, so you can get up on that stage and give the people something to tell their grandchildren about." I looked at my watch. "You've got five minutes. Forget the Blue Jays. Think of the common good. The bathroom's just over the hill – a green building behind the concession stands."

Andy laughed. "Okay, but you just wait till next year."

"You bet," I said, and I stood and watched as he ran up the hill, a slight figure with the slim hips and easy grace of an athlete. At the top, he stopped to talk to a man. I was too far away to see the man's face, but I would have recognized the powerful boxer's body anywhere. Howard Dowhanuik had been premier of our province for eleven years, leader of the Official Opposition for seven, and my friend for all that time and more. He was the man Andy succeeded in June, and there was something poignant and symbolic about seeing the once and future leaders, silhouetted against the brilliant blue of the big prairie sky. Even from a distance, it was apparent that their talk was serious and emotional, but finally the crisis seemed resolved, and Howard patted Andy's shoulder. Then, in the blink of an eye, Andy disappeared over the top of the hill, and Howard was walking toward me, smiling.

"You look happy," I said.

"I've got every reason to be," he said. "I'm with you. The weather's great. I managed to get over to the stage in time to hear the fiddlers and I got away before those little girls started dancing. What is it that they call themselves?"

"The Tapping Toddlers," I said, "and I doubt if they chose the name. My guess is that the parents who let those kids wear hot-pink satin pants and sequinned bras are the ones who came up with it. Sometimes I don't think we've come very far."

"Sometimes I agree with you." He shrugged. "Come on, Jo. It's too nice a day to despair of the human race. Let's go over and watch the chicken man. I'll buy you an early supper."

I groaned. "I've been eating all day, but I guess the damage is already done. As my grandmother always said, 'In for a penny, in for a pound.'" And so we walked over to the barbecue pit across the road from the stage. A man from the poultry association was grilling five hundred split broilers. Up and down he moved, slapping sauce on the chickens with a paintbrush, reaching across the grill to adjust a piece that didn't seem positioned right, breaking off a burning wing tip with his thick, callused fingers.

Howard's old hawk's face was red from the sun and the heat, but he was rapt as he watched the poultry man's progress.

"Jo, the trouble with politics is that it doesn't leave you time to enjoy the little things. Look at this guy – I'll bet he's cooked two thousand chickens today. He's a real artist. Go ahead and smile, but see, he knows just when to turn those things. That's what I'm going to enjoy now that I'm out of it – the simple pleasures."

"Going to find time to smell the roses, are you?" I said, laughing. "Howard, you're a fraud. Two days ago you told me that anybody who doesn't care about politics is dead from the neck down. I don't think you're quite ready to trade the back rooms for a bag of briquettes."

Across the road, the entertainment had ended and the speeches had begun. The loudspeakers squawked out something indecipherable. In the field in front of the stage, the crowd roared, and the man of simple pleasures was suddenly all politics again.

"Whoever that is onstage has really got them going," he said.

I linked my arm through his. "Are you going to miss all this?" I asked, indicating the scene around us.

"Yeah, of course I am."

"You could change your mind and run again, you know, or just stay around behind the scenes. Andy could use somebody who knows how to keep things from unravelling."

"No, I wasn't cut out to be an éminence grise – lousy fringe benefits."

The man from the poultry association was taking broilers off the grills now, grabbing the tips of the drumsticks between his thumb and index finger and giving his wrist enough of a flick to propel the chickens into an aluminum baking pan he held in his other hand.

"How about you, Jo? Have you thought any more about running? That guy who won Ian's seat in the by-election is about as dynamic as a cow fart."

"Not a chance, Howard. I'm happy right where I am. I think I'm over Ian's death. The kids are great, and I finally

have some time to do what I want to do. This year off from
teaching is going to be heaven. And, you know, the speech
writing I'm doing for Andy is going to fit in perfectly. It'll
give me some good examples for my dissertation. If I get it
done in time for your birthday, I'll give you the first copy.
Want to read a scholarly treatise called 'Saskatchewan
Politics: Its Theory and Practice'?"

"God, no. I might find out that I've been doing it wrong
all along." He looked at his watch. "Time for the main
event. Let's grab a plate of chicken. Incidentally, guess who
I strong-armed into giving the warm-up speech before Andy
comes out."

"His wife?"

Howard winced. "I'm not a miracle worker, Jo. Although
Eve is here today. I saw her in that little trailer thing they've
got in back of the stage for Andy's family and the entertainment people."

"How did she look?"

"The way she always looks when she gets dragged to one of
these things – like someone just beamed her down. Anyway,
you're wrong. Eve isn't introducing Andy. Guess again."

"Not Craig Evanson."

Howard pointed at the stage across the road and smiled.
"There he is at the podium."

"You underestimate yourself," I said. "You are a miracle
worker, especially after that terrible interview last night on
Lachlan MacNeil's show. I can't believe Andy isn't more
worried about it. I tried to talk to him, you know, but he
says people will forget about it in a week, and besides, since
everybody knows what MacNeil's like, no one'll take it
seriously."

"Julie Evanson's taking it seriously," Howard said grimly.
"She tracked me down this morning and told me Andy
should either resign or be castrated – I think she felt that as

the aggrieved party, Craig should have the option of selecting the punishment that fit the crime."

"Well," I said, "if Craig decides on castration, I might volunteer to hold his coat. Didn't you ever take Andy out behind the barn and tell him the boys and girls of the press can play rough? He should have known better. Craig and Julie had just about gotten over Craig's losing the leadership and what does Andy do? He tells Canadians from coast-to-coast that if we're elected, Craig had better forget about being deputy premier or attorney general because he's too dumb."

"Be fair, Jo, that shithead MacNeil really drove Andy into a corner. All Andy said was that when we're elected he'll find a job for Craig that's suitable to his talents. And you know as well as I do that Craig isn't the brightest light on the porch."

"Oh, God, Howard, I know. We all know Craig's limited, and I'll even grant you that he shouldn't be deputy premier or A-G. But he's a decent man, and more to the point, he almost won. Andy only beat him by ten votes. That's not much. I wish MacNeil hadn't made Andy run through that list of all the serious jobs and say Craig wasn't up to any of them. And I really wish that Andy hadn't risen to the bait when that twerp asked him to name a job Craig would be capable of handling. Minister of the Family? My dogs could handle that one. No wonder Julie was mad. Speaking of . . . we'd better get over there. Julie's always been able to look at a crowd of five thousand people and know exactly who wasn't there to hear her Craig."

The man from the poultry association opened a metal ice chest, pulled out the last bags of fresh broilers and began laying them on the grills. It was a little after four o'clock. The ballplayers were coming off the diamonds tired and hungry. The poultry man wouldn't be taking any chickens back to the city with him tonight. For a moment Howard was still, watching, absorbed. Then he shrugged and grabbed my hand.

"Let's go, lady," he said. Hand in hand we crossed the road and moved through the crowd toward the stage.

When we got close, Dave Micklejohn ran out to meet us. He had been Andy's executive assistant for as long as I could remember, and his devotion to Andy was as fierce as it was absolute. No one knew how old Dave was – certainly he was past the age suggested for the retirement of civil servants, but he had such energy that his age was irrelevant. He was fussy, condescending and irreplaceable.

That day, as always, he was carrying a clipboard. Also, as always, he was immaculate. He was wearing white, white shorts and a T-shirt imprinted with a picture of Jean-Paul Sartre.

"I like your shirt," I said.

"I tell everyone he's running for us in the south end of the province," he said. "You two were certainly no help. I run my buns off getting that bunch up there at the same time –" he waved at Andy's family and friends, sitting like kindergarten children on folding chairs along the back of the stage "– and you two vanish into thin air."

"Howard wanted to watch his hero, the chicken man," I said. "Anyway, we're here now. Did you find Andy to give him the fresh shirt?"

"Of course," he said, "I'm a Virgo. I know the importance of details."

I reached over and touched his hand. "Dave, don't be mad at us. You've done a wonderful job. How did you ever get Eve to come?"

I could see him thaw. Then, unexpectedly, he looked down, embarrassed. "Well, it wasn't easy. I had to agree to sneak a piece of quartz onto the podium today. She says the electromagnetic field from the crystal will combine with Andy's electrical field to erase negativity and recharge energy stores."

"Oh, God, Dave, no."

He squared his shoulders, and Sartre rippled defiantly on his chest. "She's here, isn't she? And look." He held up a sliver of rose quartz that glittered benignly in the sunlight. "You can put these things in water, you know. Eve says they charge up the people drinking it and bring them into harmony with their environment. Actually, we had quite a nice talk about it."

"Why don't you make Roma a nice cup of water on the rocks?" I pointed to the far end of the stage, where Andy's mother, Roma, was sitting stiffly, as far away as she could get from her daughter-in-law. "She looks like she could use some harmonizing. Actually, what we probably need is a slab of quartz dropped in the water supply for the whole city – take care of all our problems." Beside me, Howard gazed innocently in the direction of the ball diamonds.

Dave snapped the clip on his clipboard. "You don't have to be such a bitch, Jo. In fact, if you could manage to let up a little, I could tell you about our real triumph." He smoothed the crease of his shorts and looked at me. "Rick Spenser's here today."

I was impressed. "What's he doing here? I know this is big stuff for us, but it's penny ante for the networks. Why would those guys at CVT send their top political commentator to cover a little picnic on the prairies?"

"I don't know," said Dave, "but I'm ecstatic. There are a lot of nice visuals here today – all the little kids guessing how many jellybeans are in the jar, and the old geezers throwing horseshoes and reminiscing. How many points do you think all this heartland charm will be worth in the polls, Jo?"

"You'll have to ask Howard. He's the expert."

But Howard was heading behind the stage, where the major players, as they liked to think of themselves, were talking politics and drinking warm beer out of plastic cups. It didn't matter. We couldn't have heard Howard anyway because Craig Evanson had finished, Andy was walking across the stage to the podium, and the crowd was on its feet.

They had waited all afternoon for this, the moment when Andy would stand before them. Now he was here and they were wild – clapping their hands together in a ragged attempt at rhythm and calling his name again and again. "Andy, Andy, Andy." Two distinct syllables, regular as heart-beats until throats grew hoarse and the beat became thready.

We could see Andy clearly now. He was wearing an open-necked shirt the colour of the sky, and when he saw Dave and me, he grinned and waved his baseball cap in the air. The crowd cheered as if he had turned stone to gold. Finally, Andy raised his hands to quiet them, then he turned toward Dave and me and made a drinking gesture.

"Water," I said.

"Taken care of," said Dave, and he ran behind the stage and came back carrying a tray with a glass and a black thermal pitcher. When he went by me, he stopped and pointed to a little hand-lettered sign he'd taped to the side of the Thermos: "FOR THE USE OF ANDY BOYCHUK ONLY. ALL OTHERS DRINK THIS AND DIE."

I laughed. "So much for the brotherhood of the common man."

Dave passed the tray to the woman who was acting as emcee for the entertainment. She was a big woman, wearing a flower-printed dress. I remember thinking all afternoon that she must have been suffering from the heat. She handed Andy the tray with a pretty little flourish, and he took it with a gallant gesture.

I moved to the side of the stage. There was a patch of shade there, and it gave me a clear view of Andy and of the crowd.

They were arranging themselves for the speech – trying to find a cool spot on their beach towels, pouring watery, tepid drinks out of Thermoses, slipping kids a couple of dollars for the amusement booths that had been set up. Afterward, even the police were astounded at how few people had any real memory of what they saw in those last moments. But I saw, and I remembered.

Andy filled his glass from the Thermos, drank the water, all of it, then opened the blue leather folder that contained the speech I'd written for him. It was a sequence I'd watched a hundred times. But this time, instead of sliding his thumbs to the top of the podium, leaning toward the audience and beginning to speak, he turned to look at Dave and me.

He was still smiling, but then something dark and private flickered across his face. He looked perplexed and sad, the way he did when someone asked him a question that revealed real ugliness. Then he turned toward the back of the stage and collapsed. From the time he turned until the time he fell was, I am sure, less than five seconds. It seemed like a lifetime.

As I looked at the empty podium, I knew it was all over. I hugged the portfolio to me. In it was the last speech I would ever write for Andy Boychuk. The solid line of family and friends shattered into dazed groups. Eve Boychuk, Andy's wife, moved from her chair to the portable staircase. She was blocking the stairs, trying to keep the ambulance attendants from taking her husband away.

The August sun was getting low in the sky, and as she stood blocking the stairway, Eve was backlit with golden light. It was a striking picture. She wore a short sundress made of unbleached cotton and she seemed to be all brown limbs – powerful athlete's shoulders, strong arms, long, taut-muscled legs. She looked strong and invulnerable. But her face was dead with disbelief, and her eyes were terrible – vacant and unseeing.

The sirens were getting closer. Dave Micklejohn came up behind Eve, moved her from the staircase, and started giving directions to the ambulance attendants. "Bring him over to the side of the stage," he said, then he turned to me. "Come on, Jo, let's jump down over here and they can lower Andy to us."

And that's what we did. When she saw what we were doing, Eve came over and grabbed Dave's hand, and we all jumped down together. We must have looked like actors from the theatre of the absurd, but it was right that we were the ones who took Andy from the stage that last time.

They hadn't brought the ambulance up to the stage. There were so many people on the grounds, and I guess someone had told them there wasn't any hurry. We wouldn't let the ambulance people take over. They tried, but Dave, who was usually the most courteous of men, snarled at them to get away. As we began carrying Andy toward the ambulance, a woman dressed in blue came over, wordlessly took one corner of the stretcher from Dave and walked along with us.

I had noticed her earlier because she was a genuine beauty. She was, I think, close to sixty, but auburn-haired still, and she had the freckled skin of the natural redhead. As one of the attendants slid Andy's body into the ambulance, she reached her hand out toward the open doors in a gesture so poignant that Dennis Whittaker from our city paper, the *Sun Examiner*, took a picture of her that the paper used on their front page the next day.

We should have counted our lucky stars when we opened the paper and saw that heart-stopping picture. It could have been worse. Seconds after that photo was taken, the nightmare of that afternoon turned another corner.

Eve Boychuk had climbed into the ambulance before the attendants put Andy's body in. She was hunched over, sitting on one of the little jump seats ambulances have so family members can go along to the hospital with their loved ones. The ambulance had begun to pull away when a small, dark figure broke through the crowd and ran after it. She was shouting, but in a language I couldn't understand. It was Andy's mother, Roma Boychuk.

Eighty-three years old, brought from her neat little home in the west end of Saskatoon to watch her son's triumph, and we had forgotten about her. She had lived in Canada for seventy years, but she was still uneasy with English. Ukrainian was the language of her heart, and it was in Ukrainian she was crying out as she tried to stop the ambulance that was carrying her son away.

The scene was like something out of a silent movie: the round little figure in black running across the field, dust swirling around her heavy legs as the sun fell in the sky and the ambulance sped away. But the movie wasn't silent, and you didn't have to know Ukrainian to hear the anguish in her voice.

I didn't recognize the man who ran after her. He was tall and very thin. He looked like the singer James Taylor. The auburn-haired woman and I stood and watched as he reached Roma, enclosed her small body in his arms for a few moments and then, still holding her, walked across the dusty field toward us. When he came close, we could hear that he was saying to her the soft, repetitive nonsense words you use to soothe a child.

She was crying freely now, and her pain hung in the air like vapour. The auburn-haired woman felt it and reached out to Roma. She placed her fingertips under Roma's chin

and gently lifted the old woman's face so that Roma could
see her. They stood there looking into one another's eyes for
perhaps ten seconds – two women united by grief and pain.
Then Roma made a terrible feral sound, a hissing growl, the
sound of a kicked cat, and she leaned closer to the woman
and spat in her face. The man grabbed Roma and I reached
for the auburn-haired woman, but she was running across
the field toward the parking lot. I started after her, but when
I'd run a few steps I was hit by a sense of futility. What was
the point? Andy was dead. And so I just stood there as sirens
sliced the air and police cars screamed over the hill.

Then someone was holding me. Suddenly my daughter,
Mieka, was behind me; her arms, suntanned and strong,
were around me.

"Oh, Mummy." She buried her head in my neck the way
she had when she was a little girl. Over her shoulder, I could
see Howard Dowhanuik with his arms resting on the shoulders of my two sons. They were still in their baseball uniforms, and I remembered they'd had a game before Andy was
scheduled to speak.

"So who won?" I asked them. The automatic question.
Andy would have approved.

"Us," said Peter, my older son, who was a head taller than
I was. He had cried only once since he was a child, but he
came running to his sister and me, and wept.

In the west a bar of gold separated sky and land. Over
Peter's shoulder, I could see a grove of poplars. Already their
leaves were turning, and the golden light caught them and
warmed them to the colour of amber.

I closed my eyes and there, in memory, was another day of
golden light. My classics professor was standing at her desk
while the September sun streamed in the window, and she
told us about the myth of the Heliades. Phaeton, she said,
shaking her head sadly, had tried to drive the chariot of the

sun across heaven, and Zeus had struck him down and turned his sisters into poplar trees. As they wept for their dead brother, the tears of Phaeton's sisters hardened into amber.

As I closed my arms around my son, I knew that my heart had already turned to wood.

CHAPTER

2

At six o'clock the next morning I was walking across the Albert Street bridge, thinking about murder. The city was sullen with heat from the day before, and it was going to be another scorcher. Mist was burning off Wascana Lake, and through the haze I could see the bright sails of windsurfers defying the heat. Already the T-shirts of the joggers I met on the bridge were splotched with sweat, and I could feel the cotton sundress I'd grabbed from Mieka's closet sticking wetly to my back.

The heat was all around me, but it didn't bother me. I was safe in the isolating numbness of aftershock. It was a feeling I was familiar with, and I hugged it to me. This was not my first experience with murder, and I wasn't looking forward to what came after the numbness wore off.

Three years earlier, in an act as senseless as it was brutal, two strangers had killed my husband, Ian. His death changed everything for me. The obvious blows – the loss of a husband and father – had left me dazed and reeling. But it was what Ian's death implied about human existence that almost destroyed me.

Until the December morning when I opened the door and Andy Boychuk was standing there, shivering, telling me there was painful news, I had believed that careful people, people like me, could count on the laws of cause and effect to keep us safe. The absence of motive in Ian's murder, the metaphysical sneer that seemed to be the only explanation for his death, came close to defeating me.

It had been a long climb back, and I thought I had won. I thought I had vanquished the dark forces that had paralyzed me after Ian's murder, but as I stood on the bridge and looked at the sun glaring on the water and smelled the heat coming up from the pavement, I knew nothing was finished. I could feel the darkness rising again, and I was desperately afraid.

The snow was deep the night Ian died. It was the end of December, the week between Christmas and New Year. We always get snow that week, and the day Ian died was the day of the worst blizzard of the winter.

He had driven to the southwest corner of the province just after breakfast. He went because he had lost the toss of a coin. There were two funerals that day: one in the city for the wife of one of the government members and one in Swift Current for an old MLA who'd been elected in the forties. Two funerals, and the night before at a holiday party, Ian and Howard Dowhanuik had had a few drinks and tossed a coin. Ian lost.

We quarrelled about his going. I called him, dripping from the shower, to make him listen to the weather forecast. He dismissed it with an expletive and disappeared into the bathroom. Fifteen minutes later, pale, hung over and angry, he got into the Volvo and drove to Swift Current. That was the last time I saw him alive.

At the trial, they pieced together the last hours of my husband's life. He had spoken well and movingly at the

funeral, quoting Tennyson in his eulogy. ("I am a part of all
that I have met . . . /How dull it is to pause, to make an
end/To rust unburnished, not to shine in use.") After the
service, he went to the church basement and had coffee and
sandwiches, talked to some supporters, kissed the widow,
filled his Thermos and started for home. It was a little after
four in the afternoon.

It must have been the girl who made him stop. I saw her
at the trial, of course: a dull-eyed seventeen-year-old with a
stiff explosion of platinum hair and a mouth painted a pale,
iridescent mauve. Her boyfriend was older, nineteen. He had
shoulder-length blond hair and his eyes were goatish, pink-
rimmed and vacant.

They didn't look like killers.

The boy and the girl had separate lawyers, but they were
alike: passionate, unsure young men who skipped over the
death and asked us to address ourselves to the defendants'
state of mind on the night in question. The boy's lawyer had
a curious way of emphasizing the key word in each sentence,
and I, who had written many speeches, knew that if I were to
look at his notes I would see those words underlined.

"He was *frustrated*," the boy's lawyer said, his voice squeak-
ing with fervour. "His *television* had broken down. And then
his car got a flat tire on the night of the *blizzard*. And he
wanted to take his girlfriend to the *party*. When Ian Kilbourn
stopped to offer assistance, my client was already agitated,
and when Mr. Kilbourn *refused* to drive my client and his
girlfriend to the party, my client's *frustration just boiled
over*. He had the wrench in his hand anyway, and before he
knew it, it just *happened*. *Frustration, pure and simple*."

"Fourteen times," the Crown prosecutor said, leaping to
her feet. "The pathologist said there were fourteen blows.
Mr. Kilbourn's head was pulp. Here, look at the pictures."

When I saw the dark spillage of my husband's head against the snow, the old, logical world shattered for me. It was months before I was able to put the pieces together again, and it was Andy who made me believe there was a foundation on which it would be safe to rebuild.

One evening the September after my husband died, I was in my backyard cutting flowers, and I sensed someone behind me. It was Andy, and there was a look on his face that was hard to read in the half light. As always when he talked with friends, there was no preamble.

"Jo, I've had a hell of a time dealing with what happened to Ian. I know it's been a thousand times worse for you, but today something came back to me, and it's helping. When I was in high school we read *Heart of Darkness* – I guess all the grade twelves read it that year. Anyway, the woman who taught us said that Kurtz possessed a mind that was sane but a soul that was mad. I think those kids who killed Ian must have been like that. Somehow that explains a lot. The world's a rational place, Jo. Anyway," he had said, "that's all I came to say."

Much later, as I thought back to the words, they didn't seem particularly profound, but on that September night I clung to them. In isolating my husband's murderers as mutants, spiritual misfits, Andy had made it possible for me to reclaim the image of a world that made sense. But now the man who had touched my shoulder and turned me from the heart of darkness had been swallowed by the darkness himself.

I turned onto the path that curved around Speaker's Corner. "A mind that was sane, but a soul that was mad," I said. A woman walking by with her basset hound looked at me curiously. I smiled at her. "Just saying my mantra." She tightened her grip on the dog's leash and quickened her steps. I didn't blame her. If I could have managed it, I would have run from me, too.

Considering what was waiting for me at the hospital, perhaps leaving reality behind wasn't such a bad idea. Howard had called at five o'clock that morning sounding tired and worried.

"Jo, I'm at Prairie Hospital – all hell's about to break loose here. How long would it take you to get over here?"

"Howard, I was sleeping. Can't it wait?"

"Would thirty minutes be all right? If you don't want to drive, Dave'll come over and pick you up."

I looked at my clock. I had slept for three hours. Obviously, Dave and Howard hadn't slept at all. They didn't need a prima donna.

"No, I'll walk. I could use the air. Why doesn't Dave meet me in the park and he can fill me in on the way to the hospital."

"Yeah, okay. I'll tell him to meet you at the flowers."

"Howard, the park is full of flowers."

"The red ones. You know, the weird little ones – the ones that bite," he said and hung up.

In the shower, it came to me. The ones that bite were snapdragons; there was a bank of snapdragons on a little hill past the bandstand. Sure enough, when I came over the hill, Dave Micklejohn was waiting. He was still wearing the white shorts and the Sartre T-shirt he'd had on at the picnic. He must have been at the hospital all night.

I put my index finger in the middle of his chest, right on the bridge of Sartre's nose.

"Existence precedes essence," I said.

"Never truer than today," said Dave, straightening his shoulders. "Oh, Jo, this thing just gets worse and worse."

"What now?" I said.

"Well, there's no doubt at all that Andy was murdered. The pathologist is ninety-nine per cent certain Andy ingested potassium cyanide seconds before his death. They think it was in the water that he drank at the podium. You know, the stuff in the black Thermos that I filled myself and then put the little note on for good measure."

I felt a coldness in the pit of my stomach. Cyanide in the water. My instincts had been right.

Dave waited for reassurance. "Oh, Dave, the police will know the note was a joke."

"Well, for the moment they're entertaining that possibility, hence I'm still a free person. You, incidentally, are a hero, Jo. When you decked that bigwig Spenser, you saved his life. If he'd managed to get the water down, there would have been two of them dead instead of . . ." He swallowed and looked toward the marina. The striped windsocks on the poles around the deck of the restaurant hung limp in the hot stillness of the morning. Dave swallowed again.

"Speaking of heroes, Dave, you're not doing too badly yourself," I said, touching his arm gently. "What's happening at the hospital?"

"It's full of media people. Jo, you wouldn't believe the mess and the confusion in that lobby. They've already got a crew setting up a live feed to *Good Morning, Canada*. Andy's murder will be coast-to-coast by 7:05. Great coverage, kiddo." And then, smiling ruefully, he gave me the final piece of news. Eve Boychuk was insisting that she would take Andy home to their place in Wolf River and handle the burial herself. That was where I came in.

"Jo, for fifteen years we've managed to smooth over the fact that Andy was married to a person who, to put it kindly, is unusual. Now, when we've got every media person in Canada here, Eve is going to throw our leader's body into a bag, pitch him into the back of her half-ton, drive down the

Trans-Canada and bury him in the garden next to her cat."

As we walked across the parking lot to the emergency entrance, we were both laughing. We must have sounded crazy, but the laughter helped. Suddenly, Dave pointed to the emergency room door.

"Well, how about that?"

I looked. There, bigger than life, left arm in a sling, was Rick Spenser. The doctors must have kept him in the hospital overnight for observation. His beautiful cream suit was filthy, and there was a nasty cross-hatch of cuts on his forehead, but as a taxi pulled up to the door, his wave was imperious. He settled himself beside the driver, closed the door smartly and was gone.

I said to Dave, "Another myth shattered."

Dave grinned. "You mean our boy Rick in a dirty suit?"

"No, I mean our boy Rick jumping into the front seat of a taxi. A cabbie told me once that he could always spot easterners by the way they head for the back seat, even if they're alone. And there's Rick Spenser, an easterner right to the tip of his Dack's, diving into the front seat like a stubble jumper. A mystery."

"A day for mysteries, my friend," said Dave as he opened the glass door to admitting.

The hospital smell stopped me. Memories. I had come here the morning they brought Ian's body in. I hadn't believed Andy.

Dave was looking at me hard. "Jo, are you all right?"

"No," I said, "but I'm still functioning. Use me while you can."

"In that case, I'll go find Howard and meet the press and you take care of the Lady. That's what Andy used to call her, you know. He'd say, 'Well, Dave, looks like we're going to have to go to the Elstow Sports Day alone. The Lady has declined our invitation.'" He shook his head at the memory.

"They've put her in the conference room. It's just through those doors at the end of the hall. Be firm with her, Jo. Don't let her make Andy look ridiculous. This has to be first class all the way."

He gave me a hug and walked to the foyer, where media people were drinking hospital coffee and checking sound systems and lights. Two men carrying hand-held TV cameras trailed him. I watched as he picked his way carefully over the tangle of cables and wires on the floor and moved a pot of pink azaleas from the reception desk to the table where Howard would be holding the press conference; then, shaking his head, put them back where he'd found them. Virgo all the way.

Then I opened the double doors and walked down the corridor, in search of the Lady.

CHAPTER

3

The room that they'd put Eve in was in the new wing. The corridor I walked down smelled of fresh paint, and the floor was soft with carpet. The names and titles on the doors that opened off the hall made it clear that this was where the power of the hospital, medical and administrative, went to work. When I came to the door marked Conference Room, I took a deep breath, knocked and walked in.

The first thing I noticed was that, by anyone's standards, the room was luxurious. During the election campaign seven years before, the other party had promised a massive program of new health-care facilities. "A hospital for every patient," Howard Dowhanuik had scornfully called their program, but the people had bought it, and we lost the election. Now, seven years of scandals and kickbacks later, the number of hospitals in the province was exactly the same as it had been the day we left office. However, as a sop to the electorate, the government had, the winter before, begun construction on a new wing for the biggest hospital in the capital, Prairie General.

This was their showpiece, their shining rebuttal to nagging questions about available beds and state-of-the-art medical equipment. They would use this as evidence of a promise fulfilled, but we could use it too – as an indictment of a government that starved rural hospitals but emptied out the treasury for the folks in the capital. As I stood in the door of the conference room, I filed away details: the shining oak of the conference table, the deep chairs upholstered in leather the colour of a dove's breast, the handsome pieces of aboriginal art that blazed on the muted grey walls. Andy could get a great ten-minute speech out of this room . . . Then, like a blow to the temple, the correction, the change of tense – Andy could have gotten a great ten-minute speech out of this.

Andy was dead. There wouldn't be any more speeches. But I could do this much for him. I could take care of his wife. She was sitting at the head of the oak table. Her back was to a wall of windows that filled the conference room with the raw light of a city in the grip of a heat wave, but this room was cold – unnaturally cold – and quiet. Through the windows I could see the traffic on the street, but the air in the room was silent and dead.

I walked toward the window and sat in the chair beside her.

"Hello, Eve. How're you doing?"

Her voice was low and strong. "On a scale of one to ten, I'm about a minus five." She tried a smile. "They didn't want me to be alone last night, so I stayed here."

"You're looking fine," I said, and it was true. She was still wearing the unbleached cotton sundress she'd had on at the picnic, but her thick grey hair was brushed smoothly and caught in a barrette at the back, and her makeup was fresh. On the floor beside her was a bag, a large, tooled-leather bag with a shoulder strap, the kind travellers carry. With her deep tan and her Greek sandals and her self-contained, slightly abstracted look, she had the air of a traveller who suddenly finds herself inexplicably in the wrong place.

"Eve." I covered her strong brown hand with my own. "Dave thinks we should talk."

"Sort of widow to widow?" she asked and then she laughed.

"Yeah, kind of like that," I said and wondered if the doctors had given her something. "It's about –"

"It's about Andy's funeral," she said. "Dave told you he's afraid that I'll disgrace you all." She sounded distanced, ironic.

I took a chance. "Yeah, that's about it."

"Did he tell you what I want to do?"

"He said you were thinking about taking Andy home to Wolf River and having a private burial."

"And you don't think I have that right?" Her voice was low and controlled, but there was an edge in it.

"I know you have that right. It's just that Andy meant a lot to a great many people, and I think we should give them the chance to say good-bye."

She looked at me. Her eyes were extraordinary – grey-green with little flecks of yellow, cat's eyes that seemed focused on something behind me that I couldn't see, that I would never see.

"Of course," she said, "a big funeral would be good politics. All those people talking about what Andy believed in, and all of you rededicating yourselves to Andy's principles. By the time we left the cemetery you guys would be way ahead in the polls."

She was right. None of us had illusions about the next election. It was, as they say, a crap shoot. The polls were good for us now, but polls change, and it would be nice to have a cushion. A big, emotional funeral would get a lot of print, and we would use the coverage.

There wasn't a political person in Saskatchewan who

hadn't thought of the impact Andy's funeral could have. What amazed me was that Eve had thought of it. Eve hated politics. We all knew that. And she hated political people. I had known Andy fifteen years, and I could count on one hand the number of times Eve had talked to me and on two hands the number of times I'd seen her in public.

But here she was, sounding as shrewd as a party organizer. She was protean – changing shape before my eyes – and I was knocked off base. I didn't know where to take the conversation.

Eve did. "Jo, what would you do?" Another surprise. Eve asking advice, looking for a reasonable solution.

Well, I had one. Burying a murdered husband was an area in which I'd had some experience. I tried to keep the relief out of my voice. "I'd do what I did when Ian was killed. I'd ask Dave Micklejohn to arrange everything. I'd show up for the funeral. I'd do the best I could till everything was over and then I'd go home and fall apart."

Eve got up, walked to the windows and looked at the street. The minutes passed. I stored away more details about the room in case I ever wrote another political speech for anyone: the smoky glass of the wet bar tucked discreetly in the corner; the handsome oak sideboard with the circle of crystal decanters gleaming in the sunlight; the spiky beauty of the vase of prairie lilies placed dead centre on the conference table.

Eve turned to face me, picked up her bag, slung it over her shoulder and shrugged. "Okay, let's go find Dave Micklejohn."

I couldn't believe how easy it had been. I had told Dave I was functioning. Apparently, I was functioning pretty well. As I grabbed my purse and headed out the door with Eve, I congratulated myself on a job well done.

The congratulations were premature. I had forgotten what waited for us when we left the new wing and went into the centre block of the hospital. It didn't take long to be reminded. There they were – the *Good Morning, Canada* people and half a dozen others. Howard Dowhanuik and a woman wearing a white medical jacket with a hospital ID picture clipped to the lapel were standing behind a row of microphones. The woman was reading a statement. It was 7:05 and we were going live – coast-to-coast.

I'd set her up. Eve had trusted me, and I'd led her right into shark-filled waters. It didn't take long for one of the local journalists to recognize her, and the crew turned the cameras on us. Someone stuck a mike in Eve's face and asked her if she had any idea who had murdered her husband. I was furious at the predatory smile on the face of the man who asked the question, and I was furious at myself. But Eve was wonderful. She said she knew people would understand if she didn't say much, she was still shocked. She would help the police in every possible way. Funeral arrangements were in the hands of Andy's friend, David Micklejohn. I looked at Dave, who was standing out of camera range beside the hospital spokesperson. I could see the relief on his face.

I grabbed Eve's arm, pulled her along with me and said, "Let's get out of here. Walk as if you know where we're going." Together we strode purposefully toward the heavy glass doors that opened on the parking lot. After the chill of the conference room, the hot city air was like the blast from one of those automatic hand dryers in a public washroom.

Eve is tall, five foot ten or so, at least a head taller than me. As we came to the fence that divided the doctors' parking lot from the public one, she leaned down and whispered, "Do you know where we're going?" We stopped and looked around. Not twenty feet away was an old maroon Buick – Andy's car. Dave must have driven it to the hospital from the picnic. I pointed it out to Eve, and she rummaged in her purse and pulled out some keys.

"Bingo," she said. We slid into the front seat of that car as coolly as two women driving to the office. Eve slammed her door shut, then put her head on the steering wheel and began to cry great, noisy, racking sobs.

She was entitled. So was I. But it wasn't my turn. Today I was supposed to be the strong one. I sat beside her and played with the paper coffee cups that were lying on the dash. Dave and Andy and I had driven to the picnic in this car together. Just at the edge of town we'd stopped for ice cream and take-out coffee. These were our cups.

Outside in the heat, barelegged women in bright summer dresses were walking to work. It seemed like such an ordinary thing to do that I felt a stab of envy as I watched them. Inside the Buick, Eve wept and I played with the paper cups. One, two, three – one for Dave, one for Andy, one for me.

As suddenly as she had begun, Eve stopped crying. She reached over to the glove compartment and came up with a crushed box of moist towels. We each took a couple and wiped our hands and faces. Then Eve turned to me.

"Joanne, I'm going home. I hate this city, and if Dave Micklejohn is taking care of the funeral, there's nothing for me to do here. I should go and see Carey and tell him his father's dead. We never know how much he understands, but I don't want him to hear about Andy on television." She had not mentioned murder. Her mind was protecting itself more efficiently than mine was. She was devastated but she was coping. As she sat there, pulling a comb through her hair, looking critically at her face in the rearview mirror, she was, I thought, more centred than we had given her credit for being. Maybe I'd been too quick to dismiss all the New Age theories about quartz crystals and cosmic harmony.

However she managed it, Eve was a strong woman and a brave one. Her tender and unpitying reference to her son touched a vulnerability in me, because until that moment

I had forgotten all about him. He must, I thought, be in his late teens now. It had been more than ten years since the accident. I'd seen those flat, factual lines in Andy's biography so often that they didn't register any more.

"Andy and his wife, Eve, have one child, son, Carey, who is learning disabled and lives at the Pines, a special-care facility operated by Wolf River Bible College in Andy's constituency. Both parents visit their son frequently."

Did they? How would I know? I never asked. I thought of all the spring evenings Andy had taken my kids out to the lawn in front of the legislature to play baseball in the pale light of the prairie dusk. And I remembered how, when Mieka had broken her leg skiing last winter and ended up in traction for ten days, Andy hadn't missed a visiting hour. I couldn't remember ever once asking him about his son, or for that matter about his wife.

Andy was the one. We, all of us around him, had dismissed his wife and son in a paragraph and then gotten on to the stuff that really mattered – the next speech or the next meeting. I looked at Andy's widow, and I was bitterly ashamed. I knew what lay ahead of her, the empty months and weeks, but I could only guess at the horror of her next few hours. On impulse, I reached over and touched her hand.

"Eve, let me come with you. I wouldn't mind getting away from the city for a while myself. I can take the bus back later."

"Suit yourself." She shrugged. She'd pulled away again. Well, who could blame her? In fifteen years I'd never attempted to get close to her. I could hardly expect her to embrace me now. She snapped her seat belt on, turned the key in the ignition and pulled out of the parking lot. She didn't say another word till we were out of the city and on the highway.

When she spoke, her voice was small and tight with pain. "Am I going to get over this?"

I tried for the easy answer, but it wouldn't come. When finally I did speak, I told her the truth. There didn't seem to be much point in lying.

"I don't know if you'll get over it, Eve. I haven't."

She turned and gave me a curious little smile, then we both drew back into ourselves.

Outside, the heat shimmered above the fields. Most of the crop was off, and as far as I could see the land was the colour of beaten gold. It was a heartbreakingly beautiful late August day, the kind of day when you know in your bones that the long days of light and warmth are over, and the darkness is coming.

I thought about the cold, white, empty months ahead, and panic rose in my throat. Only yesterday everything had been certain, heavy with promise. And now . . . But if it was bad for me, it was ten thousand times worse for the woman beside me. I turned to ask how she was doing, but the question was stillborn. In an instant, I knew that everything had changed.

On the way out of the city, Eve had driven cautiously and well, but now the little green spear of the speedometer was trembling toward 130 kilometres. She was gripping the steering wheel so hard that the veins that ran from her wrists up her inner arm were rigid; her profile was carved with tension. Even her thick, steel-grey hair seemed charged with wild, kinetic energy. When she turned onto the overpass just west of Belle Plaine the needle on the speedometer moved past 135.

The car and the woman seemed fused. It was as if the little green spear was registering her agony in the numbers on the speedometer. The old Buick was vibrating dangerously.

"For God's sake, Eve, slow down."

She looked at me as if she had forgotten I was there. Her eyes were dull with pain. "I've tried to believe that we can be in charge of our lives, that if we focus on the desire, we can create miracles." Her voice broke. "I don't think that can be true."

I felt the wheels lose traction, and I reached across and grabbed the wheel. The heaviness of the old Buick kept us on the road as we curved around the top of the overpass. Below us was the junction where traffic from the overpass entered the highway. There were a lot of cars down there for a Monday morning.

"Please, Eve, please . . ." My voice sounded wrong – whining, not desperate.

But it did the trick. She shook herself, as if she were coming out of a dream.

"I just lost my focus there for a minute," she said. Her voice came from far away. Then she slowed and drove carefully onto the highway.

Half a kilometre down the road, she pulled the car on the shoulder, stumbled out, bent over in the ditch and retched – terrible, agonizing dry heaves. My legs were shaking so badly I couldn't go to her. I opened my door to the smell of heat and dust and hot asphalt. It smelled terrific. I was alive.

When Eve came back to the car, her face was yellowy grey, but she seemed in control.

"I think it would be better if you drove the rest of the way," she said.

I slid over to the driver's seat, and Eve climbed in and shut the door.

We drove in silence for about ten minutes, then Eve said quietly, "I need you to help me."

"If I can, Eve, anything."

"Food." She opened her hands in a gesture of emptiness. "I don't think I've eaten since yesterday morning. Nobody fed me. I think I need to eat before I see Carey."

I remembered a doctor I knew who said surgeons were always hungry just after they'd lost a patient. Something to do with the need to connect again with the life force, he'd said. I looked at the woman slumped in the passenger seat, and I thought that if ever anyone needed to be connected again with the life force, it was Eve Boychuk.

CHAPTER

4

Disciples is a restaurant on the Trans-Canada Highway just outside Wolf River. It's run by the people from Wolf River Bible College, and whatever you think of their theology, they make the best pastry in the province. If you're serious about food, it's worth the forty-mile drive from the city to sit at their gleaming white Formica tables drinking coffee and eating the pie of the day.

That's what Eve and I did. The pie of the day was raspberry, and when we finished the first piece we ordered another. Two women playing at being ordinary, while the overhead fan stirred the smells of good coffee and fresh baking and on the radio in the kitchen, Debby Boone sang "You Light Up My Life." We didn't talk, but it wasn't an awkward silence, and when I looked at Eve after she'd finished eating, she seemed tired but calm.

"Do you know how long it's been since I ate pie?" she asked. "And I haven't had a cup of coffee in ten years. I try to stay away from toxins."

"I guess we should all be more careful," I said. Even to me, my voice sounded condescending, and Eve, who was unusually sensitive to nuance, caught it.

"Don't patronize me, Joanne. From what I've seen of political people, some cleansing and enlightenment might not be a bad idea." She turned and looked out the window. Across the parking lot from the restaurant was a small motel. In front of it was a sign: "Seek Ye First the Kingdom of God." Remote again, Eve sat and stared at the motel; on the table, her hands were busy making neat little nips around the edge of the place mat.

Finally the silence got to me. "You never really knew us, Eve. You never gave us a chance."

When she turned from the window, her eyes were narrow. "*I* never knew *you*. Listen to yourself, Joanne. That incredible narcissism. You people think the world begins and ends within six blocks of the legislature. I never knew you! Well, none of you ever knew me." Her voice rose. "Oh, you had your opinions – I heard things. Believe me, people always made sure I knew what you all thought. I knew about your contempt. About how you thought I was a liability, an embarrassment. 'Keep her out there in her house in the country, throwing her pots or whatever it is she does. Out of harm's way. Out of our hair. Out of sight, out of mind.'"

One by one people at the tables around us fell silent. Even Christians like a little drama, and the late breakfast crowd at Disciples smelled blood. On the radio, Amy Grant was singing about how much she loved her Lord, and in the booth by the window Eve was giving everybody a morning to remember.

"God damn it, none of you ever took the time to know me. None of you ever tried to understand our marriage." She slid out of the booth, slung her leather bag over her shoulder, then gave me an odd smile. "You never understood me, but you know what's worse? You never understood my husband. He was the centre of your little world, but none of you knew the first thing about Andy Boychuk." She walked toward the door, then turned. "Thanks for breakfast, Joanne. Thanks for driving down with me. Now leave me alone. You people aren't good for me. None of you know shit about anything." She looked hard at me for a moment, then she was gone.

By the time I'd paid the check, she was walking toward the parking lot, her car keys swinging from her hand. I started after her, but I was fresh out of good deeds. I went back into the restaurant, ordered another cup of coffee and checked the bus schedule posted over the cash register. I had two hours to kill until the bus came.

I took a sip of coffee, but I couldn't swallow it. A memory came, and I felt my throat close with pain. Less than twenty-four hours earlier, I'd been eating ice cream sandwiches at the Milky Way on Osler Street, listening to Andy and Dave argue lazily about whether the Blue Jays had the sand to go all the way this year – good, aimless, hot-weather talk.

I managed to get outside before the tears started. As the door to Disciples slammed shut, Debby Boone's dad was singing "He's Got the Whole World in His Hands."

The sun was climbing in the sky when I turned down the road to the Bible college. The campus had the late-summer stillness that hangs in the air of a college town in the days before students, tanned and reluctant, come back for another year. The smell of pine trees, sharp with memories of cottages and corn roasts, filled the air. In spite of everything, I felt better. Here was a world that still made sense.

To the right I could see a compound of low, flat-roofed buildings that couldn't be anything but World War II military barracks. Once they must have housed the entire school. Now most of them were student residences with names like Bardon Hall and Wymilwood. One was a grocery store called

God's Provisions. That morning there was a hand-lettered sign nailed to the front door: "Closed for the Summer."

In the fifties, the college had come into some money, not an extravagant sum but enough to build a cluster of institutional buildings: smug, bland, closed in on themselves. West of the main road was a little subdivision of bungalows – faculty housing. Over the front doors, burned into pieces of cedar, were the owners' names: "The Epps," "The Wymans."

In the seventies the money had really rolled in: a classroom building, a gymnasium, half a dozen dormitories – all made of cinder blocks with slits for windows – Dachau modern, energy efficient, ugly, utilitarian. The campus was made up of the kind of unexceptional buildings any institution that has to answer to its board of governors would build.

Except – and it was an extraordinary exception – northwest of the main road where it was clearly visible from the highway – where it was, in fact, the first thing anyone driving west from Regina saw – was the new chapel of Wolf River Bible College. It was an amazing structure for an institution that prided itself on cleaving to the traditional values. It looked like a high-tech child's toy – a building made of giant Lego pieces or those intricate metal building sets kids used to play with thirty years ago.

The central building was an octagon, and four lozenge-shaped wings angled off it in an X shape. Everything was there in plain sight: steel beams, trusses, ducts, huge concrete planks, transformers; and everything was painted in primary colours, red, yellow, blue. Only the cross, which soared from the centre of the octagon, was unpainted. In the sunlight it glinted with the soft glow of anodized metal. The chapel was a brazen and innovative building as out of place in the midst of the comfortable mediocrity of the campus as a Mies van der Rohe chair in the middle of a K-Mart. I wanted to get a closer look.

The first thing I discovered was that the building had a name. A sign encased in Lucite pointed the way to the Charlie Appleby Prayer Centre. The construction was recent enough that the area around the chapel hadn't been land-scaped. Clumps of earth turned over by machines baked hot and hard in the sun. Someone had thrown down a makeshift path of concrete blocks; and when I looked in the direction of the chapel, I saw a man and a woman walking toward me. The man was pushing a wheelchair, and the woman had a stroller. When they got closer, I realized that I knew the young man. He was Craig and Julie Evanson's son, Mark. Seeing him brought a rush of memories – memories of the time before the leadership race had divided us, and Craig and Julie and Ian and I had been young together.

We had met seventeen years before – the year our party, to everyone's surprise, formed the government. This was the election we weren't supposed to win, and the months that followed were heady times – at least for the men.

The wives saw a lot of one another that first term. It was a time of birthday parties and car pools and earnest discus-sions about preschools and free schools and French immer-sion. No one was more earnest than Julie Evanson. She and Craig had one child, Mark, the same age as our daughter, Mieka. He was the centre of Julie's existence. She planned her days around him, and there wasn't an hour in the day when Mark wasn't being instructed or challenged or enriched by his mother. Once, at the deflated end of a birth-day party, all the parents began talking about the unthink-able: the death of a child. Julie had been passionate: "Can you imagine if, after all the hours and hours you put in to make them into something really special, it was over just like that?" And she had snapped her fingers defiantly at the disease or the drunk driver or the act of fate that might end her boy's promising life.

Mark Evanson hadn't died. He'd done something worse. He'd turned out to be ordinary. By the time he hit high school it was apparent, even to his mother, that Mark was average, perhaps even a little below average. Betrayed and baffled, Julie floundered for a while. Then, to everyone's amazement, she, who had had only the most perfunctory interest in her husband's professional life, threw herself headlong into advancing Craig's career.

It was, for her husband and son, as if a hurricane had suddenly changed direction. The lives of both men were thrown off course. Craig, who would have been content to be the Member from Regina–Little Flower for the rest of his life, suddenly found himself speaking at strawberry socials and annual meetings all over the province. Julie had decided her husband was going to be the next premier, and the first step was winning the party leadership.

Julie's son's life had taken an even stranger turn. He was confused at first by the sudden withdrawal of his mother's attention and affection. Then Mark linked up with a group of kids from Wolf River Bible College. At sixteen, Mark was born again. At seventeen, he became a husband and, in short order, a father. I'd bumped into Mark and his baby at an outdoor crafts show earlier in the summer. At nineteen, Mark Evanson was a solid, good-looking young man with a solid, good-looking baby. When he said he was happy, I believed him.

Craig and Julie were not happy. If he hadn't loved Julie so completely, losing the leadership to Andy Boychuk would, I think, have been a relief for Craig. He could have accepted defeat gracefully and eased into the life he had wanted all along. Except he did love Julie. Passionately, uncritically, Craig Evanson loved his wife, and her pain at losing gnawed at him. Long after the votes were counted, Craig was haunted by the knowledge that he had failed his wife.

Julie was haunted by demons of her own. Losing seemed to be like a slow poison seeping through her system. She was sullen with those of us who had worked on Andy's campaign, and she was jubilant when, late in June, Andy had answered a question whimsically and had been forced to issue an apology. Before the six o'clock news was over, she was on the telephone. "Well, Jo, what do you think of your blue-eyed boy tonight?" she had asked.

Now summer was almost over, the blue-eyed boy was dead, and Julie's boy was standing in front of me, his face glowing with pleasure.

"Mrs. Kilbourn, what are you doing here? I mean, God loves us all and everybody's welcome at Wolf River, but what are you doing here?" Mark's face was as open and without guilt as a newborn's. He stood on the path, smiling, expectant, waiting for an answer.

"I came down with Mrs. Boychuk – you remember, Andy Boychuk's wife. They're friends of your mum and dad's. I guess you heard what happened to –"

The smile vanished. Mark cut me off. "We heard, but we didn't want C-A-R-E-Y here –" he spelled carefully, then rested his hand on the shoulder of the boy in the wheelchair "– to sense that anything was wrong, so we've been walking him all morning. He loves the new chapel – all the bright colours, I guess."

For the first time, I noticed the boy. I looked into his face. It was hard to imagine him responding to anything. He was dressed neatly, even whimsically, in shorts and a T-shirt that had a picture of Alfred E. Neuman from *MAD* magazine on the front and the words "What, Me Worry?" underneath. He would have been a handsome boy. His head was shaped like his father's, and his hair was the same red-brown, but Carey's head, too heavy for his slender neck, lolled to one side like a flower after a rainstorm. His features were regular but they were slack, and his mouth gaped. A little river of spit ran from his mouth to his chin. Mark reached down and dabbed at it with a Kleenex.

I held Carey's hand and smiled at him, but he didn't respond. When I straightened, I found myself face to face with Lori Evanson. She had stepped out from behind her husband, and she was looking at me with wonder.

"Mrs. Kilbourn, we saw you on television," she said. "Such a terrible thing – an evil thing! You were very brave to save Mr. Spenser's life." Her voice was light and sweet, with a lilting singsong quality, like a child's reciting something she's learned by heart. Lori was holding a baby I knew was her own, but there was a quality about her, a sense that somehow she would never move much past adolescence.

It wasn't her body. Physically, she was mature and beautiful. She looked the way we all wanted to look when we were eighteen. She was wearing a sundress the colour of a cut peach, and her arms and face were golden with tan. Up close, she smelled of suntan lotion and baby powder. Her shoulder-length hair was dark blond and streaked from the sun. She was incredibly lovely but in her eyes, which were as blue as forget-me-nots, there was such vacancy. If the eyes are the windows to the soul, Lori Evanson's soul was spotless.

"We're so glad you're all right. 'Praise the Lord.' That's what Mark said when he heard you were fine." She stopped for a second and looked gravely at her husband, at this man who could say just the right thing; then she directed those incredible eyes at me. "You've always been so good to us – that toaster oven with sandwich grill when we got married, and the cheque for twenty-five dollars when Clay was born. Look, isn't he a precious lamb?" She turned the baby toward me for inspection. The baby was handsome and reassuringly alert. "So kind," his mother continued. "If ever there's any-thing we can do for you."

"No thanks, Lori. I was just looking around. Perhaps I'll go over to the prayer centre. Are visitors allowed?"

Her perfect brow wrinkled. "Gee, Mrs. Kilbourn, I guess so, but you know, I don't know if anyone ever asked. I mean we're all, like, very proud of the chapel. It was designed by Soren Eames in consultation with a prize-winning Regina architect." Her brow smoothed. "The Charlie Appleby Prayer Centre seats 2,800 people and is a multi-purpose area that can be converted for other uses. The building also boasts four radiating modules: a cafeteria, a gymnasium, a faith life centre and a complex of state-of-the art business offices." Her innocent blue eyes shone with happiness. She was on home ground again. I saw the care with which those vacant blue eyes had been made up – peach eye shadow blending into mauve and then a soft smudge of grey eye liner beneath the lower lashes. Suddenly, those perfect eyes focused on something behind me, and they lit up. I turned to see what she was looking at.

On the main road that led through the campus, a man was getting out of a black Porsche. He was dressed like a university kid – denim work shirt and blue jeans – but even from this distance it was apparent that he wasn't a kid. He was tall and boyishly slender but there was something defeated about the set of his shoulders that suggested this man's worries went deeper than a conflict in his class timetable. When he began to walk toward us, I recognized him. He was the James Taylor look-alike, the one who'd run after Roma Boychuk to console her after Andy died. Lori grabbed my hand.

"Here's Soren now. Oh, Mrs. Kilbourn, you have to meet him. He is so kind and good. He understands everything, and I mean everything."

But the man who understood everything walked past us with a curt nod for Lori and Mark and not even that for me. Lori's face fell, but she was quick to defend him.

"Mrs. Kilbourn, that is just not like Soren Eames. He is usually so friendly. I think he must be mourning Mr. Boychuk's passing, too."

"I suppose he met Andy when Andy came to visit Carey."

She stood very straight and looked directly into my face. "I don't know about that. All I know is that Mr. Boychuk came to see Soren almost every week, and lately a lot more than that. They were very close."

"Lori, I don't think we should be talking about this – even with Mrs. Kilbourn. When a man talks to his pastor, that's just like when he talks to his doctor. There's a trust there, like an oath."

Lori looked so shattered that I jumped in. "I guess," I said, "that he came to talk about Carey."

Mark was silent. "I guess if you two are going to talk about this, Carey and I better go down to Disciples and get a Popsicle. Lori, I'll see you and Clay at home for lunch." He kissed his son and wife and pushed the wheelchair toward the road to the restaurant.

Lori was solemn. She was attempting to analyze something, and it went against the grain. "Mrs. Kilbourn, please forgive me but I think you're wrong. Mr. Boychuk never really spends – spent much time with Carey. I mean he was like good to him and all that but, you know, Mrs. Boychuk would spend like hours with Carey – watching TV with him and talking to him about the programs and reading to him and telling him about things, but Mr. Boychuk – well, you could tell he, like, loved Carey and everything, but it just seemed real hard for him to stay with him. He'd come in and he'd sit and hold Carey's hand for a little while and then it was like he couldn't take it any more. He'd kiss him and he'd

just leave. No, Mrs. Kilbourn, Mr. Boychuk didn't come for
Carey. Anyway, Soren is the spiritual head of Wolf River
Bible College and all, but he wouldn't have been the one to
like talk to about Carey – that would have been . . ."
Suddenly a laugh as musical as the tinkle of a wind chime.
"Well, of course, it would be Mrs. Manz. She's the matron
for special care – sometimes I can be so dumb." She smiled
shyly, waiting for approval.

I gave it heartily. "Well, thanks, Lori, that's good to know.
It was kind of you to go to so much trouble." We both smiled
– neither of us seeing a barb in a comment that equated
human thought with trouble, and we parted friends.

I didn't make a conscious decision to call on Soren Eames.
It just happened. I'd turned down Lori Evanson's invitation
to have lunch at their trailer and walked down the path that
led to the chapel. Close up, it seemed to change, to reveal
itself. Somehow up close you didn't notice the hard-edged
bravado of the building as much as the simple fact that
everything fit so well.

The Charlie Appleby Prayer Centre was a fitting building
in both senses of the word. The parts fit together with the
cool inevitability of a beautiful and expensive watch. The
result, as I discovered when the front door opened to my
touch, was a building where form and function meshed
smoothly. It was a fitting building in which to worship God.

The heart of the building, the octagon-shaped chapel, was
a beautiful room. No stained glass or groined wood or silky
altar cloths – just a room in which everything was practical
and workable. All eight walls were glass – eight walls of
windows filling the room with natural light. In the centre
of the room was a simple circular altar. Suspended above it
was an unpainted metal cross. Arranged in octagons around
the altar were bright metal pews, covered in sailcloth cushions. The sailcloth was vivid: red, green, yellow, blue. I walked

down the aisle and sat in a pew. From there I could see how pieces of pipe had been joined together to form the cross. It looked functional and heavy. Suddenly, everything caught up with me. Exhaustion and grief and the familiar clutch of panic. There had been other deaths: my grandparents, my best friend from high school, my father, my husband. I had survived, but as I watched the play of light on the cross, I began to tremble.

I sat for perhaps half an hour. There were no tongues of flame. No pressure of an unseen hand on my shoulder. But after a while I felt better – not restored but capable of functioning.

"I am going to make it through this day," I said. There were no thunderbolts, so I picked up my bag and walked.

I don't know which I heard first – the man's voice or the sobbing. But as I stepped outside the chapel, squinting against the harsh midday light, I heard someone in distress. The sound was coming from one of the wings – modules, Lori had called them – that radiated from the chapel like spokes from a wheel. The crying was terrible. It seemed to spring from a pain so pure and so private that I knew there was no help I could offer.

But there was another sound – the sound of a man's voice. At first, I couldn't catch the words, but I didn't need to. The cadences were as familiar to me as my own, and I listened with my heart pounding against my ribs as the sounds shaped themselves into words. "I thought it was the right thing to do, but now I don't know." Then something I couldn't make out, then, "It would have been kinder if I'd used a bullet." The voice was tight with anguish. "Why can't we go back? Oh, God, Soren, why can't we go back?"

Then nothing except the blood singing in my ears and the knowledge that the voice I was listening to was Andy Boychuk's.

I turned and walked to the double doors of the wing where the voice was coming from. When I came to the office marked Soren Eames, I didn't bother to knock. Out of breath and close to hysteria, I opened the door.

There wasn't much to see – a slender man with a receding hairline and on the desk in front of him a portable tape recorder clicking metallically to signal that the tape had ended. I don't know what I'd expected. I was sick with anger and disappointment.

I went over and pulled the tape out of the recorder. I had a hundred like it myself: small, cheap tapes that Andy used, when he was driving, to record an idea or his impression of a meeting or sometimes just the thoughts he had driving late at night across the prairie.

"Where did you get this?" I asked.

Soren Eames's voice was so low I could barely hear it. "He gave it to me."

"What's it supposed to mean? All that about 'the right thing to do' and using a bullet."

Soren Eames looked steadily at me, but he didn't answer.

My voice was shrill in the quiet room. "I asked you a question. Why have you got that tape? What's it all about?"

"It's a private communication." He stood and walked over to me. "I'd be grateful if you'd leave me alone now." His voice was gentle. He took my arm and led me down a corridor, through a door and into the light. For a few seconds, Soren Eames and I stood on the threshold looking into one another's faces with the intensity of lovers. I don't know what we were looking for – clues, I guess, some sort of insight into what had suddenly gone so wrong. Finally, I turned and began to walk down the path toward the highway.

"Mrs. Kilbourn," he called after me, "when you're working through all this, try to remember that you're not the only one. Other people loved Andy, too." It was only later that I realized he had called me by name.

There was one cab waiting outside the Regina bus depot, and I beat out an old lady for it. I'm not proud of that, but there it is. As the cab pulled away, I looked out the rear window. She was standing on the corner shaking her bag at me.

It was two-thirty when the taxi pulled up in front of my house on Eastlake Avenue, less than twenty-four hours since Andy's death. Our dogs greeted me hopefully, and I remembered that I hadn't taken them for their run that morning.

"Sorry, ladies," I said, "it's shower time. You can come up and bark your complaints through the bathroom door." They did. By 2:35 I was in the shower, and by 3:00, clean and cool in a fresh cotton nightgown, I was lying on top of my bedspread fast asleep.

It was late in the afternoon when I woke up. The room was full of shadows, and my son Peter was standing by the bed with a glass of iced tea. He is a handsome boy, dark like his father with the Irish good looks all the Kilbourns have. His sister, Mieka, thinks it's a crime that she looks like me: "blond and bland" are her exact words. She's right, but Peter carries his own burdens. At sixteen, he is as shy as Mieka and my younger boy, Angus, are outgoing. The political life with its endless rooms full of strangers has always been torture for him, yet he has walked into those rooms and offered his hand without grumbling. He is wonderfully kind with our dogs, with his sister and brother and with me. The tea was just the kind of thing he would do.

He sat on the edge of my bed. "Mieka's down there making dinner. It looks kind of gross but it smells okay."

"What's she making?"

"Pork chops something and chocolate mousse."

"Wow."

He smiled. "Right, and Angus and I rented a movie for you. Something with Robin Williams. The guy at 7-Eleven said it's hilarious. And there were a bunch of phone calls for you but Angus took the messages so you'll probably have to wait for people to call back. Anyway, here they are." He handed me some slips of paper and grinned a little. "And that television guy – the one you decked yesterday – Rick Spenser?"

I shuddered.

"Right. Well, a delivery man came with some flowers he sent you." He gave me the thumbs-up sign and closed the door behind him. He had not mentioned the word *murder*. It was a delicacy I was grateful for. I sat on the bed, took a sip of tea and looked through the messages Angus had taken.

There were two surprises: Eve Boychuk and Soren Eames had phoned. I called Eve first. She sounded composed, and asked me to go to the funeral with her. She didn't, she said, know who else to ask. She and Roma Boychuk, Andy's mother, hadn't spoken in years. "And that," she said wearily, "leaves only Carey and, of course, you, Jo." She didn't explain the "of course." I said I would go with her. She said she'd get back to me.

Soren Eames, sounding tentative but friendly, said he just wanted to make sure I'd gotten home safely. I thanked him and told him that the next time he was in the city, I'd be pleased if he'd call me. I hung up, certain I would hear from him again. The lady whom I'd beaten out for the cab at the bus depot didn't call, but I was two for three on my morning encounters. Things were definitely looking up.

There was a call from a detective named Millar Millard of the city police. Detective Millard was out of the office but he would be in touch with me, said a young woman named

Ironstar, who added that one winter she had taken a class in human justice my husband had taught at the university.

And there were phone calls from friends. Ali Sutherland, who had been my doctor and my friend when Ian died, had called to send love and condolences. And there were invitations to dinner from two of the people in this world I would under most circumstances have liked to have dinner with – Howard Dowhanuik and Dave Micklejohn. I turned them both down. They would have talked about Andy's murder, and I couldn't face it. That night, nothing could compare with the prospect of sitting in my cotton nightgown at our kitchen table, eating Mieka's pork chops something and chocolate mousse, then curling up and watching a movie some guy at the 7-Eleven said was hilarious. Safe in my house, I could vanquish the word *murder*.

When I padded downstairs in my nightie and bare feet, I felt virtuous – all those phone calls answered – and I felt hungry. What Mieka was cooking smelled of ginger and garlic. As I entered the kitchen, she was putting a loaf of sourdough bread into the oven to warm, and Angus was chopping vegetables. When Mieka told me to fix myself a drink and check out the dining-room table, I kept walking.

The table was set with the knives and forks reversed – Angus again – but in the centre of the table was a crystal pitcher so exquisitely cut I knew it was Waterford. It was filled with gerbera daisies. Half were that vibrant pink we used to call American beauty, and the others were rosy orange. The late summer sunshine poured in the window, turning the facets of the crystal to fire. It was a centrepiece from a Van Gogh picnic. There was an envelope propped against my water glass. Inside, on hotel stationery, was a note from Rick Spenser: "On November 22, 1963, Aldous Huxley died. His death will always be merely a footnote to the Kennedy assassination. Thank you, my dear Mrs. Kilbourn, for keeping me from becoming a footnote. I have never liked seeing my name in small print." It was signed "RS." I called the hotel and left a message thanking him.

All things considered, it was a happy evening. Mieka's dinner was great, and after we ate I made myself a gin and tonic and plugged in the fan and we all sat and watched the movie. The guy at the 7-Eleven had been right. It was pretty funny. Angus fell asleep on the couch, so when the movie was over, I brought down a blanket and pillow for him, tucked him in, kissed the big kids and went up to bed.

The light from the little brass lamp on the bedside table made a warm pool in the darkness. Under the lamp, a stack of novels in bright dust jackets sat unread and inviting. The bed was turned down and the pillows were fluffed against the headboard. Peter again. Obviously today he was bucking for sainthood. He had my vote.

When I walked toward the bathroom to brush my teeth, I noticed a splash of material on the chair by the window – my dress from the picnic. I picked it up to throw in the laundry hamper. Under it was Andy's blue leather speech portfolio. Printed in gold Gothic type on the cover were the words "Property of Every Ukrainian Mother's Dream." Dave Micklejohn and I had given it to Andy for Christmas, when he'd announced that he was running for the leadership.

When I opened the folder, I expected to see that last speech. What I saw was not my words triple spaced on the familiar buff paper, but a single sheet of dove-grey paper – expensive paper. A third of the way down the page, hand-written in elegant calligraphy, were eight lines of poetry:

O rose, thou art sick.
The invisible worm
That flies in the night,
In the howling storm,

Has found out thy bed
Of crimson joy,
And his dark secret love
Does thy life destroy.

At the top of the page, centred the way they would be on engraved notepaper, someone had drawn the letters *A* and *E*. But they weren't separate; they were linked with little swirls and flowers the way they would be on a wedding invitation.

"His dark secret love/Does thy life destroy." Those had been the last words Andy Boychuk had read before his death, the last image retained on his eye. The warm, familiar room suddenly seemed alien, violated. My hands went slack, and the portfolio slid off my knee to the floor.

That night I dreamed of roses the colour of dried blood and of gold Gothic letters that refused to arrange themselves into coherence. I awoke with my mouth dry and my heart pounding.

"Who killed you, Andy?" I whispered in the dark. "Who killed every Ukrainian mother's dream?"

CHAPTER

5

Inspector Millar Millard had done what he could to make his office human. The fluorescent lights overhead had been disconnected, and the room was lit by a reading lamp on his desk and an old standard lamp in the corner. Along one wall was a bookshelf with some interesting names on the book spines: Dostoevski, Galsworthy, Thomas Mann, C.P. Snow. On either side of the low round table by the window were two chairs, real chairs, overstuffed and comfortable looking. In the middle of the table – a surprisingly domestic touch – was a fat yellow ceramic teapot.

There was a folder on the table in front of one of the chairs; Inspector Millard motioned me to the other one.

"Would you care for tea, Mrs. Kilbourn? Or I could send out for coffee if you prefer."

"Tea would be fine," I said, sinking into the chair.

On the bottom bookshelf were a dozen or so coffee mugs, each with the orange and yellow sunrise logo of *Good Morning, Canada*. They were given as mementos to people who appeared on the show. As I looked across the table at the man pouring tea, I thought I must have watched him earn all those mugs, and a dozen more besides. His face, weary and decent, had flickered across TV screens for twenty years. It was comforting to see him sitting across from me.

He was a tall, courtly man, white-haired and sunburned. His clothes were off the rack: lightweight trousers, not expensive but nice, and a white golf shirt. When he handed me the mug of tea, I noticed that the tips of two of his fingers were missing. The tea was good, and I said so.

"Earl Grey," he said. "I change blends during the day but I like Earl Grey for mornings – a good, no-nonsense tea."

"Yes," I said, and we lapsed into an awkward silence.

"Well," he said finally, picking up the folder, "it's about this business, of course." Across the file in blue marker was the name "Boychuk." "I'll need you to tell me about some things. Why don't you just start at a point you feel is useful, and I'll stop you if I need help following your line of thought. Would it irritate you if I smoked?"

"No, of course, not. I used to smoke myself."

"Everybody's smoking is in the past tense but mine," he said gloomily, opening a fresh pack of Kools. "You deserve praise for quitting."

"Thanks," I said. "It's been a while." If the city police force trained its officers to do the good cop, bad cop procedure, then Millar Millard must have been the prototype for the good cop.

Two hours later I knew he could also be the prototype for the smart cop. I had described that last day hour by hour, minute by minute. I had begun with Dave Micklejohn picking up first me at my house then Andy at the apartment on College Avenue where he stayed when he was in the city, and I had gone through our stop at the Milky Way for ice cream, the time at the picnic, the people we saw, the things we ate and drank. Millar Millard had been gentle and encouraging. After about an hour he had made us a fresh pot of tea, and brought out a box of Peek Freans biscuits, which he arranged carefully on a plate before offering them to me. I began to relax. We were friends, two intelligent people working out a problem together. At least that's what I thought, and that's why what happened came as such a shock.

I had found giving a narrative of that last day painful but bearable until I came to the moment when Andy walked across the stage to the podium. When I remembered how happy and certain he had been in those last minutes, I felt my throat closing. I had to look out the window to keep from breaking down as I told the story of the last minutes of Andy Boychuk's life. When I finished, I turned from the window and looked into the face of my new friend Millar Millard. I guess I expected some sort of commendation. I had, after all, gotten a pat on the head for quitting smoking. This had been worse, but I'd managed to give him a thorough, controlled account of those last awful minutes on the stage. Praiseworthy.

But there was no praise.

Inspector Millar dragged deeply on his cigarette. He had changed. We had changed. I was no longer someone helping the police with their investigation. I had become something else. Millard's blue eyes had lost their weary amiability, and his voice had lost its warmth. He leaned toward me.

"Just two more questions, Mrs. Kilbourn, but I want answers: How did you know there was poison in that water Andy Boychuk drank at the podium?"

I was thrown off base. I babbled a long and aimless story about being in Florida when my children were little and how one day on the beach my daughter had instinctively recoiled from a poisonous man-of-war even though it was as blue as a jewel. "It was as if Mieka just knew that thing was a killer," I finished lamely. "When I bent over to give Andy mouth-to-mouth, I knew the smell on his lips was deadly, and I knew I couldn't let Rick Spenser drink from the glass Andy had drunk from. Call it atavistic, if you will . . ."

"Oh, I will, Mrs. Kilbourn," he said dryly. "I will note in my report that you were obeying a primal response when you tackled Rick Spenser." He stubbed out his cigarette, looked hard at me and said, "Shall we abandon this area for the moment and look at another puzzling aspect of your behaviour that day?" His eyes were the hostile grey of a March sky. "What was it that you took from the podium before the police arrived? There are, I should mention, a dozen witnesses, albeit reluctant ones, who will testify that they saw you remove something from the area in which the murder had been committed."

"I believe they call it the scene of the crime," I said, smiling.

"I believe they do," he said, not smiling.

I took a deep breath, reached into my bag, pulled out Andy's speech portfolio and handed it to Inspector Millard. "This," I said, "is what I removed from the scene of the crime."

It was his turn to be knocked off base. He read the words on the cover aloud: "'Every Ukrainian Mother's Dream.'" Mrs. Kilbourn, I'm at a loss here. Is this some kind of joke?"

"Yes," I said, "that's exactly what it is – or was. That's Andy Boychuk's speech portfolio. The inscription was a private joke."

His eyes were glacial. "Private between whom and whom?"

"Between Andy and the people who worked for him. The portfolio was a gift to Andy from Dave Micklejohn and me last Christmas. One of the Ukrainian newspapers in the province had run a picture of Andy and used the Ukrainian mother's dream thing as a caption." I hesitated. "It seemed pretty funny at the time . . ."

He lit another Kool and rubbed the area between his eyes. "I'm sure it did. These little whimsies always look a bit tawdry when there's been a murder."

"You have more experience of that than I do, Inspector," I said.

He looked at me wearily. "Mrs. Kilbourn, let's cut the crap. Why did you take the portfolio from the stage that day? You're a clever woman. You knew better than that."

"I guess I wasn't thinking clearly. If you want to dismiss me as hysterical or stupid, go ahead. But there was nothing devious in my taking the portfolio. I had given it to Andy. It contained the last speech I'd ever write for him. He was dead. At that moment I suppose I just thought I was taking something that was mine."

"Mrs. Kilbourn, you amaze me." He shook his head sadly. "Well, let's have a look at the last speech." He opened the portfolio. The poem was still in place. He read it without expression and when he was through, he looked up at me. "William Blake," he said. " 'The Sick Rose.' "

"Yes, I know."

"What's it doing here?"

I was angry. I picked up my bag and stood. "I guess that's for you to find out, Inspector. Thanks for the tea." I started toward the door. I think I expected him to stop me. He didn't.

But when I opened the door, he said very quietly, "Any time, Mrs. Kilbourn. And, Mrs. Kilbourn, I'm certain I don't have to tell you this, but we'd appreciate it if you didn't leave the city for a while."

That patronizing "we" ignited something in me. "You seem to forget, Inspector, I have a funeral to go to. I'm not the kind of woman who leaves a friend to go to his grave alone."

It made no sense, but at that moment it was the best exit line I could muster.

The police station was air conditioned, but by the time I got to the street where I'd parked the Volvo, sweat was running down my back. There was a parking ticket on my windshield. Somehow, I wasn't surprised. When I reached into my bag for car keys, I pulled out a sheet of orange paper – the list of school supplies Angus needed before they'd let him through the door to grade eight. That didn't surprise me, either. I wanted a shower, a cold drink with gin in it and a novel in which an inspector of police was first humiliated then killed. But I was not a free agent; I was Angus's mother. I peeled the ticket off the windshield, put a quarter in the meter, crossed the street and went into the Bay.

I like the way stores look in the last days of summer: the stacks of fresh notebooks, the bright new three-ring binders, the crayons sharp with possibilities. I like the "Back to School" signs – cardboard cutouts of shiny red apples and cartoon bookworms suspended above the school supplies. And the "Back to School" clothes cut from heavy fabrics in deep and glowing colours reassuring us that, after a light-weight summer of ice cream pastels, life is about to begin again in earnest. It's a time of hope, and that morning, in spite of everything, I could feel my spirits rise as I ticked off items on Angus's list.

I saw her by accident. When I was walking toward the boys' department, I happened to look up and spot the televisions, a bank of them, different makes and models and sizes. And on the screen of every one of them was the face of Eve Boychuk. Twenty Eves looking out at me through twenty pairs of unreadable eyes.

I walked over and turned the sound up on one of the TVs. She was amazing – no other word for it. She was reeling from the murder of her husband, but she was opening up her fragile and private world to public scrutiny. Tanned and handsome in a simple blue cotton dress, she was leaning forward, telling the interviewer that she wanted her husband's funeral to be something people would remember all their lives. The camera pulled in for a close-up, and there, in the large appliance section of the Bay, Eve was saying that her "dearest wish" was that her husband's body lie in state in the rotunda of the legislature.

I couldn't believe my ears. Twenty Eves coolly rebuffing the interviewer's timid reminder that lying in state was an honour reserved for premiers and lieutenant governors.

"So many people loved Andy," said all the Eves, "that I'm sure the premier wouldn't be mean enough to deny people the chance to come to the city to say good-bye." Oh, she was smooth. For the first time since his party had booted us out of office seven years before, I felt sorry for the baby-faced ex-linebacker who sat behind the big desk in the premier's office. Eve had flummoxed him.

She had, as it turned out, flummoxed us all. When I walked in the front door of our house, Angus barrelled into me. He was on his way to play baseball, he yelled over his shoulder. I made him come inside to check out his new school supplies.

"Awesome," he said, deadpan. Then on the porch he turned. "Mum, Mr. Micklejohn has called about eighty-three times and he sounds like he's going to cry."

When I picked up the telephone to call Dave, he was already on the line. Not a word about the coincidence of my trying to call him when he was calling me, not a word of greeting. The man who prided himself on taking care of details was starting to crumble. There was no preamble, just, "Jo, something's going on with Eve. I thought she was going to leave everything to me, then this morning, before I'd even had time for my morning ablutions, she was on the phone giving me directions about the funeral. She is intruding in everything from the choice of pallbearers to the food at the reception. 'No perogies, no cabbage rolls.' That's what she says. Can you imagine? Did you catch her act on television this morning? She is not the woman we thought she was."

"Fun is fun till somebody starts to mutate," I said. "Angus has that written on his science notebook."

"Kids," said Dave. "Anyway, what do you think's up with Eve?"

"I think she's showing us she can play the game, too. I think she's showing us that we underestimated her because she wasn't part of our little circle. And don't forget, she's suffering."

"All of us are suffering, dear. But we're professionals. We know how to do things right. I don't think we should have to restructure Andy's funeral as a confidence-building experience for Eve. However, I don't know what options we have. The frame of mind she's in – who knows what she'd do? I need some guidance here, Jo.

"In that case, my advice is to go along with her. Let her give us some general ideas and tell her we'll work them out. We've got the organization. You saw to that."

At the other end of the phone, I could feel Dave preening. He had a right to.

In the last year of his life, Andy Boychuk had the best organization the province had ever seen, and in large part it was due to Dave Micklejohn. We were as attuned to one another as partners in a trapeze act or a good marriage. We knew one another, and we knew Andy. We loved his strengths, but we also knew his weaknesses, and we worked to make sure no one else did. We all had our reasons for working for Andy Boychuk, and we all had our areas of competence, but the working life of each of us was fuelled by one desire: the need to make our guy look good. So strong was that drive that neither Andy's death nor Eve's intrusions stopped us. In those days before the funeral, we kept on going to the Caucus

Office; we kept on working on plans to make sure our guy looked good. "Man makes plans, and God laughs," said Dave Micklejohn sadly, but we kept on. Planning was a way of thumbing our noses at a universe where a bright and decent man could stand up to give a speech and be murdered before our eyes. And so Dave, who had been, among other things, Andy's advance man, advanced the funeral – making sure that the routes from the legislature to the cathedral would be lined with people but not congested, that the cathedral could handle an overflow, that the women who were preparing the lunch had ovens that heated and refrigerators that cooled – making certain, in short, that the final public event of Andy Boychuk's life didn't blow up in all our faces.

Kelly Sobchuk, who had done itinerary, planned the times and places all of us would be the day of the funeral. Lorraine Bellegarde, who had done correspondence, kept track of the memorial donations and flowers and letters that poured into the office first by hundreds and then thousands. Janice Summers, who had been Andy's principal secretary, made certain that out-of-province VIPs and in-province political powers had hotel rooms and schedules and transportation. And there were a half-dozen more of us working at a half-dozen other jobs efficiently and bleakly.

Every so often a kind of wild gallows humour would erupt. Around five o'clock one steamy afternoon before the funeral, I walked into the offices of the Official Opposition. A bottle of Crown Royal was open on the desk and another was empty in the wastebasket. About five of our people had gathered to hear Lorraine Bellegarde read the mail: a man in Ituna promised to deliver thirty thousand votes for us in the next election if we sent him Andy's clothes, "since I am his identical size and he has no further need for same"; a woman in Stuart Valley had made Andy a pair of slipper socks out of white flannel. She made them, she said, "for all my departeds because I don't like to think of them going over the line with bare feet, but let's call a spade a spade: there's no point in wasting good money on shoes for them." Two men who had seen Eve on television sent proposals of marriage, and one woman who was a cosmetologist from the southwest of the province told Eve she would look ten years younger if she had her hair cut into a "soft bob" and dyed it a colour called Hidden Honey. A stubby sample of human hair – like a paint-brush – was taped to the page. I had a drink and walked out of the building into the heat. I couldn't seem to get into the spirit. There were no more speeches to write, but I couldn't see beyond the day of Andy's funeral. Maybe I didn't want to.

My life between Andy's murder on Sunday afternoon and the Friday morning of his funeral had a shapeless, anarchic quality.

"I'm walking around doing things but none of them seems very real," I said to Dave Micklejohn one sweltering morning when I met him outside the legislature.

"Here," he said, slapping a five-dollar bill into my hand. "Do you want a sense of reality, Jo, dear? Go downtown and get Eve a pair of pantyhose for the funeral – taupe, all nylon, no spandex, cotton crotch, queen size – not, you understand, because our Eve is fat but because she is tall." He was joking, but I went. You didn't have to be a psychiatrist to see that he was close to cracking.

There was no pattern at home, either. The boys didn't go back to school till after Labour Day, and Mieka was to start university in Saskatoon in the middle of September, so our lives were ad hoc, listless, like the lives of people who are stuck in a strange city by an airline strike or bad weather.

Part of the sense of strangeness could, I knew, be traced to the fact that on Tuesday, two days after the murder, the kids and I had moved into the granny flat. It was Peter's idea – a way for us all to get away from the heat.

Our house on Eastlake Avenue was built in 1911, and like all old houses it had dozens of cracks and crannies through which winter and summer air passed freely. Air conditioning would have been a waste there. But the granny flat was another matter.

There was a sprawling double garage behind our house, and the previous owner had had a flat built over it for his mother. It was one large room with a kitchenette and a bathroom. She had allergies, so it was sealed tight as a tomb. With a flick of a switch you could have it cool enough to refrigerate a side of beef or hot enough to slow cook it.

The granny flat had been the place where Ian worked on lectures for his human justice class, and on more than one lazy afternoon, a place where we made love. When he died, I moved in the books and notes for my dissertation. Now it was my office, but for me it was more than that. The granny flat was a place where I could mourn or sit staring into space without fear of worrying the children or of being seen to look like a fool.

When Ian had had his office there, he'd panelled the walls in knotty pine and had bookshelves built along one wall. There was a desk, a good leather chair for the desk, a reclining chair for reading, a brown corduroy couch that made up into a hideaway bed, and that was it. The decorating was fifties *Argosy* magazine, but the room had a cottagey feeling I liked.

The Christmas before Ian died I'd ordered a braided rag rug from Quebec as a surprise. It is a joyful splash of colour in that sombre room. The rug and a wall full of photographs Ian's mother sent me after he was killed are the only changes I've made. The pictures are a chronicle of Ian and his brother, Jack, growing up. I don't know what a grief counsellor would say about the hours I spend standing in front of the pictures, but it helps. There is something comforting about the neat and inevitable progression of those young lives: from babies who stare wide-eyed, then beam as they sit, then walk, to boys who hold dogs and play baseball and ride bikes, to young men, faces suddenly serious under strangely dated haircuts, who hold the arms of girls in billowy dresses, and graduate, and receive awards.

I wonder now if Peter didn't believe we all needed the healing power of those pictures when he suggested we carry our sleeping bags into the cool peace of the granny flat until Andy's funeral. Whatever the reason, we moved. And in those still, hot evenings before the funeral, we turned up the air conditioner, ate ice cream from Bertolucci's and worked hard at doing nothing. The boys watched baseball on the portable TV, and they brought the VCR over so they could watch movies when there wasn't a game. Mieka and I read through a stack of old women's magazines she'd bought at a garage sale.

It seemed in that cool apartment we could, for a few hours, seal ourselves off from the hot world of pain and insanity that surrounded us. And it was in those rooms that I decided to write Andy Boychuk's biography.

It was a decision that almost cost me my life.

It began on the morning of the Taber corn. At around seven o'clock, somebody started pounding on the door. When I opened it, Howard Dowhanuik was standing there. Over his shoulder, Santa style, was a gunny sack of corn.

"Jesus, Jo, I thought you guys were all dead. I just about smashed down the front door of the house, and then I remembered this place. What're you all doing up here, anyway?"

"It's cooler for sleeping."

"Well, it's not going to be for long if we stand here with the door open. Aren't you going to invite me in?"

"Howard, would you like to come in?"

"Yeah, I would, and I'd like some coffee. Look, I brought some corn for breakfast. A guy was setting up a stand at a gas station out on Dewdney. He drove in from Alberta this morning – first Taber corn of the season. Let's get some water boiling. I'm starving. Peter, go over to the house and get a pot. Angus and I'll start husking this. C'mon, c'mon. Let's look alive, everybody."

Laughing and grumbling, we began to look alive. The kids had always liked Howard, and since Ian's death, they seemed to treasure his rough kindnesses. They liked to be with him. So did I.

I made coffee. Howard cooked the corn and it was wonderful, indescribably delicate and sweet. Mieka unearthed a half gallon of peach ice cream and a Mieka cheesecake from the deep-freeze. It was an oddly comforting meal, and after Howard left to go to the legislature, I poured myself another cup of coffee and sat back in the reclining chair.

The room was filled with sunshine and the sweet smell of corn and butter. The boys were playing canasta – that summer they'd exhausted the possibilities of every card game but that one. Mieka, barefoot and in her cotton nightie, was sitting in the window seat, a stack of *Ladies' Home Journal*s and *Chatelaine*s beside her. It was a moment of rare peace.

Mieka's glasses were balanced at the end of her nose. Suddenly she looked over them at me.

"Mum, did you know Margaret Trudeau made her own wedding dress?"

"Good Lord, Mieka, how old is that magazine?"

She flipped it closed and looked at the cover. "June 1971 – five months before I was born."

"Yeah, I remember when you were born, and I also remember that dress. It was a caftan, white, of course, and he had a rose in his lapel. She was so beautiful. Livvy Scobey, who was our MP then, told me Margaret went all over Ottawa talking about how she made all her own clothes. The seams were all crooked and the hems were coming down, Livvy said, but no one had the heart to say anything. Margaret was so young and pretty and, of course, according to Livvy, everyone just felt so sorry for her being married to 'that man.' You know, all the years they were both in Ottawa, Livvy could never bring herself to say his name."

"Oh, Mummy, you guys are awful."

"Not me, Mieka. I thought he *was* terrific. He was terrific. At least, he was terrifically interesting. I suppose now that you're grown up and going to university, I can tell you this. The first time I ever voted, I voted for him."

Mieka twirled her glasses and grinned. "Oh, no. I was counting on you getting a nice cushy job when we get to be government again. But with that kind of skeleton in your closet, I don't know . . . Of course, you do have friends in high places."

"I'm not sure about that any more, Mieka. I'm not so sure about that at all." Suddenly the golden morning was edged in black. I swallowed hard. "Pitch me one of your magazines, would you?"

But she didn't pitch the magazine. She brought it over with a hug. "Are you going to be all right, Mummy?" I hugged her back, but I didn't say anything. I didn't trust my voice; besides, I didn't know the answer.

The magazine she'd brought me had a picture of a very young Natalie Wood on the cover, and inside was a memoir of JFK. The date on the cover was February 1964, a time before the truth had made its cruel revision of Camelot. The article was uncritical and sentimental, and it brought a flood of memories: a grey November day in Toronto, coming out of political science class in the Sidney Smith building and someone saying Kennedy'd been shot and someone else saying they'd shot Johnson, too. Then numbness – walking across Queen's Park with a boy from my class, both of us crying, plodding our way through sodden leaves while old newspapers whipped wetly at our ankles. Then a pub on Yonge Street that smelled of urine but didn't check ID too carefully, and sitting at a table in the back near the television and drinking and drinking but never getting drunk. After that, a weekend of flickering black and white images on a television that had come from my grandmother's basement. The vertical was stuck so you always had the top half of the picture on the bottom and the bottom on the top. It had seemed a reasonable enough way to watch what happened in the next few days. Now there was another loss, and I wasn't eighteen any more.

It would be nice to say that the memoir of Kennedy I read that day in the granny flat inspired me to write about Andy. It would be nice, but it wouldn't be true. The decision to write about Andy's life and death came out of a need more jagged and more complex than nostalgia. I was at risk, and I knew it. If I was going to be safe again, I had to prove somehow that life, life with a capital *L*, was a coherent narrative with a beginning, a middle and an end. Somehow I convinced myself that if I understood Andy's life, I could make sense of his death. I had already lost a husband to the abyss. I couldn't lose Andy, too. There had to be logic there – cause and effect. The alternative was unthinkable. And so even before my friend was buried, I was deep in the puzzle of his life.

CHAPTER

6

Andy's funeral was Friday, September 2, in the morning, so people could get away for the Labour Day weekend. "No point," said Dave Micklejohn, "in having it later in the day and ticking people off. Next week they'll be over their grief and all they'll remember is that Andy's funeral loused up the last long weekend of summer." He was right, of course, and we all agreed. But when the telephone rang that morning in the granny flat, I was disoriented. For one thing, it was still dark. I propped myself up on my elbow and grabbed the receiver. Dave Micklejohn was on the other end.

"Wake up, dear. It's show time!"

I looked out the window. "Dave, it's the middle of the night. It's still dark out there."

"Look again, Jo. It's seven a.m. That dark you see is a rainstorm. It's coming down in sheets."

As Dave talked, I got up, picked up the phone and walked to the window. The sky was the colour of pewter, and the rain really was coming down in sheets. There were already pools of standing water in the backyard, and my sad, stunted tomato plants had been flattened.

"Dave, the sky's falling in. What are we going to do?"

"Well, Henny Penny, when it's a funeral you're putting on, it's a little hard to give people a rain check and call it off. Did Kelly get the marching orders to you? You know where you're supposed to be and when?"

"They're right on top of the suit I'm going to wear. Don't worry, I'll be all right. And Dave, I'll buy you a drink afterward."

His voice sounded very far away and old. "There isn't enough liquor in the whole world to help with this. Damn it, Jo, I had such hopes for him . . ."

The receiver clicked down, and I was standing in the still, dark room listening to the sounds of my children sleeping.

I flicked on the coffee machine, walked into the bathroom and stepped under the shower. In an hour and a half the front doors of the legislature would be closed to the public. Twenty minutes after that a limousine would pick me up and take Eve and me to the legislature for her private good-byes to her husband. Why Eve had chosen me for this painful and intimate duty was a mystery, but Eve was full of mysteries. She had asked, and I had agreed. So we two widows would accompany Andy's body from the legislature to Little Flower Cathedral for the funeral mass then to a reception at the parish hall (catered, I had noticed on Kelly's marching orders, by the ladies of St. Basil's Ukrainian Catholic Church – one in the eye for Eve there; I'd bet my last dollar there would be perogies on that table) and finally to Wolf River for a private burial.

I towelled off, put on a robe and poured a cup of coffee, then looked through the rain across the yard to our house. From this angle, it always looked big and foreign. Upstairs on my bed was my outfit for the funeral, my "sad rags," Mieka had said with a small smile when I showed them to her. But she approved. A creamy silk Alfred Sung suit that I'd bought from the "Reduced to Clear" rack at Drache's, a shiny, cream-coloured Italian straw bag and a pair of leather pumps, miraculously the right colour and on sale. I had some good gold jewellery Ian had given me over the years, and the night before, when I tried everything on, I was pleased with how put together I looked. But today the thought of getting dressed or even leaving the granny flat filled me with an exhaustion so complete I wanted to sink down in the nest of sleeping bags with my children and drift back to sleep. I was tired of being responsible. I was tired of being a grown-up. I wanted out. The rain continued to fall. The yard would be muddy under my bare feet. But part of being a grown-up is knowing that most of the time there aren't too many options. I pulled my robe tight around me, whispered to Peter to remember the dogs and went down the stairs that led to the rainy, pain-filled world.

When the limo from the funeral home pulled up outside my house, I was waiting. The undertaker, a sad-faced young man in a hot-looking wool suit, ran up the walk with a big, black umbrella to shield me. When I slid into the limo, the Alfred Sung was still bandbox fresh. Eve was already in the car. Surprisingly, she was dressed in green, a beautifully cut suit the colour of a new leaf.

She looked my outfit over thoughtfully. "Maybe white would have been better," she said, "but green is supposed to raise the vibrations of the body above the vibrations of pain." She tried to smile. "I don't think it's working." Then without another word, she leaned forward, tapped the driver on the shoulder and told him to go.

The rain was lashing the windows so hard that all I could see was the soft fuzz of the streetlights, still lit although it was almost nine o'clock. The limo was as quiet and set apart as the confessional.

"I like the rain," Eve said, as much, I think, to herself as to me. "It rained on my wedding day, too. Do you know what my mother-in-law said?" She switched to a burlesque Eastern European accent. "'Rain good. Means lotsa babies, lotsa babies for Andrue.' Oh, God." She laughed then choked. "Lotsa babies."

"Eve." I reached out to her, but she pulled away from me and pressed her face to the window.

We'd pulled into the circular drive in front of the legislature. Ahead of us, gleaming whitely in the powerful bank of lights that illuminated the entrance to the legislature, was the hearse that had come to pick up Andy.

No people – just that silvery hearse and the empty stairs in the rain. All week, from early morning till mid-evening, the stairs had been choked with people. The line, patient and endless, had stretched down Legislative Drive, past the banks of marigolds and zinnias fading in the baking heat, out onto Albert Street. Each time I went to the Caucus Office, I walked beside the line. I was amazed at how many faces I recognized. People I'd seen at party potlucks or rallies or picnics – people who, year after year, paid for their memberships and made a pan of brownies for a meeting or brought their roaster full of cabbage rolls for a dance and felt as connected to the party as any cabinet minister. They were the people who defended the party to their neighbours and tore it apart at conventions. Political people sometimes call them the foot soldiers. The soldiers were at home this morning getting ready for the funeral, and Eve and I were going to be alone with the leader.

When I looked at those empty stone stairs I felt a spasm of pain as acute as a blow from a fist. I thought of all the times I'd seen Andy, always late, pulling on his jacket, bounding up the stairs to get to the House. And now he was lying in a box in that building, and it was over, and I'd never see him again. I couldn't move. I sat there and let the sense of loss wash over me.

Eve had already climbed out of the limo when the man from the funeral home discreetly tapped at my window. All the way up the stairs he and his colleagues dodged around us with their black umbrellas, trying to keep us dry.

When we opened the doors and stepped into the warmth of the building, everything was still. The premier, in response to one of Eve's televised pleas, had given everyone who worked in the building the day off. Without the knots of tourists and the click of heels on the marble halls, the building was alien, like a house after a family comes back from a long holiday. Until that moment, I hadn't realized how much that building was home for me.

Andy was in the rotunda. There were pots of marigolds and chrysanthemums banked along the far wall, and their smell, acrid and earthy, was reassuringly familiar – a smell to come home to on a wet September day. Except for a commissionaire sitting in the corner reading a newspaper, Andy was alone. His casket was oak, and it gleamed warm and golden like the woodwork around it. The top half was covered with the provincial flag, bright yellow and green with an orange prairie lily blooming at its centre. At the foot of the coffin was a spray of prairie lilies. Three years before, when Ian died, I had counted the panels of the disciples in the altar behind his coffin, and I had been able to shut out reality for a while. But there was nowhere safe to look here. The staircase to the left led up to the opposition offices – our offices. The one to the right was the one Andy and the kids would sit on for pictures when a school group from our constituency came to meet their MLA. He used to do a nice thing with them: after the pictures and refreshments, he'd take them outside and show them how they could use a paper and pencil to make rubbings of the fossils embedded in the limestone walls of the legislature. He had been a good man.

A good man, but not a perfect one. He was reluctant to offend, to make enemies. He didn't want to be the bad guy. Often, too often, when the hard decision was made, one of us was left to enforce it. It was a serious flaw in a human being and a worse one in a politician, but death seems to bring a moratorium on critical thought – at least for a little while. I sat staring at the casket gleaming dully in the soft light. After a while, a terrible sob cut through the silence. I was surprised to realize that the cry was my own.

For me, Andy Boychuk had two funerals. There was the one I went to with the chief mourners, Eve Boychuk and her son, Carey, an event so painfully emotional that it will always exist for me in jagged and surprising flashes of memory. And there is the funeral on videotape I saw rerun many times on television, a coherent ceremony in which all of us seem to move through our parts with a grim composure. On that day, more than most, there was a gap between perception and reality – between the way things seemed to me at the time and the way they were.

Double vision. What the camera shows first is a sullen sky and a street that, except for the police van on the north side, is empty. The white hearse, shiny with rain, and the mourners' car, also white, arrive at the cathedral. Eve and I walk behind as the men from the funeral home carry the casket up the endless stairs. Two women alone, one in white, one in green. Incongruously, there is indoor-outdoor carpeting on the cathedral steps. It is sodden with rain. The honorary pallbearers are inside and dry; the working pallbearers must climb those endless steps slick with water, and the load they carry is a heavy one. I can hear them talking to one another under their breath.

"Shit, I almost fell."

"Watch that one."

"Have you got him?"

Later, I learn that they are not from the funeral home; they are city cops. Eve and I plod after them, the water squishing under our shoes. The camera shows none of this.

When the door to the vestibule is opened, a gust of wind comes out of nowhere and sweeps us inside. Roma Boychuk is there – all in black, of course. She is with an older man, a distant cousin, we learn later. She and her daughter-in-law do not speak. The casket is placed on its carrier, and we stand behind it, waiting. None of this is televised. Instead, the camera picks up the priest and the servers as they process down the middle aisle to meet us. I recognize Father Ulysses Tilley – Mickey to his friends. I'm glad he's the one. He would never have voted for us in a thousand years, but Andy liked him, and I did, too. Across the coffin, Mickey Tilley smiles at me and begins.

"The grace and peace of God our Father and the Lord Jesus Christ be with you."

The casket is sprinkled with holy water. Mickey Tilley has a good voice, an actor's voice that projects without strain. "I bless the body of Andrue with holy water that recalls his baptism." On television, Eve is magnificent, chin high, grey hair coiled regally under the lace mantilla, spine ramrod straight, gloved hands smartly at her sides, every inch the graceful public widow. But up close, I can see the muscles of her athlete's body tensed for flight. As the white pall is spread over the coffin, Eve begins to tremble.

"Consciousness. Energy," she says under her breath.

Finally, Mickey Tilley turns and Eve and I follow him and the coffin up the centre aisle of the church. As we walk, there is a soft babbling and a swishing sound behind me. Mark Evanson is pushing Carey Boychuk behind us. A surprise, at least to me. About halfway up the aisle Carey begins to cry. When I turn, I see Mark calmly stopping to give Carey a hug of reassurance. Eve marches, head high.

The Mass of Resurrection drags on – the confession, the prayers. Beside me, Eve drums her strong fingers on the prayer book. Legs crossed, she swings the toe of her black pump against the kneeler. It makes a small pucking sound. Every so often, she takes a deep breath and sighs audibly. Behind us Carey babbles, and Mark Evanson's low voice whispers reassurances.

There are three readings from the Bible. The camera pulls in for a tight shot of the readers. Dave Micklejohn, solemn and suddenly old, reads from the Book of Joel ("Your old men shall dream dreams, and your young men shall see visions"); a student lector from the Catholic college, her voice break- ing, reads the Epistle; and Father Mickey Tilley reads, well and movingly, the Gospel ("No one who is alive and has faith in me shall ever die").

When Howard Dowhanuik steps to the lectern to deliver the eulogy, he stands, head bowed, for a heart-stoppingly long time. Finally he lifts his head and looks at the congre- gation. In the half light of the cathedral, his impassive hawk's face with its hooded eyes looks almost Oriental. Later, when he embraces me, there is, beneath the light, citrusy smell of his expensive cologne, the smell of Scotch. Up close his eyes are red with weeping or liquor or both. But on television none of this is apparent, and his voice, when he speaks, is deep and assured – the voice of a man accus- tomed to being listened to, a man worth listening to.

Howard's memories of Andy are warm and personal – stories of law school, of campaigning in forty-below weather, of flying through thunderstorms in tiny private planes and finding six people at the meeting.

Andy is so alive in Howard's stories that the people seem

to forget where they are and the cathedral is filled with laughter. When he is finished, his place is taken by an old man from Sweetgrass Reserve, in Andy's constituency. The man wears a baseball cap, a plaid shirt and work pants. He looks like Jimmy Durante. He takes off his glasses, coughs, closes his eyes and begins to sing the honour song in Cree. His voice is strong and pure – a young man's voice. For the first time, Eve seems to connect with what's going on around her. She leans forward in her pew, and when the man is finished and goes to his seat, Eve turns with frank curiosity to watch him.

After he goes, Eve stares straight ahead, and I can almost feel her breaking. The TV camera shows none of this, of course. Her bearing is regal, and when she turns to embrace her son during the kiss of peace, she looks contained and engaged. She is neither. As the bread and wine are brought forward, Eve lapses into lethargy. When the altar and casket are incensed, she smiles a private smile. She takes no part in the communion, and as Mickey Tilley goes through the post-communion prayer ("O Almighty God, may this sacrifice purify the soul of your servant, Andrue"), she drums her fingers and taps her foot. When Father Tilley says, "Grant that once delivered from his sins, Andrue may receive forgiveness and eternal rest," Eve leans forward, head reverently touching the gloved hands that grip the wooden rail ahead of us. When I lean forward, I can hear her desperately repeating her own prayer. "Consciousness. Energy. Consciousness. Energy."

Finally it is over. "May the angels lead you into paradise." Our little party of mourners follows Andy's casket down the centre aisle of Little Flower Cathedral and into the vestibule. This is where our role in the television version ends. The camera pulls away from us and focuses on the faces of the people in the church.

The cameras missed the best part. At first, everything went smoothly. The pallbearers carried the casket smartly toward the door and waited. Roma Boychuk and her cousin took their place near the casket. Mark Evanson pushed Carey's wheelchair beside Roma and stood with his sweet Christian smile, waiting for whatever the Lord directed. Eve and I stood off to the right by a rack of pamphlets from Serena and the Knights of Columbus, waiting, I thought, to thank Father Tilley. I turned my head for a second, and Eve was gone.

It was simple enough. She had pushed past her husband's coffin, her son and her mother-in-law and slipped out the door. Mark and I followed her, but by the time we got out the door, Eve was headed for the street. The rain had stopped pelting down. It was falling in a soft mist – a gentle rain – and Eve was standing in it in the middle of the cathedral stairs, taking her shoes off. Ten minutes before, hair swept into an elegant French braid, face carved with pain, Eve had been the prototype of graceful suffering.

Not any more. She had ripped off her mantilla, and the French braid had come undone. She had tried to stuff the mantilla into her purse, but the bag wouldn't close and the lacy edges of the mantilla hung over its edges. She stood in her stocking feet, arms outstretched, a fashionable leather pump hooked onto the forefinger of each hand. She yelled something to Mark.

"Mark, I just can't . . . Sorry. Take Carey to Wolf River, and I'll meet you at the cemetery." She turned and ran down the steps and along Thirteenth Street. I looked to see if there were any media people there to witness her performance. For once, we were lucky. They were still inside packing up, getting quotes, making head counts. But Mark and I weren't alone.

Three doors open on the cathedral staircase, and the stairs are broad – I would judge about fifty feet across. Mark and I had come out the west door, and we were standing by the railing on the west side of the top step when a woman came out of the east door.

At the picnic she'd worn a dress that was the colour of cornflowers. She wasn't in blue today. She was in full mourning – expensive black from head to toe. But there was no mistaking the still, perfect profile or the dark auburn hair. She was the woman who had walked with us as we carried Andy's stretcher to the ambulance, who had tried to comfort Roma and who had run when Roma spat in her face. She stood and looked around uncertainly in the soft, misty rain. Then she was joined by a man. He put his arm protectively around her shoulder, and together they walked down the stairs and disappeared around the corner. Beside me, Mark watched with the frank curiosity of a child.

"Who was that lady?" he asked.

"I don't know," I said, "but she was at the picnic when Andy – when Mr. Boychuk died. Her picture was in all the papers, but I don't know who she is. I do know the man, though. That was Dave Micklejohn. Your mum and dad know him from politics. Dave Micklejohn was one of Mr. Boychuk's best friends."

While Mark and I stood and watched Dave Micklejohn and the mystery lady disappear into the parking lot, the camera crews and the news people came out of the church. I knew most of the local news people, and they waved or smiled or said they were sorry. They were a nice enough bunch, but they were young, and Andy's funeral was just one of the day's stories for them. It was time to move to the convention centre to interview delegates from the CLC, or to the teacher's club for a feature about how teachers felt about school beginning on Tuesday. The press thought the show was over. But they were wrong. Act Two was just about to begin.

CHAPTER

7

Because it serves the sprawling inner-city parish of the cathedral, Little Flower Hall is bigger than most. Apart from that, it looks like all church halls. A room as big as a gymnasium and about as warm, lined with stacking chairs and heavy tables with collapsible legs, the kind of tables that can be easily set up for banquets or potlucks. At one end of the hall is a stage; at the other is a large kitchen with a long counter open diner-style to the hall, a cloakroom, and off it the bathrooms. The hall was a place for modest wedding dances and parish fiftieth-wedding anniversaries and occasions like this, except I don't think there had ever been an occasion like this.

The ladies of St. Basil's Ukrainian Catholic Church had, they explained, "gone in with" the ladies of Little Flower to put on the funeral lunch. They had planned for five hundred people to come and go. There were three times that many, and the people came but they did not go. They stayed and stayed and stayed. The ladies did their best. Weaving their way through the crowd, they carried black enamel roasting pans filled with cabbage rolls or perogies or turkeys or hams already sliced in the kitchen, and casseroles of scalloped potatoes and chili and macaroni and cheese. But as soon as the women put down the food, it was gone; and at the end, I noticed platters loaded with an unmistakable brand of fried chicken.

I was standing at the end of a line waiting for a cup of tea when Howard Dowhanuik came up behind me.

"I'd give the next two hours of my life for a drink," he said.

I leaned close and whispered, "I'd give the next two hours of your life for a drink, too."

"Jo, you have a cruel tongue," he said but he smiled.

"Hey, this will cheer you up," I said. "The pie eater is here." I pointed to the corner where a man in a red open-necked shirt and too-big pants held up by suspenders was working away at a dinner plate piled high with pie. "The ladies have already been at me about him. They say he has eaten three whole pies in less than half an hour. That must be his fourth."

Howard turned to look at him. "What did you tell the ladies?"

"I told them their pies must be better than St. John's Norway because the pie eater only ate two there, and he left quite a bit of the second one."

"A very political answer. You sure you won't run for Ian's old seat?"

"Positive. You know, Howard, I'm kind of glad he's here. The pie eater, I mean. He came to all Andy's stuff. Do you think he votes for us?"

"Of course, he votes for us. All the slightly bent ones do, and when we're government, they're all there demanding jobs and justice. Speaking of justice, did you notice all the guys in grey windbreakers trying to look inconspicuous? My God, there were cops all over the place. I talked to the police chief on the way over. They had two cops in every pew during the funeral, and cops in the choir loft filming. That must explain some of the low notes the girls from the abbey hit during the hymns. And there's an unmarked van out front filming the comings and –"

He never finished the sentence. A cabinet minister who had lost his seat in the last election came up and greeted him. Howard sent the man to the dessert table and told him he'd be with him in two minutes. Then he turned to me.

"Jo, I hoped I'd find a quiet minute to tell you this, but no such luck. I'm off to Toronto tonight for a few days. Something's come up. I won't be back till Wednesday – the late flight."

"I'll miss you. Howard, look, why don't you let me pick you up at the airport Wednesday night and bring you back for supper? I can make a pot of chowder, and we can open a bottle of Riesling and catch up on the news. Except it'll have to be an early night. I'm taking Mieka up to Saskatoon on Thursday to get her settled in for school."

Howard turned away for a minute to say hello to an expensively dressed man who looked out of place in the old church hall. "My dentist," said Howard. "Andy's, too, come to think of it. Nice enough guy but a bit of a dandy. Look at that suit. I'll bet it cost him five hundred bucks. Anyway, here's an idea about next week. I have to go up to Saskatoon and do a bit of politicking sometime soon, anyway, and I've got the van. Why don't I drive you and Mieka up? We can get her settled and go somewhere for steaks. I'll buy. Then you can take me down to the river bank and have your way with me in the moonlight."

"Sounds good to me," I said, "especially the part before the moonlight."

He grinned, gave me an awkward hug and walked off to find the cabinet minister.

I was still smiling when someone came up and touched my elbow. I turned, and Soren Eames was standing in front of me. He was all in black, too, but in his turtleneck and beautifully cut cotton slacks, he looked more like an actor than a mourner. I hadn't noticed before what a handsome man he was. But as everybody's grandmother says, "handsome is as handsome does," and, at that moment, "handsome" wasn't doing much for Soren Eames. He looked ill and harried.

"Mrs. Kilbourn, I need your help. Mark Evanson and I were in the cloakroom getting Carey Boychuk into his coat when Mark's mother came in. She wants Mark to go home with them. She says it's important for everyone here to see they're a family. Forgive me, but I think her concern is less personal than political." I could see the pulse beating in his throat. He took a breath and continued. "Anyway, whatever her reasoning, Mark doesn't want to go with her, but, of course, she won't listen to him. There's no way I can get through to her. She's very negative about me. When I saw you, I thought perhaps she might listen to you because you're –"

"A woman?" I asked.

"No," he said, "I thought she might listen to you because now that Andy's gone, Craig Evanson will run for leader again, and your good opinion of him would carry a lot of weight."

"For someone not involved in politics, you know a lot, Mr. Eames."

"I had a good teacher," he said softly.

He looked about as miserable as I felt.

"All right," I said, "I'll give it a try."

Julie had her back to the door, so she didn't see me come into the cloakroom. She was so intent on her son that I don't think it would have mattered if she had. As always, Julie looked impeccable in a dress that she had, no doubt, sewn herself. It was black with a pattern of pale green leaves and white roses. As she pleaded with her son, the roses on her dress shook as if in a summer storm. But the platinum cap of her hair remained perfect – it always did.

Her voice was low. She was trying not to make a scene, but it was an effort. "Mark, please, let me run through it one more time. Slowly. There are some people coming to the house for drinks, and it would help Daddy if you were there. It's just for a couple of hours, but it's important for you to come. People say things if families aren't together at a time like this."

Mark listened quietly, his hands resting on the handles of Carey's wheelchair. He looked perplexed, as if he were trying to work through the possibilities in his mind.

Finally he said, "I'd like to help Daddy, but I have a job. I have to make sure that Carey is okay. He's my responsibility."

When she was at her cruellest, her most cutting, Julie Evanson had a little trick. She would laugh. I was never sure whether her laughter was intended to lessen the sting of her words or to suggest her disdain. At that moment, when she laughed at her son, there was no doubt. She was laughing to show her contempt for him and his life. It was an ugly sound.

"Mark, you don't have a job. You're just a babysitter." She looked quickly at Carey. "You're a babysitter for a halfwit. Do you know how humiliated I was when you walked up the centre aisle of that church today with your little charge? Everybody we know was there. Can't you at least try to make it up to me? Damn it, we're your family. You owe us something, don't you?"

Mark listened quietly, then he said, "No, Mama, I'm sorry. I'm a family man myself, and I have responsibilities. I'm sorry I disappointed you," and he bent forward and gently did up the zipper on Carey Boychuk's raincoat.

"Can I help you with anything, Mark?" I said. Even to my ears, my voice sounded stilted.

Julie wheeled around and looked at me. Then without a word, she walked past me into the hall, and I knew I'd just moved up another notch on Julie Evanson's enemies list.

But when I looked at Julie's son standing quietly and expectantly, I knew there was no time to worry. I took a deep breath, pasted on a smile and said brightly, "So, Mark, do you need some help?"

His face lit up with its sweet born-again smile. "No, we're just fine, Mrs. Kilbourn, thank you." He thought for a moment. "Well, actually, you could help us with one thing." He leaned forward and whispered confidingly, "You can help us find Soren so we can go home."

I found Soren, then, in one of those small moments that seem significant in retrospect, I saw Rick Spenser.

He was standing with his back to the stage and he was being spoken to by an old woman with savagely cut red hair and lipstick that was a bright fuchsia streak across her face. It was Hilda McCourt, Andy's high-school English teacher. Andy had introduced me to her at the picnic. During the tribute-to-Andy part of the program, she'd given a little talk. It hadn't been the usual "I knew he was marked for greatness" stuff. She'd given a good, dry and professional account of Andy's strengths and weaknesses as a student, and I had liked her.

I joined them. "Miss McCourt, I don't know if you remember me, but –"

She cut me short. "My memory is excellent, Mrs. Kilbourn, as I was trying to explain to Mr. Spenser here. I was telling him that some time in the past I met him; he insists I'm wrong."

"You know, Miss McCourt, media people are in our living rooms so often that they do seem like acquaintances." From her look, I knew I'd taken the wrong tack, but I blundered on. "A couple of times I've gone up to someone and felt so certain I knew her. Then she's turned out to be someone I'd seen on television."

Hilda McCourt's brown eyes were bright with anger. "Mrs. Kilbourn, if your thought processes are muddled, you have my sympathy. Mine are not. In future, you'd do well not to ascribe your shortcomings to others. I hope you and Mr. Spenser will excuse me if I find more congenial company." And off she clipped on her perilously high heels, leaving Rick Spenser and me face to face.

What was surprising was how attractive he was. He was undeniably a big man. Even the skilful cut of his beige linen suit didn't disguise that. From hard experience I have learned that television is not kind to people whose features are not well defined, but the camera really did not do Rick Spenser justice. On television he looked cherubic and bland; in person, his face was both less innocent and more interesting. He was, I remembered reading somewhere, forty-three, but he looked younger. There was a boyishness about the way he wore his dark blond hair – parted at the side and slicked down, the way mothers and Ivy League academics slick down hair. He wore round glasses of light tortoiseshell, and his eyes behind the lenses were hazel and knowing.

Most of the men I know are politicians or professors – notoriously lousy dressers both – but I recognized that Rick Spenser dressed with elegance. He was six foot two or so and at least three hundred pounds, but his clothing was just right. He had style. It was a pleasure to look at him and a pleasure to listen to him. He pronounced words the way someone who loves the possibilities of language does. Even that day in the church hall of Little Flower Cathedral with Hilda McCourt's assault still vibrating in the air, Rick Spenser seemed to savour the words he spoke.

"That's twice you've saved my life in five days. I'm in your debt, Mrs. Kilbourn. She really is a formidable person."

"That's what Andy always said. She was his high-school English teacher, and I think that even after he became leader she intimidated him."

"Not one of those sweet old things who invites the class over for tea and cakes on the Bard's birthday?"

"She seems more the three-fingers-of-gin-for-Dorothy-Parker type to me. But Andy thought highly of her. There was some sort of bad patch in high school that she helped him through . . . I'm sorry, Mr. Spenser, I shouldn't be rambling on. How are you? You look great – no cast on your arm, and that bruise on your forehead looks much less angry."

"I'm fine, and Mrs. Kilbourn – Joanne – I'm not good at this sort of thing, so I'll just say it once. I am deeply grateful to you for saving my life." He reached out one tanned and beautifully manicured hand and touched the top of my hand for a split second, then he withdrew it and smiled. "Now let's hear the gossip about Hilda McCourt."

"I haven't got any, really. I just wish I hadn't hurt her."

"Conscience?"

"Partly. And partly something less admirable. I'm mulling over the idea of writing Andy Boychuk's biography and I don't think alienating Hilda McCourt was the smartest way to begin. She knows a lot, I think."

Rick raised an eyebrow. "A biography?" He reached over and picked something off my suit jacket. "Lint," he said, putting it carefully in an ashtray at the end of the table. When he turned to me, I couldn't read the look on his face. "A biography," he repeated. "Not a bad idea. You certainly have a gripping final chapter. And, if memory serves, some other gripping chapters as well. There was an earlier tragedy, wasn't there?"

"You surprise me, Mr. Spenser."

"I do my homework, Mrs. Kilbourn. Now the accident . . . ?" He looked at me expectantly.

"It's public knowledge. It was about ten years ago. Eve Boychuk was driving. They were all in the car, Andy and Eve and their two children. Their daughter was killed instantly. Carey had terrible head injuries. He'll never be capable of living a normal life. Andy was thrown clear. Eve was injured, but she recovered. Well, I guess a mother could never recover from a horror like that. Anyway, she survived . . ."

Standing in the middle of that hot room filled with smells of turkey and coffee and cigarette smoke and people, I suddenly remembered sitting in my kitchen on a sweet spring day and opening the paper and seeing those pictures: the blackened metal of the car, Eve's eyes, dazed like the eyes of an animal caught in a headlight. Andy standing on the side of the road with the two stretchers . . . and something else. In the background, the swoop of the overpass at Belle Plaine.

"That's where the accident was . . ." I had spoken aloud. Rick Spenser was looking at me curiously. "I'm sorry," I said. "Two pieces of a puzzle just clicked together for me."

"I'm glad," he said. "That is, if you wanted them to fit."

"I don't know if I did, but I guess it's always best to know the truth." Eve's eyes dull with pain as the Buick pulled onto the Belle Plaine overpass. "I've tried to believe that we can be in charge of our lives, that . . . we can create miracles." In that close, hot room, I suddenly felt a chill.

"Are you all right, Joanne?" Rick Spenser's face bent close to mine, concerned.

"I'm fine, just . . . I would like to change the subject, though. How long are you staying in the city?"

He sighed. "I'm here till Sunday night. I couldn't get a flight out because of the holiday weekend. The young woman on the phone assured me they always reserve a few seats for those who might need a flight out for compassionate reasons. Apparently the fact that I was suffering from terminal boredom didn't excite her compassion." He looked so woebegone that I fell into what my daughter calls "the mummy mode."

"Why don't you come over and eat with us tomorrow night? I've promised the kids a barbecue, and I am a serious cook."

He brightened. "I accept, but since the promise of dinner tomorrow will bring to three the number of times you've saved my life, I insist on preparing a meal for you. I, too, am a serious cook, Joanne." He raised a finger to silence any protest. "You'll be doing me a service. Truly. It will give me something to do."

"I'm convinced," I said. "You're on. Now, we're in the book. J. Kilbourn on Eastlake. Give me a call when you're ready to shop and I'll pick you up and take you to Piggly Wiggly."

"Piggly Wiggly?" he said, eyebrows raised.

"Piggly Wiggly," I said. "This isn't Ottawa."

He looked at me hard, then he grinned. "You know, all of a sudden, I don't care that this isn't Ottawa. I really am looking forward to tomorrow night, Joanne."

"Yeah," I said, "me, too," and I meant it.

CHAPTER

8

When I got home after the funeral, there was a note from Mieka saying she'd taken the boys for haircuts. I made myself a pot of tea and a plate of toast, stuck a casserole in the oven for the kids and went upstairs to my bedroom. I turned on the radio to listen to the news, but I never heard it. By six o'clock, I was asleep.

I slept fitfully at first, dreaming dreams that in the strange world of the subconscious had their own peculiar logic. I can remember only fragments of one of those dreams. I was at a wedding and I was dancing with Andy. I could smell the odour of almond paste on his breath, and I tried to warn him not to eat any more wedding cake. I knew he was in jeopardy, but he wouldn't listen to me. Then Rick Spenser and I were in my kitchen and he was making little marzipan doves that carried gossamer strands of spun sugar in their beaks. And then Andy was there, but I don't remember the rest. Finally, I fell into a dreamless sleep and I slept deeply and well.

When I woke up, my bedroom was filled with the pale light of early morning. The digital clock on my radio said 6:00 a.m. I had been asleep for twelve hours.

I went downstairs, let the dogs out, made a pot of coffee and turned on the radio. It was, said the voice of the man buried in the windowless basement room of the glass broadcasting building across the park, going to be a beautiful Labour Day weekend. Bright, warm and breezy – perfect weather for late sailing and football and barbecues.

I showered, pulled on some cotton sweatpants and a T-shirt, stuck my head in Peter's room and asked if he wanted to come with me to take the dogs for a walk around the lake.

Of my three children, Peter is the most restful to be with. Mieka is bubbly and witty. When you are with her, you are, like it or not, drawn into the maelstrom of her exuberance. Angus is the one who questions everything. He is dreamy and stubborn and inventive. When he was six, he came back from Good Friday service at our church and lashed together a broom handle and a piece of two by four. Late that afternoon, I walked into our bedroom and saw him standing in front of the full-length mirror, head lolling to one side, arms gripping his cross. "This is how it must have looked," Angus's image in the mirror said to me. Indeed.

Peter is neither exuberant nor stubborn. He is content just to be. He loves sports, animals, and his family in an order that changes constantly. That morning what I needed more than anything was an hour with his quiet goodness.

When he came down, we put the dogs on their leads and headed toward the lake. The city had that lazy holiday feel to it – light traffic, a few joggers, but generally pretty quiet. There was a breeze from the southwest, and for the first time in a long while, the windsock in the marina showed some life. The little waves on the lake flashed in the sun, and as Peter and I walked along the shore we could hear the water lapping against the rocks. In the sky, some geese were trying out a preliminary V, and my son and I turned to one another and said, "Fall's coming" at exactly the same moment.

By the time we turned up the walk in front of our house, I felt healed enough to start the day. I made pancakes as I do every Saturday, then we went to the Lakeshore Club, also as we do every Saturday. Over the years, the boys have gone through every racquet sport imaginable, and Mieka has graduated from Moms and Moppets to high-impact aerobics, but my routine never varies. Every Saturday morning I put on my never-quite-fashionable bathing suit and swim laps. Then I shower, get dressed and take the kids to McDonald's for lunch. The high life.

Rick Spenser turned out to be an accomplished, considerate, no-nonsense cook. If the meal he prepared for us wasn't the best meal I'd ever eaten, it was certainly in the top ten.

He called just before two and asked me to meet him at the fish counter of the Piggly Wiggly. When I arrived ten minutes later, there he was, a striking figure in rough-weave cotton pants and an open-necked shirt the colour of bark cinnamon. Next to him a woman with a print dress pulled too tight over her small, round, pregnant stomach was looking speculatively at a slab of whitefish. An adolescent boy on yellow roller skates glided up to the counter, filled a clear plastic bag with oysters in the shell and skated toward the front of the store. Rick Spenser didn't see either of them. He was wholly absorbed in something he was pointing to inside a closed glass case.

Behind the counter a bored young woman wearing surgical gloves stood holding a fish.

When I touched Rick on the arm, he didn't even turn toward me.

"Good, you're here," he said. "What do you think of that pickerel? This young woman tells me they were caught last night and flown in from the north this morning."

"From the way the eyes are bulging I'd say she's telling

the truth. I think twenty-four hours ago that pickerel was probably swimming in Lac La Ronge planning her new fall wardrobe."

"What?" He looked puzzled.

"I think the fish looks great, Rick."

"Oh, good." He was still distracted. "That's what I thought, too. Now, do your children like pickerel?"

"I don't think anyone's children like pickerel."

He didn't miss a beat. "We'll get them steaks. Children like steaks." He wrote something in a little pocket notebook, then spoke to the woman behind the counter, who was still holding the fish. "We'll take that one and the third one from the left."

While she was wrapping the fish, he handed me his notebook. "See if there's anything you'd like to add." It was a splendid list: chicken livers, cream, butter, nutmeg, watercress, baguettes, pickerel, beef tenderloin, new potatoes, fresh dill, walnut oil, blueberries, and at the bottom in tiny letters, "Does J have a garden?"

"How can you add to perfection?" I said, handing the notebook to him, "and, yes, I have a garden."

For the first time since I'd come into the store, he looked at me. "I hope you're going to like me, Joanne."

It was such an intimate and revealing thing to say that I was taken aback. "Of course, I'm sure I will . . ." We both stood there, embarrassed, until Rick had the wit to get us moving.

"Good, that's settled. Now let's leave the Piggly Wiggly behind and get to your place and start cooking."

From the first, we were easy with one another. When we were taking the grocery sacks out of the trunk I said, "Do you like kids?"

He turned and looked hard at me. "Honestly?"

"Honestly."

"I hate them. They scare me."

"Mine won't."

"Well," he said, sighing, balancing the French bread delicately on top of two bags of groceries, "I'm willing to be convinced."

I guess one of the reasons we fell in together so easily was that we shared two passions: food and politics.

Rick had bought an apron that he unwrapped with great ceremony before we began to cook. It was a huge red-and-white striped affair – a butcher's apron. When I laughed, he produced a duplicate – but in a smaller size – for me.

"Jo, you said you were a serious cook, so I thought perhaps we could cook together." He tied my apron at the back, then scrutinized me closely. "I just can't imagine why these would have been on the clearance table. Now let's have a glass of something cold and get started."

"There's some Carta Blanca in the refrigerator."

"You really are perfect," he said. I could feel my neck colouring with pleasure.

We cooked well together. Rick would run through what he had in mind, then, without even discussing it, each of us took a couple of tasks.

There was one odd note. As we stood with the bowl of chicken livers between us, I realized that the recipe for pâté Rick gave me was my own. Not like mine, but mine to the smallest detail. I'd come up with it when I was pregnant with Mieka and I'd had a problem with anemia. Our doctor had prescribed liver, liver and more liver, and the pâté had been one of the ways I'd come up with to make it tolerable. I could close my eyes still and remember standing in that gloomy kitchen in our house on Avenue B and trying out different combinations of herbs and spices till I'd hit upon thyme and allspice. And I could remember Ian's expression when I'd used the last of his Christmas cognac to moisten the pâté. It had been a wonderful addition, but in those days we saw brandy once a year, so I'd switched to cream and melted butter, cholesterol be damned, and that was the way I made pâté to this day. But here was a man who was almost a stranger, and he had my recipe right down to the last cracked peppercorn.

When I spooned the pâté out of the blender bowl into a round little dish, I said to Rick, "This is terribly deflating. All those years believing this was my own invention. Anyway, I'm glad we made it today – it was one of Andy's favourites."

He broke off a heel of bread, spread it with pâté and handed it to me. "Here's to Andy Boychuk," he said with a smile.

"You need one, too," I said. So I broke off the other heel of bread, spread it with pâté and handed it to him. "Here's to Andy Boychuk. Here's to Andy." And very solemnly, we both ate.

For someone who hated children, Rick was thoughtful and generous with them. While we were cooking, he gave Peter money to get a bag of ice cubes and a case of soft drinks, and he threw the ice into an old washtub on the deck so the drinks would keep cold for the kids during supper. And, perhaps even more telling, just before supper, when Angus came in to say we had an hour, tops, to eat and be at the ball diamond because his game had been rescheduled, Rick accepted Angus's need without question. "Really, Joanne, it's all right. Everything's prepared. We just need to get the coals ready. We five can be full and happy and sitting in the dugout in an hour."

"I don't think Angus's coach would be wild about all of us sitting in the dugout, but I can teach you the terminology when we get there. Are you sure you don't mind? We could feed the kids and eat after they leave, you know."

"And miss your son's performance? Never. Let's have another glass of burgundy and get the steaks on. We can come back for dessert. I think people in Ottawa will be impressed to hear that I went to a Little League game. You know," he said happily, "baseball on Labour Day weekend does have a certain cachet."

And so we went and sat in the bleachers and drank terrible coffee while the baseball mothers around us chanted their litany for their sons: "Come on, Brandon, buzz like a bee . . . You got him . . . Hum, baby, hum . . . Bring it in, Brandon, bring it in!" And the sun slipped down on the horizon and the sky glowed with streaks of pink and peach and purple. And I thought about Andy and how much he would have loved this evening. He would have been down on the field, volunteering to coach third base, yelling for the kids. I could feel the anger gathering. He should have been there. God damn it, he shouldn't be dead. Then the tears started.

Rick didn't say a word, just reached inside his breast pocket, pulled out a new handkerchief and handed it to me. I mopped my eyes and blew my nose.

"Sorry."

"Don't be, Joanne. Don't try to hold on. It's been one hell of a week. Now, look. There's Angus putting that helmet thing on, so he must be going to get another turn . . ."

The evening ended in muted triumph. In his last turn at bat, my son hit one out of the park, but the Gulls still lost thirteen to one. Sort of like winning your poll but losing the election. We ate our blueberry tart by moonlight. It was an evening that seemed to flow. Rick and I sat on the deck with a pot of tea, and the kids drifted in and out of the house. Mieka came out to ask if there were any sheets and pillow cases she could take with her when she went to Saskatoon to start university. Angus came out to talk about owls. Did we know the burrowing owl was smaller than a person's hand? Peter came out to thank Rick for a great meal and to ask me sotto voce if I'd seen his jockstrap. And, in between, Rick and I sat and drank tea and talked. Or rather, I talked.

There was something cathartic about sitting in the dark with someone I barely knew. As Rick said, it had been one hell of a week. From the minute Andy lifted the glass that killed him, I had done what needed to be done. But now Andy was buried in a pretty little Catholic churchyard a few miles outside Wolf River. I had done the best I could for Andy's wife and child. As a party, we would deal collectively with the question of who would be the next leader. Everything had been taken care of. There was nothing left to do. Tomorrow Andy would have been dead a week. It was time, time to give in, time to rage against the dying of the light.

I didn't bother trying to be brave or strong. In all likelihood, I'd never see Rick again, and if I did, he'd know I wasn't a paragon. I could live with that. So I talked about Andy and the book I wanted to write about him, and every rambling, incoherent memory brought a fresh stab of pain and an awareness of loss. But still, a week after his death, there was one area of pain I couldn't touch in front of a stranger. I wasn't ready yet to ask the question that was at the heart of everything: Who had killed Andy Boychuk?

Rick Spenser was a good listener, and when I stopped talking, we didn't say anything for a while. We sat, two people who'd come too close to the lip of the horror that lies at the edge of our rational lives. Finally, Rick touched my arm, and I turned toward him. In the moonlight, he looked – strange words for such a substantial man – delicate and vulnerable. I wanted him to keep touching me. I wanted to touch him. It had been almost three years since my husband's death, and as Rick's hand rested warm and strong against my arm I felt the remembered stirrings of sexual heat. But after a few seconds he took his hand away, and when he spoke it wasn't about passion.

"Joanne, let me help you with this book. You know all the people, and you're here, but I don't think that will be enough for this job. You've been around politics long enough to know how far the biography of a prairie politician will go in this country if there's not a familiar name attached to it. And I can offer you something more concrete than a name on a dust jacket. I'm not without resources, contacts, file footage. A project like this can be easy or it can be difficult. I have access to the kinds of things that can make it easy. Let me help."

I was astounded, and I said so. Finally, I asked the question that needed answering. "Rick, what's in it for you? I know that's crudely worded, but why would you want to be part of this?"

He shrugged. "I'm not sure that I know myself. But I think it has something to do with discharging a debt."

For me, that was exactly the right answer.

"Rick, let's have a glass of brandy and drink to Andy's book, to *our* book. I have a bottle of something really special that Andy bought for my husband the last Christmas Ian was alive. I've been waiting for an occasion, and I think we are occasion enough. Come on. Let's go over to the granny flat and we'll open that bottle."

"Sounds great, but what in God's name is a granny flat?"

"You're looking at it. It's that apartment on top of the garage. I use it for an office." I reached for his arm. "Come on. It's easier to show you than tell you."

He followed me through the dark garden and up the wooden staircase that led to the little balcony outside the door of the flat.

"Should I carry you over the threshold?" he said.

"I don't think it's that kind of collaboration," I said, turning the key in the lock.

When the door opened, we were met by an arctic blast of cold air. I was annoyed at myself.

"Damn, no one's been in here since the morning of the funeral, and the air conditioner's been on high all that time."

"It's certainly efficient," said Rick, rubbing his hands.

"No more than most. I guess this place is just sealed up so tight it seems that way. Anyway, here's the cognac. Look at the label. Andy was always a generous man. And here are the glasses, but let's take our drinks out on the balcony. It's freezing in here."

Rick poured and we stood on that ridiculous little balcony and looked at one another in the moonlight.

"Here's to Andy Boychuk," he said for the second time that evening.

"To Andy and to sane minds and souls that aren't mad," I said, and I sipped and felt the heat of the cognac spread through my veins.

In the morning I picked him up at his hotel and drove him to the airport. He wouldn't let me get out of the car. "An airport is a grim place to say good-bye," he said and he reached out and traced the lines of my cheekbones with his fingertips. When finally he spoke, his voice was husky. "I'll call you tonight."

He did, and he called many nights afterward. The thing to remember about my relationship with Rick Spenser is that he came at the right time in my life.

CHAPTER

9

The word "bittersweet" is not part of my working vocabu-
lary, but that's the word that seemed to hang in the air that
week as my daughter was getting ready to go to university.
From the day she was born I had dreaded the day Mieka
would go away to school, but suddenly, that September, her
going seemed not just inevitable but right.

My relationship with my mother had always been so
uneasy that I'd worried about how I'd be with a daughter.
Mieka made it easy. From the first day she was level and
sunny, and she had grown into a confident and optimistic
woman. She has had her share of sadness and often more
than her share of responsibility. In the months after Ian died,
I had leaned on all the children but, because she was the
oldest, I had leaned on her most. On the black days when I
would awaken so tired and dispirited that all I could do was
turn over in bed and watch the morning light on the wall-
paper, it was Mieka, cheery and practical, who would get
the boys off to school and run in with a cup of coffee for
me before she caught her bus to high school. I'm not proud

of that time, but it's there. And Mieka didn't need a rerun.

. That September was her time to move into a place of her own and cook and go to classes and do laundry and dream dreams. She had genuinely liked Andy, but she was not yet nineteen, and he had been peripheral to her life. She was sad he was dead, and she was sensitive to my grief, but a new part of her life was going to begin in less than a week, and she was bright with joy.

Because I loved her, I was happy for her. But as I stood and watched my daughter earnestly compare guarantees on toaster ovens and look critically at no-iron sheets, it was hard not to feel a sense of loss – not just of her, but of me.

It had been twenty-eight years since I'd carried my suitcase up to the third floor of the house opposite Victoria College at the University of Toronto. And it was a quarter of a century since I'd invited my seminar group in political science to my flat on Charles Street for dinner, and we'd eaten spaghetti and drunk Italian wine out of fat bottles in straw baskets and argued all night about the meaning of *Last Year at Marienbad* and the philosophy of Ayn Rand. That was the year I met Ian. On our first date he took me to dinner at his logic professor's house in north Toronto. The logic professor, who was smug and reputedly brilliant, was in his late thirties. His wife, whose name was Betsy, was twenty-one, like me, but she already had three little children. Her father had been a mathematician at MIT, and the logic professor had married her when she was sixteen, so he could, he said, "help her grow." Besides the children, Betsy had two cocker spaniels. She called one Professor and one Wife.

It was winter but a beautiful starry night, and Ian and I walked home miles along Yonge Street. I held his arm, and even through his heavy winter coat, I felt a sexual charge. I knew that night I wanted to marry him, but not the rest, not

Betsy's hot domestic world of babies and dogs and casseroles
out of the *Good Housekeeping Cookbook*. We would be
different, Ian and I – twin stars, separate and brilliant and
eternal . . . We would be different . . .

And now it was Mieka's time to turn the key of the door
of her first private home, to cook her own suppers for
friends, to make her own choices, and I knew how I would
miss these two: that daughter of mine, that younger me.

That week wasn't all elegiac. Politics, like nature, abhors
a vacuum, and our party had, for ten days, been without a
leader. In politics, you do what you have to do. Once when
our party was in deep financial waters, I went to a funeral
where the best friend of the dead man stood outside the
funeral chapel with a fried-chicken bucket and took up a col-
lection for the party. No one was shocked. Even the widow
wrote him a handsome cheque before she left for the cemetery. Life goes on.

I was not surprised that the person who came to ask my
support was Craig Evanson – "that floppy man," Peter had
called him once when he was little, and in our family, the
name stuck.

Craig Evanson *was* a floppy man. Tall and shambling, his
body was as loose-limbed as his wife's was clockwork tight.
I had always liked Craig, and on Wednesday morning, when I
came to the door, barefoot and without makeup, and saw
him kneeling there talking to my dogs through the screen
door, I remembered why.

He was always full of hope, even now when, in my eyes at
least, his life had turned out badly. He had wanted three
things. I knew this because years before when our children
were small, Craig had told me what he wanted. That was the
kind of dopey, ingenuous thing he was always doing. He said
he wanted to be close to his wife and son, to have friends to

talk law with and drink with, and he wanted to serve as the member for Regina–Little Flower till he was sixty-five years old and could retire and write his memoirs. It was, I guess, not much to want from life.

They were modest dreams, but Julie Evanson had undercut them all. Her love for their son, at first so consuming and then so conditional, had driven Mark away in confusion. Her ambition had coarsened Craig's relationship with his friends, and her need to make Craig leader of the party had jeopardized his seat in Little Flower. She had made her husband's name synonymous with all those terms we smirk over: wimpy, spineless, henpecked. She had made him into a joke, but as I saw him with the golden September light behind him, bending to soothe my dogs with his words, it was hard not to feel the old tug of affection.

He was so happy to see me, so grateful to be invited to stay for coffee. And as we sat in the middle of the chaos of Mieka's packing and talked about our children it was like the old easy days. I told him I'd spent a little time with Mark and Lori and had seen their baby, and it was as if someone had thrown a switch inside him. We talked about Mark's gentleness and Lori's beauty and the baby's brightness, and Craig glowed with happiness. Then, suddenly, the switch was shut off.

"You know that Julie thinks Mark has betrayed her," he said.

We sat in awkward silence. Even her name was enough to take the shine from the morning. Finally, he shook himself like an old dog. "Anyway, Jo, I'm here for a reason, and you know what it is. I'm running for leader. If you're committed elsewhere, or you want to wait and see who else announces, that's okay. I just want to be considered."

"You'll be considered." I tried to sound gentle.

"But not for long and not seriously," he said flatly.

"Craig . . ." I tried to find a way to take the sting out of turning him down. "You're such a good constituency man – everybody says you're the best. It's just that you know how tight and how dirty this election's going to be. I think we need someone . . ."

"Smarter." He supplied the word for me.

I didn't say anything.

"God damn it, Jo. After all these years, that hurts. I wish Andy hadn't given that last interview. It just about killed Julie." He looked at his watch. "Well, I should be getting home." He stood up – the floppy man making his exit. "Thanks for the coffee and the talk."

Sad and embarrassed, I walked him to the door. He started to leave, then he turned.

"I can't disappoint her again, Jo."

"I know that, Craig."

"She's given up everything for me," he said simply, then he went down the walk, got in his car and headed home to a marriage that I couldn't even begin to imagine.

The story has a postscript. The next morning, after we finally got everything loaded in Howard's van, I ran into the house to get my sunglasses. The phone was ringing. I was going to leave it. Then I worried that it might be some problem with the boys or maybe with the college kid I'd hired to stay with them while I was in Saskatoon. But it was a woman's voice.

"Don't stand in his way, Jo. Craig might not be tough, but I am." Then her humourless laugh and she hung up. So he had told her.

When I got in the van, Mieka said, "Mummy, you're white as a ghost."

"Nothing, just a nasty telephone call."

"A crank caller?" asked Mieka, all concern.

"No, sweetie. Remember Mark Evanson? Well, it was his mother, Julie." I put on my sunglasses. "I think Julie is about ready to start her own coven."

Mieka smiled, but Howard didn't. "Be careful around her, Jo. She's got a wicked temper."

"I'll be careful, Howard. Now come on, old man, let's get this show on the road."

Mieka, house-proud, didn't want to eat with us. Her new place was a two-storey frame house on Ninth Street. She and her boyfriend had come up earlier in the summer and rented it from a woman who was spending a year in Dublin studying Lady Gregory. It looked perfect to me when we opened the door, and more perfect after we'd spent the afternoon switching furniture around and unpacking Mieka's stuff. But my daughter is not me. She said she wouldn't enjoy dinner when she knew that things "at home" – and she used the word "home" to describe the house on Ninth Street – weren't quite right yet. So she waved Howard and me off, told us to have fun and invited us for a spaghetti dinner the next day before we drove back to Regina.

"So," I said standing on the sidewalk in front of my daughter's new home, "are you ready to take a broken-hearted mother out for dinner?"

"You'll love this place," said Howard.

"I'll bet it has leather menus," I said.

Howard looked off in the distance thoughtfully. "You know, I believe it does."

Howard is not adventurous when it comes to food. Years ago a nouvelle cuisine place opened in town, and Ian and I dragged Howard there between meetings. He'd eaten without complaint, but his despair as he searched the menu for something more substantial than slivers of sole had been palpable. Since then I had let him pick the restaurant, and we always went to places where the beef was cut thick, and the bar Scotch was top of the line.

Tonight, as we drove to the west side, he said, "You'll like this place, Jo. They grow their own vegetables."

"Do they rope their own steers, too?"

Howard snorted. "No wonder Mieka's glad to get rid of you for the evening."

The Hearth did turn out to be a very good restaurant – lots of oak and dark leather and candlelight and a big functioning fireplace, which felt good on a cool September night. The waiter brought the menus, and Howard ordered a double Glenfiddich on the rocks. I ordered vermouth with a twist, and when our drinks arrived, Howard took a long, satisfied pull on his Scotch and settled back in his leather chair.

"Well, how are you doing?" he said.

"Okay, I guess, but I don't want to talk about me, I want to talk about Andy."

"I've got no problem with that."

"You know, the police have that portfolio Andy always used for his speaking notes – the blue leather one with –"

"'Every Ukrainian Mother's Dream' on it in gold." Howard finished the sentence and smiled.

"Millard found a poem in there. It wasn't there earlier, I know, because I checked the speech just before Andy went on the stage. Someone had copied out William Blake's poem 'The Sick Rose' – it's pretty standard stuff, I think, on most freshman English courses. Anyway it was beautifully written in calligraphy – is that redundant? At the top were two letters – initials maybe – A and E, and they were joined by a bunch of little curlicues like the initials of the bride and groom on a wedding invitation. I can't get those initials out of my mind."

Howard finished his drink and put the empty glass carefully on the centre of his coaster.

The waiter came and asked if we were ready to order.

Howard looked at me hopefully. "They are reputed to do a first-rate Chateaubriand here, but it's a dish for two and I'm always a one. Would Chateaubriand be acceptable?"

"Absolutely."

"Well, then, we'll have that and –" he pointed out a bottle of Bordeaux on the wine list "– a half litre of that."

When the waiter left, he turned back to me. "About the initials – what do you make of them?"

"I guess the most obvious assumption is that they're wedding initials – Andy and Eve. But whoever put that poem in the portfolio killed Andy. I'm sure of it. Do you think Eve Boychuk is capable of murder?" It was the first time I'd said the words aloud, and I felt a shiver of apprehension.

We had chosen a table close to the fireplace. The rosy light turned Howard's drink to fire, and cast flickering shadows across his old hawk's face. He looked like a man to talk to about murder.

"I don't know, Jo. I'm not one of those cynics who says that everyone's capable of murder. There's a threshold there that most of us could never cross. But Eve's had such a hell of a life, I just don't know."

The waiter brought our wine. Howard absently gave it his approval, and the waiter filled our glasses. "You know, Jo, I'm glad we're talking about this. It may ruin our dinner, but since Andy died, I've had more than a few ruined dinners. You see, I think if it weren't for me, Andy would never have met Eve."

The salad arrived and Howard brightened. "Now does this meet with your approval? You will note, recognizable chunks of everything, a good garlicky dressing, and they have the wit here to bring your salad before dinner when you're not too loaded to eat it.

"Anyway, back to the beginning, and the beginning was my thirtieth birthday, April 17, 1963. That was the day I arrived in Port Durham, Ontario, and that was the day I met Eve Lorscott."

When he said that name, I felt as if I had lit up a pinball machine – lights and bells everywhere. "You mean Eve is a Lorscott – one of the Lorscotts of the Lorscott case? I remember it from when I was at U of T, but how come no one ever told me it was Eve?"

Howard speared a piece of tomato and smiled. "Because, my friend, it was none of your business. Really, Jo, it was no one's business. After all, Eve hadn't committed a crime, and she had come out here to make a new beginning, so what was to be gained?

"Anyway, on April 17, I arrived in Port Durham, and for a Ukrainian boy from Indian Head it was like landing on the other side of the moon. Two days before, Ray Lewis had called me from Toronto. He was my prof at the law school in Saskatoon, and he'd followed my career a little so he knew that I'd made a bit of a specialty of the laws governing the insane. Not a bad preparation for politics, come to think of it. Anyway, Ray called and said he had a case that he thought I could be a real help with and, in the process, make a name for myself in the east. It seemed like a hell of a great idea at the time.

"Anyway, I was on the first plane out. Ray picked me up at the airport and drove me to Port Durham. You know, Jo, I'll remember that drive till the day I die." He sipped his wine and smiled. "Rural Ontario on an April day. It's hard to believe the same God that made the prairie made those gentle hills and the little rivers and the ditches filled with wildflowers. And those farms –" he shook his head in disbelief. "All those farms with the new paint on the barns and the fuzzy sheep and fenced-in fields – they looked like something you'd give a kid to play with. We got into Port

Durham around noon – pretty little place, have you ever been there, Jo?"

"Once, for a weekend with a friend from school."

"Well, Ray took me to the hotel for lunch and filled me in on what I could expect to find at the Lorscott house. Tudor Lorscott, the father, was in Port Durham Hospital. He was badly hacked around the face, neck and groin, but he was going to live. His wife, Madeline, had lost four fingers on the left hand when she tried to stop the attack. The fingers were gone – kaput – but she would be released from hospital later in the week. Nancy Lorscott, the daughter who had, as the papers said, 'wielded the axe,' was in the hospital ward of the Port Durham Correctional Centre, a two-years-less-a-day provincial jail, which also served as a remand centre. Nancy was crazy as a bedbug but physically okay. Eve Lorscott, the younger daughter, the one who had called Ray and asked him to handle things, was waiting for us at the house.

"The 'house' – Ray tossed that word off so casually, but it was wholly inadequate. I was thirty years old but I had never been in a rich man's house – God, Jo, that house made you see why people get the hots for money."

I smiled. Howard had, since I'd known him, lived well, but he always talked as if he had to return his pop bottles to pay for his next meal.

Howard caught my smile and grinned. "I know, I know, Jo, but you should have seen the Lorscott place – another order of things altogether. The house was a beauty – clapboard, I guess, and painted a shade of grey that looked sometimes grey and sometimes – what's that shade of light purple?"

"Lavender?"

"Yeah, lavender. And lilacs. The lilacs were everywhere – great masses of them all around the house – white and purply pink and . . ." He smiled. "Lavender. Gentle – a gentle house for gentle people, but a week before in this gentle house, the twenty-five-year-old daughter had tried to hack her old man's head and nuts off with an ax and, when Mum tried to stop her, had chopped off Mum's fingers."

"Oh, God, Howard, no."

"We rang the bell and, as we were standing there in the sunshine waiting, Ray Lewis said something I've repeated to myself a thousand times. 'Don't let the splendour get to you, kid; when they're scared, they dirty their drawers just like the rest of us.' Words to live by, I guess, but when I stepped into that front hallway, it was hard to believe anybody ever dirtied anything around there. Marty and I had just bought our first house – it was about three blocks from Mieka's new place, close to the Catholic school, of course, for Marty. Anyway, we were fixing it up and we thought it was really special, but next to the Lorscott place it was pathetic – a real dump.

"The housekeeper walked us down a hall as long as a bowling alley. The walls on both sides were hung with discreet pictures of the family – the ancestral line, I guess. I was feeling more and more like the dumb bohunk from the sticks, when I saw yellow police tape blocking off the entrance to a room with a big desk and a globe and a lot of books – the old man's office – the scene, as we say, of the crime. But the housekeeper just marched us right on by and at the end of the hall, she opened a door and we were in the sunroom – the atrium, she called it. In the centre of the room was a bunch of wicker furniture, some chairs with flowery cushions and a round table. Sitting there waiting, as sweet as a little girl at a birthday party, was Eve.

"And here," he said, "is our dinner. Do I get to pick the restaurant from now on?"

"Till the day we die," I said. "That is a beautiful piece of meat."

The Chateaubriand was nicely charred on the outside, pink inside and covered in a good Béarnaise sauce made with fresh tarragon. The waiter sliced the beef and arranged it and our vegetables well and without fuss on oval pewter plates.

"You know, whatever you want to say about Eve, and over the years we've all said plenty, she is a beauty. That day she was beautiful enough to stop your heart. She must have been about twenty, and her hair was still black. It didn't turn grey until after the car accident. She wore it kind of fluffed out the way women did in 1963. The housekeeper – Mrs. Cartwright – God, Jo, half the time I can't remember where I parked the car, but I can remember the name of a house-keeper I met for maybe three minutes more than twenty-five years ago. Anyway, Mrs. Cartwright brought us our scones and tea, and everything was very civilized. Eve was cool as a cucumber, pouring the tea, passing the butter, all that stuff, and she told us the history of the house and then, in that same flat little voice, she told us what happened that night."

"How did she deal with it?"

"She made one hell of a witness – every detail, no stum-bling, no hysteria. She even put in all the disclaimers, 'and then I believe my sister said,' and, 'then, to the best of my recollection, my father moved rapidly toward the window.' Anyway, she told her little story, and it wasn't very nice. Her sister alleged, to use Eve's word, that the old man had made improper advances to her – Eve's words again – from the time she was a little kid and now she couldn't hold her head up and then, so help me, Jo, Eve kind of giggled the way you do when you're getting near the punch line, and said, 'My sister said if she couldn't hold her head up, my father shouldn't be allowed to, either, so she took this axe and started whacking at his head and his private parts.' Then she laughed, and I swear, Jo, she was surprised when we didn't join in.

"Anyway, apparently when the mother tried to stop Sister Nancy, Sister Nancy chopped her through the fingers."

I swallowed the rest of my wine and filled our glasses. "And Eve saw it all?"

Howard was grim. "And Eve saw it all, but here's the kicker, Jo. She wouldn't let us use any of it. She said, 'Now you know the truth, and that should help you arrange' – that was her word, 'arrange' – 'what they tell you. But what you've heard here must not go out of this room,' and she walked out and left us sitting there, the hired help smelling the pretty flowers."

Howard speared the last of his steak, and the waiter came to remove our plates. Howard asked him to bring us both coffee and B&B, and sat back contentedly.

I was on the edge of my seat. "Well, what happened?"

"Not much. Ray and I tried every tack we could think of, but Eve wouldn't testify. Mum and Pop and Sister Nancy lied through their teeth – said it was an accident, some sort of aberration. Little Nancy had always been delicate, blah, blah, blah, so that was that. Nancy went to a toney sanitarium in upper New York State – the kind of place where you can stash your resident psycho if you've got the money. The Americans are better at understanding that kind of thing than we are. And Mum and Pop went back to the house at the lake and lived happily ever after. Every so often I still see Old Man Lorscott's picture in the *Globe* – appointed to the board of this or that." He shook his head, then looked up. "Jo, do you want to split a piece of cheesecake? They make one with Amaretto here that you would really love."

I groaned. "Howard, if we have cheesecake, that will push the number of calories for this meal into six figures."

"Jo, forget the calories tonight. Yes or no?"

"Yes – now tell me, how did Eve get here?"

"She just came. After the trial I got a cheque signed by Eve

Lorscott. If I hadn't needed the money so much for the new house, I would have framed it, but it was a generous cheque and Marty wanted to fence in the backyard. Anyway, I'd see Ray Lewis at bar association meetings, and the first few times I saw him we'd talk about the Lorscotts and then, you know how it is, we both had other stories. Anyway, the Lorscotts kind of drifted to the back of my mind.

"Then one day, about five years later – I think it must have been 1968, or one of those years when the world was blowing up, I was walking across the university campus. There was a demonstration against the war in Vietnam, and there, marching along together, were Eve Lorscott and Andy Boychuk. They were a striking couple. Andy looked pretty much the way he did when you knew him – longer hair, of course. Eve in 1968 was very different from the woman we know now. Remember how the kids then used to talk about being free? Well, that day Eve was free. She wasn't the wound-up little doll Ray Lewis and I had met in Port Durham, and she wasn't the fragile woman you and I know. She was free and she was very beautiful.

"Andy was in my criminal law class. He waved, came over and introduced Eve. You know, Eve always surprises. I was prepared to play dumb and ignore the connection, but Eve – cool as you please – slipped her hand into mine and said, 'Howard and I have met. In fact, he's the reason I'm here. After all that trouble with Nancy, I needed a place to escape to – and I was sitting there one day, and Saskatchewan just came to mind. I mean whoever would pursue anybody here?' And she beamed and put her arm around Andy's waist and lay her head on his shoulder. They were such a striking couple. Then they got married, and you know the rest. That awful accident . . ." He picked up the little lamp that had a candle burning inside it. "As I said, Eve Boychuk has had one hell of a life."

"I wonder how she survived," I said.

"That's a question for a shrink or a philosopher, Jo. I'm just a washed-up politician; I don't have answers for questions like that."

I reached across the table and squeezed his hand. "Not so washed-up," I said.

The Amaretto cheesecake was as heavenly as Howard promised it would be, but he was subdued as we ate it. When we finished, he leaned across the table and looked at me hard.

"Jo, I guess everyone at that picnic is a suspect. Did you have any special reason for asking about Eve?"

"No – at least no more reason to ask about her than about any of us. And don't forget, there were five thousand people there. I know the police have got the big push on, and I keep hoping I'm going to turn on the radio and hear they've arrested some poor crazy person who killed Andy because he got out of the wrong side of the bed that morning or because God told him to. But we have to face facts. It's been eleven days now, and the police are still coming up empty. What if it's not some anonymous psycho? What if it's somebody we know? What if it's one of us?"

Howard tossed back the last of his drink. "I don't know, Jo. Do you remember that TV show that used to open with the police sergeant saying, 'Be careful out there'? I guess that's all you can do. Be careful."

Mieka, perfect Mieka, had unpacked my suitcase and hung up my skirt and blouse for the next day. She had even thrown my nightgown and robe on the bed.

"Where's the chocolate on my pillow?" I asked.

"You don't deserve one. I'll bet you and Howard ate and drank everything that wasn't nailed down. Where is he, by the way? I thought he might come in for tea."

"Not tonight, little girl. He was a bit tired and I have to get up early tomorrow because I'm going out to see Roma Boychuk."

"Andy's mother?" Mieka said. "Well, don't give her a clear shot at you."

"Mieka, what an awful thing to say. And you don't even know her."

"Oh, but I do. One night I'd had it up to here with you nagging at me about my grades, and I complained to Andy. You know what a nice guy he was. Anyway, that night we had a long talk about mothers."

I was surprised. "When was that?"

"After mid-terms when I was in grade eleven. Remember when you told me I'd end up scrubbing toilets at the bus station if I didn't pass chemistry?"

"Well, you did pass chemistry."

"With a fifty-three. Anyway, Andy took your side, of course. Said you guys do nag at us because you love us so much. But in the process of defending mothers collectively, he said some pretty interesting things about his own mother."

"Such as?"

"Such as nothing. It's bedtime. You'll be seeing Andy's mother tomorrow. Howard would say I was prejudicing the witness. But you should know" – and she grinned and bent to kiss me good night – "that there are some mothers who devour their young."

CHAPTER

10

Roma Boychuk still lived in the Junction, on the west side of town, in the house Andy grew up in. The west side is where you go if you want used furniture or real Szechuan or twenty minutes of romance. Farther out, toward the railway station, is the area called the Junction. It's a neighbourhood of onion-domed churches and mom-and-pop grocery stores with names like Molynka's or Federko's. The Junction was, Andy said, a great neighbourhood to grow up in. As I walked along the quiet streets where the leaves on the elm trees were already turning yellow, I tried to imagine Andy running along these sidewalks to school, and I tried to remember what I knew about Roma Boychuk.

It wasn't much. Andy had been born when his mother was forty. His father died just before or just after Andy's birth. I don't remember Andy ever speaking of him. Roma doted on her son. I once handed Andy an article about the disproportionately large number of political leaders who were the favoured children of strong, domineering mothers. I had expected him to laugh, but he hadn't.

"They think they're doing you a favour, you know – all that love. But you spend your whole life trying to keep the love coming. That's why so many politicians are so screwed up – and Jo, the demands . . ." His sentence had trailed off.

The fear of his mother's disapproval was something everybody who worked for Andy had to deal with. He always spoke Ukrainian to his mother, and when our party announced a policy that was at odds with his mother's beliefs, Andy would be on the phone with her for hours. I didn't need to understand Ukrainian to know he was explaining, rationalizing, justifying. He would come from these phone calls shamefaced and telling a joke on himself, but he never stopped calling. Once somebody, I think it was Dave Micklejohn, had come back from Saskatoon raving about how generously Roma had welcomed him into her home. Andy had laughed and said, "Just don't cross her or they'll find you at the bottom of the South Saskatchewan with a crochet hook driven through your heart."

I had the address in my notebook, and Howard had given me directions. I didn't need them. I knew the house at once because I recognized the place next door – the home of the Sawchuks, Roma's arch-enemies. The families had lived next door to one another for sixty years, and they had fought for sixty years.

"Why doesn't somebody move?" I'd asked Andy once.

"And lose their reason for living?" Andy had shrugged. "Jo, if my mother gets a new brooch or if I get my picture in the paper, her pleasure isn't complete until Mrs. Sawchuk – 'that Sawchuk' as my mother calls them all – sees it, and I'll bet it's the same for them. Anyway, the Sawchuks have their revenge. You should see their house."

In truth, the Sawchuks' house was unremarkable except for the colour: a neat, rectangular wooden bungalow painted egg-yolk yellow with green trim. But the lawn in front was spectacular. It had sprouted a bumper crop of lawn ornaments. White plastic lambs whose innards had been hollowed out to hold red geraniums; scale models of wooden airplanes with propellers that hummed in the wind; painted plywood cutouts of little German boys with round pink cheeks and stiff wooden lederhosen; a family of wooden ducks, a mother and the babies; a pair of plywood Percherons that pulled a wooden cart full of petunias past a miniature – perfect in every way – of the egg-yolk and green Sawchuk bungalow.

Compared to the Sawchuks', Roma Boychuk's place, 82 Joicey Street, was a model of restraint. The house was white with red trim. On each side of the walk to the front door was a half an oil barrel painted white. The raw edges of the barrels had been smoothed into scallops, and the barrels were filled with bright red geraniums.

I had told Roma I would be there by ten. It was five past when I knocked on the door, and she was waiting for me. When I called I had told her I was working on a book about Andy's life; she had been interested and pleased.

Less than two weeks before, her only child had died and I expected full mourning, but she was dressed for company. She was a stocky little woman but not fat, and she dressed with the care of a woman who has, all her life, been proud of her looks. Her black skirt was cut carefully to slim the line of her hips, and she had a brooch of china pansies at the neck of her lacy white blouse. Her hair was mauve-rinsed, and she had braided it and twisted it into two knots, one at the nape of her neck and one just above it. She had secured the knots with flowered combs that looked vaguely Japanese. Her cheek, when she placed it in front of my lips for a kiss, was smooth and unlined. "Vaseline every night," Andy told me once when he saw me buying some expensive night cream. "That's what my mother uses, and she has skin like a baby. Of course, she goes to bed looking like a channel swimmer, but she hasn't slept with anyone in forty years, so . . ." And he'd shrugged and laughed.

Roma didn't smell like a channel swimmer; she smelled pleasantly of something masculine and familiar.

"You smell good," I said.

"Old Spice," she said, "the only thing that covers the onions. I make shishliki this morning. I give you some to take when you go." She gestured me into the front room – a place of heavy drapes, heavy furniture covered in plastic slip-covers, and pale, dispirited light. "You'll have coffee," she said, then, brushing aside my offer to help, she left me alone in that gloomy room.

Through the door I could see the kitchen – a room flooded with sunlight and potted plants and good smells. If I had been a friend, I would have sat at the kitchen table and sipped coffee from a thick mug and talked to Roma as she sliced cabbage for soup or twisted dough into circles for poppy-seed bread. But I was company and I sat on the stiff plastic, which kept Roma's living room suite as free of spot or blemish as it had been the day the men from Kozan's loaded it onto the truck and delivered it to Joicey Street. When my eyes grew used to the light, I saw that the room was full of pictures. Half were of the Blessed Virgin and half were of Andy.

Most of the pictures of Andy as an adult I had seen before. They had been in campaign literature or newspaper articles and then we replaced them and forgot them. But Roma hadn't forgotten. She had clipped these pictures of her son and framed them and hung them on her wall next to pictures of the Annunciation or the Sacred Heart. There were pictures of Andy as a child – dozens of them. I walked to the wall by the window to look at these more closely. There was Andy at school, a succession of ever larger Andys sitting,

hands folded in front of him, in a series of dim grey classrooms with the pictures of the Pope and the King and Queen
and then the new Queen behind him. There was Andy with
his friends, grinning, face bleached almost into nothingness
by the sun as he stood with his baseball team; Andy sitting
in a canoe, waving at the person who stood behind the
camera on the shore of some forgotten northern lake.

There were none of Eve and Andy. None of Eve and Andy
and their children.

"You like? I get more." Roma's voice behind me, star-
tlingly loud and strong. She set the tray she was carrying on
a wooden tea wagon, disappeared and was back almost
immediately with a box of photo albums. The one on top
had a cover of palest powder-blue satin. In the centre was an
oval indentation with a picture of a tired-looking Jesus surrounded by little children. Across the top of the album in
raised Gothic letters was the legend "My Baptism."

"I get our little lunch while you look at Andrue's pictures
for your book," said Roma as she placed the box on the floor
beside me. Then, magician-like, she fluttered a lace tablecloth out of nowhere, covered the coffee table and began
arranging cups and plates. As I went through the pictures,
Roma moved from kitchen to living room, bringing first a
pot of coffee and cream and sugar, then a plastic lazy Susan
piled high with breads, poppy-seed and zucchini and carrot,
then a tray with butter and cheese and dishes of pickles and
jams and jellies. And finally another plastic lazy Susan, this
one heavy with cookies and squares.

She handed me a dessert plate and a bright paper napkin
that said, "No matter where I serve my guests they seem
to like my kitchen best," poured our coffee and began her
narrative on the albums in the box. She told me about the
pictures in "My Baptism" and "My First Communion,"

then she handed me four fat scrapbooks, each of which was labelled, "My Life in the Church."

"These," she said, "perfect for that book you do on Andrue. Just copy them out."

The scrapbooks were filled with the work Andy had done at school, drawings and poems and essays on subjects like chastity and obedience and piety. *Many* essays on chastity.

"Here," Roma was saying. "Here is the picture for the book – on the front. Andrue with the bishop. This is Andrue's confirmation picture from Saint Athanasius. That bishop dead now, but a good man, very kind and patient with the children."

The bishop did not look kind and patient. He had the bulbous nose and the paunch of a serious drinker. But then pictures often lie.

"You take it," she said. "I have copies. Use it in your book to show Andrue brought up in the church. That baby-murder stuff . . . abortion." She made a spitting sound of derision. "He must have picked it up from that one he married." Again the spitting sound of dismissal. "You write the truth in your book. Andrue did not believe in that stuff. No." And she shoved the confirmation picture in my purse and went to the kitchen for more coffee.

The rest of the morning passed pleasantly enough. Roma wanted to talk about Andy, and I wanted to listen. When I left, she kissed me and gave me an ice cream pail of lamb shishliki for Mieka.

As I started to walk down Joicey Street, the enemy Sawchuk came running after me.

"So how is she?" He stood, blinking in the sunlight, a barrel-chested man with iron-grey hair and a voice that had ordered a hundred thousand packages of smokes. "What do you make of it?"

"It's a very sad thing," I said.

His eyes were bright with spite. "I suppose she's been carrying on like crazy now that the big shot's been killed off." He laughed a wheezing, sucking kind of laugh that touched a nerve in me.

"Mr. Sawchuk, I hope you're never unlucky enough to lose a child – especially your only child."

His face came alive with malice, and I knew immediately that I'd walked into Sawchuk's trap. He wiped his mouth with a handkerchief before he answered me.

"Is that what she told you? That the big shot was her one and only? Next time, ask her about the girl – the one she threw out."

Suddenly the fun seemed to go out of the situation for him. He sounded distracted, as if his focus had shifted somewhere deep inside himself. "Probably dead now, too, or worse. Such a beauty. The old man, the father, he doted on that girl. Every year he made her a skating rink out back. Hours he'd spend, standing in the cold, holding the hose so the ice would always be smooth for her. She would skate and skate. My wife used to stand by the kitchen window and just watch her. She said it was better than the ice show. She's gone, too, now – my wife." The spite had puffed Sawchuk up. Now he looked depleted – small and old.

"Mr. Sawchuk," I said. But I'd lost him. He was somewhere in the past, standing at the kitchen window with his wife, watching the neighbour girl skate.

"Mr. Sawchuk," I said again.

He looked at me, and suddenly his eyes were as blue and untroubled as the September sky. "Elena," he said. "That was the Boychuk girl's name." He turned, and without another word, he walked away – to his fabulous yard and his empty house.

As I stood waiting for the bus, I was confused and off balance. I had known everything about Andy. And yet I hadn't. A sister. Andy had a sister. But he couldn't have known. He would have mentioned it. He couldn't have known.

But how could he not know?

And behind me, sweet with the singsong of the street chant a little girl's voice.

> I am a pretty little Dutch girl
> As pretty as pretty can be,
> And all the boys on Joicey Street
> Are so in love with me.

> My boy friend's name is Tony.
> He lives in Paris, France.
> And all the boys on Joicey Street
> Watch me and Tony dance.

CHAPTER

11

Mieka's spaghetti sauce was lighter than mine, but full of fresh basil and very good. Her boyfriend, Greg, joined us for dinner, and he was deferential to Howard, courtly with me and adoring of Mieka. It was a fine party but, as pleasant and courteous and civilized as we all were, it was apparent that Mieka and Greg wanted to be alone. There was a hum of sexual tension in the air as soon as supper was over, and it wasn't coming from our end of the table. When I announced that Howard and I should leave as soon as we did the dishes, Greg was up in a snap, putting the dishes in the sink with one hand and helping me on with my coat with the other.

Howard and I were on Circle Drive and out of the city when I realized I hadn't said any of the tender and wise things I'd planned for nineteen years. I snuffled a bit when we pulled onto the highway, and Howard looked sharply at me.

"Are you okay, Jo?"

"Fine. It's just everything happened so fast, and I think I've been done out of my big scene. Howard . . . I'm going to miss her so much. I can't imagine going back to that house without her." I could feel my throat closing and the tears gathering in my eyes. I seemed to be doing that a lot lately. The skyline of the city faded behind us; ahead the highway was a ribbon in the darkness. Howard turned on the radio, and we listened to a half-hour program on the problem of gridlock in downtown Toronto.

When the lights from the town of Davidson loomed on the horizon, I caught my breath. Andy and I had gone to a bonspiel there last winter. It was the first time I had ever curled, and I loved it. Andy, in an awful, too-big curling sweater, had volunteered to skip our rink. Standing at the end of the ice, shouting encouragement, he had grinned ruefully when my rocks sailed past him into the wall or, inexplicably, stopped halfway down the ice. A good friend.

And someone had killed him. But who? His wife? Poison is a woman's weapon, the mystery novels say. And there was the poem by Blake with its hint of inner corruption. (Eve turning in the door of Disciples the day after the murder and saying, "None of you knew the first thing about Andy Boychuk.") Most damning, those letters *A* and *E* intertwined like the bride's and groom's initials on a wedding invitation.

We passed a gas station. Howard's profile was thrown into sharp relief, and I thought of his terrible story about Eve Lorscott and her tortured family. I was reeling. There had been, as one of my sons had once said tearfully, "just too much day." I didn't want to think any more.

The sky was black and starless between towns. There wasn't even a farmyard in sight. Howard turned off the radio, and the miles slipped by in silence. Finally, he turned and looked at me.

"Are you up to some news, Jo?"

"No, but don't let that hold you back."

He laughed and reached for my hand. "You really are a nice woman. Anyway, no use beating around the bush. I'm going away for a while. When I was in Toronto last week, that old law-school buddy I mentioned asked me to teach a session in criminal law at Osgoode Hall. It's not a real appointment, just a couple of classes to help out a friend. They hired some hot-shot whiz-kid from Montreal, but at the last minute he got a chance at a TV contract interpreting the law as a background man, whatever the hell that is. Anyway, this came up and I took it."

"But that's wonderful. It'll be a good change for you."

"Yeah, I need to get out of Regina. A big part of it is because Andy's gone. Without him in the picture, the possibilities just don't excite me, but there's more . . ."

"I thought there must be," I said. "Is it Marty?" Two years before, Howard's wife, Marty, had left him and moved to Toronto. He never spoke of it, at least to me, but I'd heard rumours – the kinds of things that always seem to float in the wake of someone else's misfortune.

"Yeah," he said. "It's Marty. She's the good Catholic, but I'm the one with the guilt."

"Do you still love her?"

"I don't know. I don't know if love has anything to do with it. But somehow it doesn't seem right to me to pack up thirty years of marriage and say, 'Well, thanks so much, I've got other plans.'"

"How does Marty feel?"

"She says she has a job she likes. She says she has friends. She says politicians make lousy husbands. She says it won't work unless I change. She says a lot of stuff, but it all boils down to the same thing – she thinks it's over."

"And you don't?"

"I don't know. I think I'm too old to change, but that business about politics is just crap. You and Ian had a good marriage."

"Ian and I had a good marriage because we both lived Ian's life." I was surprised at the anger in my voice, and I was surprised at what I'd said. Until that moment I don't think I'd acknowledged how much everything had been for Ian.

"So that's the way it was." Howard's voice was gentle. "You know, Jo, it never seemed like that from the outside."

"It didn't start out that way."

"How did it start out? All the years I knew you and Ian, I guess I always just thought of you as a unit – the Kilbourns. Maybe Marty's right about me. I am obtuse."

"No more than the rest of us when it comes to understanding what goes on inside other people's marriages. And Ian and I were a unit, so you were right there. It's just that we didn't – I didn't – plan to be part of a unit. Did you ever read D.H. Lawrence?"

"A thousand years ago."

"Well, Ian and I were going to be those fiery twin stars Lawrence talks about, separate and dazzling. And then . . ."

"Ian got into politics," Howard finished for me.

"And I got pregnant. Scratch one star. We were twenty-eight that first election. Mieka was born on E-day, remember?"

Howard laughed. "Sure. I always tell Mieka she showed great wisdom in waiting for the New Jerusalem to be established before she was born."

"It didn't seem like the New Jerusalem to me. Suddenly I was a mother, and I was married to a twenty-eight-year-old who was attorney general of the province and who didn't have a clue about how to run the A-G's office."

"Jo, none of us had a clue about anything. All those kids we ran – we figured the young guys could lose their cherries on that first campaign and the next time out, well, maybe we'd get close, and then, well . . ." He reached over and patted my knee awkwardly. "Do you remember the results coming in that night? Did they bring you a TV into the delivery room?"

"Howard!" I groaned.

"Yeah, I guess not. Anyway, when I watched the results that night I just about dirtied my drawers. My God! First of all to win, and then to win and have nothing but kids to form a government." His voice grew serious. "Ian was always so good, Jo. I can count on one hand the number of times he screwed up when he was A-G. And he was smart enough to keep the constituency stuff humming. Except –" he looked at me quickly "– that was because you were there, wasn't it? I'm sorry, Jo. I should've known that."

"Howard, it was too long ago to feel guilt about, and I'm too old to enjoy making you feel guilty. It just happened. The political stuff came my way by default. I liked it. I was good at it, and it was something I could do while I was having kids. Another thing – it really mattered. It was important work. But Howard, Marty knew that, too. She really did. No matter what she says now. We're all revisionists when it comes to our own lives."

"Tell me, Jo." Howard's words were so quiet, I could barely hear him above the hum of the engine and the swish of the miles passing by. "Tell me how Marty was in the old days."

"Let's see. I guess the first time I saw her was a couple of weeks after the election. It was my first outing after Mieka was born, so of course I brought her along. Do you remember? Somebody had the bright idea that we should go out into the rural areas to show off the new team. A bunch of us went to hell and gone out into the country . . ."

"McCallister Valley," he said. "Remembrance Day. I remember. The year it rained right up until Christmas Eve. Damnedest thing I ever saw. Of course, the opposition made a big thing of it. Charlie Pratt was still leader then and he made one hell of a speech in the House. All about God's anger manifesting itself because the people had turned their backs on the one true party, and about how Charlie and his gang would have to build an ark to save the province – metaphorically, of course. The old bastard . . ." He was laughing.

"Anyway," I said, "you and Marty had been to some formal thing in the city, and she hadn't changed."

"And" – Howard's face softened at the memory – "just before we got to McCallister Valley, our car got stuck in the gumbo, and Marty took off her shoes and stockings, jammed a shoe in each coat pocket and walked barefoot through the mud."

"Ian and I were waiting in the hall," I said, picking up the story, "and someone yelled, 'Here's the premier.' I'd never met you, and my heart stopped. The premier and his wife! They threw open the doors to the Elks' Hall, and there you were and there was Marty with the skirt of her evening gown hiked up to her thighs. She was solid mud from the kneecaps down, but she had such a great smile."

We were both laughing. Howard wiped his eyes. "You should have heard her on the way home in the car – but not a peep out of her at the dinner. I'll give her that. She was always the gracious lady in public. Not like . . ."

"Not like Eve."

"No, not like Eve." His voice had a familiar edge of exasperation.

For a while we reminisced about old times, then Howard turned the radio on. We listened to it and gossiped till Howard pulled up in front of the house on Eastlake Avenue. The place was still standing, and I sighed with relief.

"All's well in Jo's universe?" Howard asked.

"No," I said, "but I'll survive. What flight are you taking tomorrow?"

"The 1:30 – gets you into Toronto in time for the rush hour along the 401 – all the charms of metropolitan life Marty's always talking about."

"Need a lift to the airport?" I said.

"Yeah," Howard said, "that would be nice."

"Well," I said.

"Well," he said, gently mocking.

"Well," I said, "I'd better get in there before the boys start flicking the porch light on and off at us."

Howard reached over and covered my hand with his. In the moonlight his face was silvery grey – like an image on black and white television. "I'm really going to miss you. Ian was a lucky man."

I leaned over and kissed his cheek. The smell of his body was familiar and comforting – Scotch and lemony after-shave. "I'm going to miss you, too, Marty's a lucky woman. Damn it, everybody's leaving me." I grabbed my bag and ran up the stairs before he could see I was crying.

The kids had managed fine. The house was clean enough. The tuna casserole I'd left for dinner the first night was in the refrigerator next to the freezer container of chili I'd left for the second night. There were two pizza boxes and a half-dozen Big Gulp containers in the garbage, but the boys were showered and in bed watching *M*A*S*H* reruns and being civil to one another, so I counted my blessings. I sat on Peter's bed and watched the end of the program with them. When it was over, I filled them in on Mieka's new house, showered and got into my robe. I was careful to look the other way when I passed Mieka's room. I went down-stairs, put on the kettle for tea, changed my mind, pulled out a lemon and some honey and made myself a hot lemon and rum. Just as I poured the hot water into the mug, the phone rang.

Mieka, I thought, or Howard, knowing I was having a hard time. But it wasn't either of them. The voice was male and familiar, but I couldn't place it.

"Joanne, do you use smoked or barbecued salmon in that mousse?"

"Whatever's cheaper."

"What a sensible woman you are. Sorry to call so late, but I'm having people in for breakfast and I'm not a morning person." I still couldn't place that voice. Keep him talking.

"It bakes two hours. You'll be up all night."

"I'm setting the alarm so I can lumber out of bed and grab it out of the oven. Although why I'm going to all this trouble for that preening cow of a minister is beyond me."

That sleepy, intimate voice that curled around words with such affection – "Rick. Rick Spenser. I'm sorry. I just didn't make the connection with your voice for a minute."

"Joanne, I'm the one who should apologize. Damn. I hate people who assume you know who they are. Forgive me for being a narcissistic ass. Let me start again. How was your day?"

"We were on safer ground with the mousse. My day was lousy. I just left my beautiful little girl alone with her new housemate who is also her boyfriend. And Howard Dowhanuik, who is, I guess, my best male friend in the world, just told me he's moving to Toronto to teach a class at Osgoode Hall."

The voice on the other end of the line was suddenly alert and professional. "Is that for public consumption?"

"I don't see why not. Classes start this week, and he's leaving tomorrow. I feel like Little Orphan Annie."

"Then I'm glad I called. I wouldn't dream of trying to fill Mieka's place, but do you think I could try out for temporary status as your best male friend?"

I laughed. "Well, they're not exactly standing in line here."

"I warn you, Joanne. I take my obligations as a friend seriously."

I took Rick at his word, and brought him up to date on everything that had happened since the last time we'd talked. At the end of it all I said, "That business about the sister really threw me. There's something terrible about discovering people's secrets. It's such a violation. If you want out, I'll understand."

"No, no, certainly not." He sounded as if he meant it. "Joanne, if I were there with you, I'd open a vein and become your blood brother, but since I'm in Ottawa, I'll do what our senators do. I'll swear an oath holding onto my testicles."

We both laughed, the balance between us restored. "I think that was the Roman senators, not our guys."

"Well, whoever held onto whatever . . . I, Rick Spenser, do solemnly swear to be friends with Joanne Kilbourn."

"Till death us do part?" I asked, laughing.

"Till death us do part," he repeated, but he didn't sound as if he were laughing.

CHAPTER

12

The next three weeks went by in a haze of activity. Angus hated his grade-eight teacher on sight, but we decided dealing with her would be character-building. Peter made the football team, and I started to research Andy's biography.

We all missed Mieka.

Our routine was the same as ever: a morning run with the dogs, breakfast, school, an early supper, ball, homework, bed. Saturday mornings we went to the Lakeshore Club. I added another fifteen minutes of laps to my time in the pool because I didn't have Mieka to gossip with in the dressing room any more.

Life went on.

Before I opened my eyes on the first morning in October I knew it was raining. The air that came in through my bedroom window smelled of wet leaves and cold. I turned on the bedside lamp, and it made a comforting pool of yellow light in the room. I switched on the radio and a woman's voice, chuckling and ersatz matronly, said it was raining cats and dogs in Regina and Saskatoon. Raining on me and Mieka alike – it seemed like a good sign. I hollered at the boys to hit the showers and went downstairs. The kitchen door had blown open in the night and the floor was wet and cold on my bare feet. I coaxed the dogs out for a run in the rain, turned on the coffee and picked up the telephone. It was 7:00 a.m. If I called right away, I could catch Dave Micklejohn at home. He answered on the first ring.

"Dave, have you eaten yet?"

"No, I was just dropping an egg in to poach."

"Well, don't poach. Let me get the kids fed and off to school and I'll take you out for breakfast."

"Jo, it's so good to hear your voice. How about the clubhouse at the Par Three in half an hour? There won't be a soul there today, and they make great cinnamon buns."

"Sounds good to me, but make it an hour," I said, but he'd already hung up. Dave hates to use the telephone.

The Par Three clubhouse is the best-kept secret in the south end. It's a queer-looking six-sided building with lots of glass so you have the sense of being on the greens when you eat. It's a mom-and-pop operation – on one side of the building Mom takes greens fees and rents clubs; on the other, Pop runs a little restaurant that offers breakfasts and sandwiches. Mom's and Pop's real names are Edythe and Al. I know this only because they have twin leather belts that have their names burned cowboy style into the backs. Why they bought the Par Three is a mystery. They are people who do nothing to encourage the loyalty or affection of their clientele. However, they have pride in what they do – Edythe's greens are always as perfectly manicured as the flawless ovals of her mauve nails, and Al's baking is the best in the city.

When I pulled in behind the clubhouse, Dave's Bronco, as shiny and red as a Halloween apple, was the only vehicle in the parking lot. Through the window, I could see Dave behind the counter pouring coffee. It didn't surprise me that he was on terms of trust with Al and Edythe. Dave was finicky, too. He handed me a cup as soon as I walked in the door.

"Saw you coming, Jo, and thought you could use some warming." He put his hands on my shoulders, stood back and looked at me critically. "You're looking weary."

"Dave, you always tell all of us that – I'm fine, honestly."

The window over the table Dave directed me to was open and the table was wet with rain but the air smelled so fresh that I left the window open. The rain splashed down on the empty golf course and the sky was grey with clouds, but we were safe in the warmth, and it felt good.

We ate our cinnamon buns and talked small talk – news about my kids, gossip about the leadership convention, which had been set for December. Craig Evanson had announced the day before, and already was the odds-on favourite. Apparently Andy had been right about how long people would remember his dismissive comment about Craig. When we finished eating, Dave brought the coffee-pot over from the counter, filled our cups, put it back, sat down again and looked steadily at me.

"Well, Jo, what can I do for you?"

"I don't think it's going to be too hard, Dave. I just need some information. It's about that auburn-haired woman you were talking to after Andy's funeral – you know, the mystery woman that the paper got such a great shot of the day Andy died."

Dave's eyes shifted toward the window. "Look at that bird out there in the parking lot, Jo. Can you tell what it is from here? It looks like a little Hungarian partridge, but it's hard to tell with all that rain."

I didn't say anything.

Dave didn't look at me. He kept his eyes focused on the parking lot where the bird was hopping through the water that was pooling in a little depression near my car.

We sat in silence for a few minutes, sipping our coffee, waiting. Finally, he shrugged. He seemed to have made up his mind about something. "I guess it doesn't make any difference now that Andy's gone. I never could understand why there had to be a big mystery anyway. The woman's name is Lane Appleby. Her husband was Charlie Appleby. They're Winnipeg people. At least, Charlie was from Winnipeg. He died a couple of years ago. A lot of money from real estate, I think, but, of course, people recognize his name from hockey. He used to play for the Montreal Royals, but when he retired, he went to Manitoba, made a bundle and bought the Winnipeg team. He poured about a million dollars into it and got them some slick new uniforms and a new name."

"The Red River Royals," I said.

He looked up, surprised.

"I may not be a jock, Dave, but I am a Canadian."

He smiled. "So you are. Sorry, Jo. Anyway here's the story. Really it's not much. It started during that first election in 1970, just after Andy was first nominated and Howard Dowhanuik was head of the party. Howard called me and said he had some money for Andy's campaign. You know how you have to put a name on all contributions over a certain amount? Well, I can't remember what the amount was back then, but this was over it. I assumed the money was Howard's. Andy had been Howard's student, and Howard had really pressured him to run. So it made sense to think the money came from Howard and he just didn't want others thinking it was favouritism.

"I donated the money in my name and got a really nice letter from Andy after the election – handwritten. Funny thing, but I guess that money I didn't contribute was the beginning of my friendship with him. Well, every year it was the same story. In years that there was no election, I'd just give the money to Andy's constituency association, and when there was an election I'd give the legal limit to the campaign. Andy was always grateful. Then as the years went by and we became friends, it was harder and harder to say anything other than, 'You're welcome – hope it helps.' That's how it was until last year, when Howard stepped down as leader and the race was on.

"Just after he resigned, Howard came over to the Caucus Office. He had a really substantial sum of cash – it was always cash. This time Howard came, not just with the money but with an explanation. He said it was time I knew the score, that I might feel compromised if I believed that he was favouring Andy over the other candidates for the leadership. And then he told me the story of Lane Appleby. That morning in my office Howard was edgier than I ever remember him being. But as he said, from the outset, it had been a queer arrangement. Nothing illegal or immoral or unethical, just peculiar.

"It had started when Andy had been in a class Howard taught. About two months into the term Howard got a call from an old friend in Winnipeg. The guy did Charlie Appleby's legal work and he said Charlie had heard great things about Andy, which was strange, because Andy was, according to Howard, a solid but not exceptional student. Anyway, Charlie wanted to know if he could contribute to Andy's education, anonymously, of course, perhaps through a scholarship. Well, as you would know, that sort of thing has to go through all sorts of official channels, and that wasn't what Appleby's lawyer wanted at all. So Howard, who wanted to help a promising Ukrainian kid and who could see nothing wrong with taking money when there were no strings attached, agreed to set up a couple of ongoing projects that Andy could help with – in return, of course, for a stipend." He shook his head in amusement. "Only academics could come up with that word.

"Anyway, that was the start, and Howard made sure the Appleby money got to Andy through one channel or another till the day Andy died. In fact, about twenty minutes before Andy was murdered, Lane Appleby gave me an envelope of cash for the campaign. That's what I was talking to her about after the funeral. She didn't want to take it back."

"What did the Applebys get out of it?"

"I honestly don't know, Jo. It seems so fishy when I sit here and lay it all out for you. Even my alarm bells are going off. But it happened a little at a time, and Andy never knew. I promise you that. There were never any special favours – never. Not from Andy, not from Howard and not from me. I wish you would just let it go, Jo. I've told you everything you need to know. There's nothing to be gained by digging up the past."

"I can't let it go, Dave. There's been a murder. Our friend was murdered. What if Lane Appleby knows something that could help us find the person who killed Andy? I need to see her, Dave. I need to see a lot of people if I'm going to get to the bottom of this."

He looked old and defeated. "Isn't it bad enough the police are questioning everything about Andy's life? Six times they've been to see me, Jo. Asking about everything from Andy's finances to his toilet habits. Isn't it bad enough they're violating his life? Can't his friends let him rest in peace?"

"That's not fair. Dave, please . . ."

But he wasn't listening. He'd pulled out a pen and a pocket diary and he was scribbling something on a napkin.

"Here, Jo." He slid the napkin over to me, and his face was indescribably sad. "I have a feeling you're going to be very sorry you started this. I hope I'm wrong. I'll pay for the breakfast."

I'd hurt him and I didn't understand why, but as I watched

his jaunty figure trudge through the rain to his Bronco, I felt my throat tighten. When the red truck left the parking lot, the tears started. I sat and looked out the window until Al came over and started ostentatiously wiping the table for lunch. I grabbed the napkin just in time. On it, in Dave's neat, schoolteacher's hand, was:

> Lane Appleby
> 824 Tuxedo Park
> Winnipeg, Man.

There were two telephone numbers. After the second, he had written "her unlisted number – your best bet."

The day after I talked to Dave Micklejohn I drove to Wolf River. I had set up an office in the granny flat the night before. The boys and I ate supper, then I'd spent a quiet, happy evening sharpening pencils and labelling vertical files and notebooks. And I'd made some phone calls. The first was to Ali Sutherland. I hadn't talked to her since the day after Andy died, but I'd been thinking about her open invitation to visit her in Winnipeg from the moment I'd seen Lane Appleby's address. Thanksgiving was in a week and two days, and I decided to call and see if we were welcome. Her voice at the other end of the line was warm and delighted.

"Oh, Jo, the answer to my prayers – a real Thanksgiving with real food and a real family. Oh, God, I sound like something out of a Walt Disney movie, but I thought we were going to end up getting takeout from the deli and calling an escort service. Do those people do just plain friends for family holidays, do you think?"

Even during those black months after Ian died, Ali had been able to make me smile.

"I can't imagine you two without friends," I said.

"Believe. It's been that kind of summer. Mort's been up to his elbows and I think I'm treating half of South Winnipeg. Lord, now I'm whining and you won't come. Call me with a list, Jo. I'll get Mort to shop. We can sit and talk and I'll do all the menial stuff like chopping while you excel. Anything at all, as long as one course is your salmon mousse. No, as long all the courses are your salmon mousse. It'll be like old times – terrific! There goes my beeper – call with the list. Take care of yourself, Jo."

I almost didn't get through to Lane Appleby. Her house-keeper was as protective as a housekeeper in a Gothic novel. Mrs. Appleby was resting and shouldn't be disturbed. I looked at my watch. It was 7:00 p.m. in Winnipeg. "Tell her please that it's Joanne Kilbourn calling about Andy Boychuk." Lane Appleby was on the phone almost immediately, but she did sound as if she should not have been disturbed. Her voice was listless and her responses not entirely coherent. She sounded drugged or drunk. Yes, she knew who I was. Yes, she'd see me at Thanksgiving. I repeated the dates I'd be in Winnipeg four times to make sure they registered with her.

When I hung up, I wondered if in the morning she'd even remember that I had called. But somehow I was going to get to ask my questions. Now I just had to know which questions to ask. I had to find out who knew what about Lane Appleby, and the place to start was Wolf River.

It was time to see Eve again. I needed answers, and I had a feeling Eve had them. She was worth a call.

I also wanted to call Soren Eames. He might know why Lane Appleby had decided to spend millions endowing a chapel in the middle of the constituency where Andy Boychuk had his home, his son and his political base.

When I called Eve, she sounded distracted. Yes, sure, I could come. She'd be in her pottery studio all day. No, it

didn't matter when I came, she was just throwing pots –
more pots that nobody wanted.

I didn't have to call Soren Eames. He called me. His voice
was boyish but edgy. He had meant to call earlier to apologize, but it had been a difficult time. Could I come sometime
soon and let him show me through the college? He'd come
into the city and drive me down if that would be better for
me. He seemed immensely relieved when I said I'd drive
down the next day and see him after lunch. His words,
before he hung up, made me think that perhaps it was more
than just a social call. "This means a lot to me, Mrs.
Kilbourn – Joanne. I'm grateful to you – very grateful."

I looked at my daybook for the next couple of weeks. In
addition to my big three – Eve Boychuk, Soren Eames and
Lane Appleby – I'd pencilled in appointments with the provincial archivist, with the president of Andy's constituency and
with eight of the people who'd served in the Cabinet with
Andy. Things were shaping up. On a whim, I picked up the
telephone and dialled Ottawa. Rick Spenser answered on
the first ring. Four for four. This was my lucky night.

"Rick, hi. How did your friend the cabinet minister like
the salmon mousse?"

"She went at it like a pack of jackals and gave me nothing
in return but some mouldy rumours that I'd heard before –
a waste of your fine recipe and twelve dollars' worth of
Lefkowitz Nova Scotia smoked salmon. Joanne, it's good to
hear a sane voice."

"You sound beleaguered."

"I am beleaguered. This place is steaming. Record tem-
peratures for October in case you haven't heard, and the
humidity is unbelievable. Between the weather and rumours
about an election call, people are foaming at the mouth. God,
Jo, why do we ever get involved with this stuff? Somewhere

civilized people are listening to Ravel string quartets and talking about Proust, and here I am driving all over this town in the heat chasing down some halfwit whose brother-in-law knows somebody who works for an ad agency who says the government has block-booked media time for October and November and the writ will be dropped any minute. God, everybody's gone nuts. The politicians are foaming waiting for the PM to call on the governor general, and we're foaming waiting for something, anything, to happen so we'll finally have a story. Sorry, Jo – referential mania, the Ottawa disease. And oh, God, it *is* hot here. How're things with you? How's the project?"

"Good. I'm cool and organized – sitting in the granny flat with the air conditioner humming quietly and a shelf full of virginal vertical files, a box of fresh paper and a jar of sharp pencils, ready to begin –"

"No word processor, no personal computer – Jo, who would have suspected you were a dinosaur?"

"Anyone who ever saw me dealing with a device that had more than two moving parts. Anyway, dinosaur or not, I think I'm making some headway. Dave Micklejohn told me some stuff that suggests a definite connection between Andy and Lane Appleby – the mystery woman in that picture of Andy's body being put into the ambulance after he was . . . well you know, after . . . Howard says the Applebys have been smoothing Andy's financial path since he was in uni-versity, and that seems to be a giant lead to me. I called Winnipeg tonight and Lane Appleby has agreed to see me over the Thanksgiving weekend."

"Thanksgiving? Joanne, that's forever."

"Only for Americans. This is Canada, remember? We have to give thanks before everything freezes on the vine. It's a week from Monday, my friend – October tenth. Life is just moving too quickly for us, I guess. Anyway, between now and then I'm going to see what I can dig up on the Appleby-Boychuk connection. I want to be able to ask the right questions. I'm going to see Eve tomorrow."

His voice was laconic. "How's she doing?"

"Well, to be honest, she sounded a bit out of it on the phone, but even at the best of times, Eve tends to be unfocused."

"And, of course, these are not the best of times."

"No, they most assuredly are not. Not for anyone, I guess. I had a phone call from Soren Eames tonight. Remember him? The mystery pastor? Anyway, he was just about abject when I agreed to go out and see him. I wonder why."

"What's he like, Joanne? What's your sense of him?"

"Well, the only times I've seen him he's been terribly upset. I can't be sure, but I think I saw him for a moment near the ambulance that day at the picnic. He took care of Roma after the ambulance left. Then I saw him in his office at Wolf River the next day. And I talked to him briefly at the reception after the funeral. Emotion-charged times, but even then he was pretty riveting."

"Pretty what? I didn't hear your adjective, Joanne."

"Riveting. He had presence – the kind of person you can feel in a room. He's gorgeous, you know. He looks like James Taylor, the singer – very tall and dark and slim. And he has a sense of drama. He dresses all in black. He's a man you would notice – very sexual."

There was silence at the other end, and I wondered if we'd been cut off.

"Rick, are you there?"

"Yes. I'm here. Sorry . . . Look, I'd better go. I'll call you tomorrow night." His voice was strained, and I found myself smiling when I thought about the reason for his sudden awkwardness. Jealousy – I had gone on too long and too enthusiastically about Soren Eames. Tall, dark, slim, riveting, gorgeous – I had, as we used to say in high school, laid it on

with a trowel, and Rick didn't like it because – and I grew
warm with the thought – because he was interested in me.

It had been so long since I'd been romantically involved
with a man that I'd forgotten the vanities and the vulnerability.

"Rick, it'll be good to talk to you again tomorrow – any
time, it's always good."

"Good night, Joanne, and thanks." The connection was
broken, and I was alone in the granny flat remembering the
interest in Rick's voice, smiling . . .

As I drove along the Trans-Canada to Wolf River I tried to
remember the second line of "To Autumn." "Season of
mists and mellow fruitfulness" and then something about
the maturing sun.

I looked at the scorched fields and the stunted crops –
there wouldn't be many farmers in our province reciting
odes to the maturing sun this fall. It had rained on and off
for a week after Andy's funeral, but the earth had sucked
up the moisture without a trace. The rain had come late
and the land had been dry. Still, Keats could have made a
poem of this morning – brilliant sun, the sky lifting big and
blue against the land. It was, I reminded myself as I drove
slowly and safely off the Belle Plaine overpass, a good day
to be alive.

It was just after nine o'clock when I drove down the lane
beside Eve's house and parked in front of the little building
she used for her pottery. The neat three-bedroom bungalow
that had been the unhappy home of Eve and Andy Boychuk
was, I noticed as I drove by, immaculate: the storm windows
gleamed hard in the sunlight, the shrubs by the house were
wrapped in sackcloth, and the flower beds had been turned
over. It was the house of a person who set deadlines and kept
them. Eve's studio was a different story. The grass outside

was uncut and yellowing, and there was pottery everywhere. Pots and vases covered makeshift trestle tables, and a family of cats stalked each other around bowls and plants stacked in the dying grass. Even to my untrained eyes, all these unsold, unsalable pieces spoke of pathology.

As I stood squinting into the sun, Eve came from a lean-to at the back of the pottery. She looked tense but handsome. Her long grey hair was parted in the middle and fell in heavy braids over her shoulders. Her feet were bare, and she was wearing blue jeans and a denim work shirt so faded they were almost white. She was carrying two blocks of fresh clay wrapped in clean heavy plastic that was looped and tied to make a handle.

The sleeves of her shirt were rolled back, and you could see the muscles of her arms taut with the weight of the clay. She dropped the clay blocks in front of me.

"Jo, carry these inside, would you? I need to get a couple more." I slid my hands through the plastic loops and lifted. The clay didn't move a centimetre, but I could feel my vertebrae creak. Tomorrow I would be forty-six. I didn't plan to celebrate the day in traction.

I left the clay on the ground in front of me. "Sorry, Eve – I'll hold the door for you, but that's my limit."

"Oh, Jo. Those things can't weigh more than forty pounds apiece." She slipped her hands through the loops and carried them easily into her workroom. I followed behind her like a puppy.

Eve's studio was a surprisingly pleasant and functional place. It was square, high-ceilinged and cool. There were windows all around, but set high on the wall. The autumn light poured in through them and turned the dusty air of the studio to a yellowy haze. Beneath the windows were shelves filled with pottery that was finished but unfired. In the centre of the room there were two slab worktables and a potter's wheel. Along one wall was a long table filled with stuff: plastic bleach bottles cut back to hold sponges, gallon ice cream buckets full of cutting tools and garlic presses and other odds and ends that could press decorations into wet clay. In the corner were a hot plate and an old-fashioned sink.

Eve bent and picked up clay from the potter's wheel – small pieces that hadn't worked out. "It's called reclaiming," she said, but I noticed when she began to wedge the clay that her hands, always so capable, were shaking. "Damn," she said, "sorry, Jo, I'm not good for much today."

"Is there anything I can do to help?"

"No, same old thing," she said vaguely. "Unless . . . Jo, there's a little exercise I do that sometimes brings me down. Do it with me."

I was uneasy. Eve was always quick to sense the moods of others. "Are you worried playing with the loony will make you loony, too? No permanent damage, I guarantee. Come on, Jo, it might even do you some good."

She rummaged around in a box of tapes and with a swift and decisive movement ejected the Hindemith that had been playing when we walked in and replaced it with something that sounded like relaxation music from the dentist's office – waves pounding and a flute. She pulled two chairs side by side and said, "Now just sit and listen. Try to close everything out but the music and my voice.

"Take a deep, cleansing breath – good – now let your hands rest in your lap. Feel the air around them."

On the tape the waves pounded and a seagull squawked. "Close your eyes . . . Think of all the hands you have known." (Above the waves, the flute notes rose sweet and sad. In the Old Testament the flute is the instrument of death.) "The hands you will never forget . . . your father's hands . . . your mother's hands . . . your grandmother's

hands." (Ian's hands warm in mine that first night . . .
Mieka's baby hand curled around my finger . . . Peter's hand
surprisingly strong when he gripped my hand and led me
up the aisle of St. Anselm's for his father's funeral.) "Now
think of your hand . . . Think of all the things your hand
has done . . . Think of how it learned to lift a spoon . . . grasp
a pencil . . . tie a shoelace . . . all the tasks your hand has
done." (No flutes now, just the sound of whales singing.)
"Working, playing, loving.

"Touch my hand now, Jo." (Her hands are large, strong,
the fingertips rough with dried clay.) "Hands are the reaching out of the heart . . . Experience my hand. Grasp it tight
. . . now release it . . . The touch is gone, but the imprint will
be there forever." (Seagulls, flutes, the whales singing their
death song.) "Forever and ever in your heart."

And we sat in silence, side by side, until the tape was over.
Eve looked serene, one hand cupped in the other, palms up,
in her lap, her chest rising and falling evenly, her eyes half
closed. I was embarrassed. I never seemed to be able to get
into these things the way other people could. In the sixties,
I was never very good with dope – the magical mystery tour
always seemed to leave without me. But the exercise had
transformed Eve. When she turned to me her face was wiped
clean of pain but her green eyes seemed slightly unfocused,
and I wondered, not for the first time, how much dope she
had done when she was young. When she spoke, her voice
was light and dreamy. "You know, I am so filled with peace
that I think I could sleep now if you wouldn't mind . . . Or
was there something special . . . ?"

I felt ridiculous, Nancy Drew meets Timothy Leary – but
I'd played her game. She owed me at least a turn at mine.
"Just one question, Eve. Do you know a woman named
Lane Appleby?"

"I don't think so."

"Eve, you must remember her. She was the one who . . ."
I looked at Eve's face. She was almost serene. I couldn't
finish. I couldn't throw those shattering words against the
fragile peace she'd drawn around her – the one who walked
with us to carry Andy's body to the ambulance, the one who
stood motionless when your mother-in-law spat in her face,
the one who endowed the chapel they wheel your vegetable
son into every day of his dim and shapeless life.

"The one who what, Jo?"

I put my arm around her shoulders. "Nothing, Eve. Come
on, let me walk you up to the house."

As I followed Eve into her shining, empty house, I thought
of all the questions I hadn't asked. But one question at least
had been answered. I couldn't prove it in a court of law, and
Inspector Millar Millard would not applaud the process by
which I had arrived at my conclusion, but I was certain that
Eve Boychuk had not killed her husband.

CHAPTER

13

I had told Soren Eames I'd see him early in the afternoon. When I left Eve, it was 10:15 and the morning yawned emptily ahead of me – not enough time to drive to the city, but too much to waste hanging around the Charlie Appleby Prayer Centre.

I decided I'd drive over to Wolf River Bible College and see if I could find Lori and Mark Evanson. Eve had worried me. The meditation or whatever it was had helped temporarily, but no relaxation technique in the world was a match for Eve's demons. Lori and Mark would, I knew, keep an eye on Eve if I asked them. They were limited kids, but they were decent and reliable. Most important, because of Mark's connection with Carey Boychuk, they saw Eve regularly. She would not feel violated by their concern.

When I drove through the main gate of the college, I felt like I'd driven into an old Metro-Goldwyn-Mayer musical. The students were back. They were everywhere and, by some people's criteria, they were an appealing bunch: boys with razor-cut hair and button-down shirts and vivid corduroy pants, girls with shining hair and careful makeup and

skirts and sweaters the colours of autumn. Perfect . . . and
yet on this sultry October day, their perfection was jarring.
They had the bright, unreal look of a casting director's idea
of students. There was, I remembered, a dress code at Wolf
River, but this studied perfection went beyond that. I
thought of my own students in their jeans or cutoffs or cords
or dashikis, and of their hair, spiked or crewcut or frizzed or
bleached or removed entirely, but all of them fumbling,
however awkwardly, with an identity. Peter has a phrase
that is both final and withering. "He looks as if his mother
dressed him." The kids at the Bible college looked as if their
mothers dressed them. It was kind of sad.

Lori Evanson wasn't hard to track down. I asked one of the
perfect boys to direct me and, with a flash of flawless teeth,
he did. Lori, he told me, had a new job. She was helping people
"get orientated," and she was working out of the CAP Centre.
I looked blank. He smiled and said carefully, "The Charlie
Appleby Prayer Centre." Poor Charlie – all that endowment
money and he ended up as the first two-thirds of an acronym.

She was in the central reception area, sitting at a table
piled high with student handbooks. On her desk was a sign,
"Please Disturb Me," and there was a picture of a cartoon
turtle with a grin on his face and a happy-face button on
his shell.

When she saw me, her face lit up with pleasure. "Oh, Mrs.
Kilbourn, you are just the person I was supposed to see, and
now here you are. God always hears us." She stopped for
breath and looked at me confidingly. I'd forgotten how compelling that lilting singsong voice could be.

Lori Evanson was a compelling young woman. If the other
college students looked like extras in a movie musical, Lori
was the homecoming queen. Her dark blond hair was swept
back into a thick braid that fell between her shoulder blades
straight as the pendulum on the college clock. The braid was

tied with a broad corded silk ribbon, the same russet red as her angora cardigan and the stripe in her tartan skirt. Her face and neck, still tanned from summer, glowed apricot against her white eyelet blouse. She was beautiful, especially now that this mission to talk to me was about to be accomplished.

"I have a nutrition break in –" She looked carefully at her watch. "Why, my break is right now." Her voice trilled with good fortune. "Let's go to Disciples and – please, Mrs. Kilbourn, let me buy you some pie."

So we walked together through the leafy streets. We made slow progress. Every few feet Lori stopped to welcome someone back or to volunteer news about Mark and Clay. She told me how they'd chosen their son's name. "You know, like in Jesus is the potter and we are the clay," she said matter-of-factly.

Lori Evanson seemed to float in a little globe of uncomplicated and undifferentiated joy. She was as filled with delight at a girlfriend's cute new school bag as she was when a thin, freckled boy told her that since June his cancer had been in remission, or with the news that the pie of the day at Disciples was deep-dish green apple.

When we settled into the booth she chose near the windows, she reached across the table and squeezed both my hands. "I prayed for guidance and here you are."

Suddenly I felt cold and impatient. "What is it, Lori?"

But her vacant lovely eyes continued to look steadily into mine. "I have to ask you something, and I've prayed that my words will be the right words."

"Lori, what is it? Just ask. If I can help, I will."

"Well, here goes . . ." The pleasant, lilting voice rose into the singsong of a child reciting. "Will you support my father-in-law, Craig Evanson, for leader of the party?"

I was astounded. I had been so absorbed with Andy's death that the leadership race just wasn't there for me. Across the table, Lori Evanson looked at me with eyes as guileless as a child's, and I was furious that Julie had put her daughter-in-law up to this. "Damn it, Lori, no! I told your mother-in-law no; I told your father-in-law no; and I'm telling you no. No! I will not support Craig Evanson for leader of the party. How many times do they have to be told, anyway?"

Lori's eyes filled with tears. I could see that each of those startling turquoise irises was encircled – contact lenses. She pulled her braid around and began chewing on the end to keep from crying. I felt like I had kicked a puppy.

"Oh, Mrs. Kilbourn, I'm sorry. It's my fault. Mark's mother's right. I'm stupid. But I wanted to do my part and she said I should ask you and now I've made a mess of everything, and I'm sorry. Please don't be mad at her. It's my fault. I knew I shouldn't ask you. Will you forgive me, Mrs. Kilbourn?" She was crying noisily now, and heads were turning in our direction. This seemed to be my restaurant for scenes.

"Lori, please call me Joanne . . . and of course I forgive you if you'll forgive me." She was nodding energetically, so I kept on. "I just thought it was mean of her to make you do it. Lori, look at me. If you thought it was the wrong thing to do, why didn't you say no?"

She wiped the tears from her face with the back of her hand. "Because I have to trust other people to decide for me." She leaned over confidingly. "You know, Mrs. Kilbourn, I'm not very smart. Soren says most of the time I can decide myself what's right and what's wrong, but if it gets too hard for me, well, I just have to trust the people around me."

"Like who, Lori?"

"Like Mark and his mom and dad and the teachers at the college and, of course, I have to trust Soren."

"Is Soren a good man?"

A look of rapture crossed her face. "Next to Mark, he's the best man I know."

"What exactly does he do? Is he the principal or the head of the church here?"

"He cares for us, Mrs. Kilbourn. He does everything. He preaches and he helps the counsellors and he makes sure everyone's fair and he gets our money for us. Before he came, this was just a little backwater Bible college, but Soren Eames had a vision." (You could almost hear the violins soar on that one.) "Soren has made the college really special. He changes people's lives – kids on drugs and runaways, but really just anybody. He could," she said shyly, "change your life if you'd let him."

"Lori, about the money. Where does Soren get the money for all this? Is there a central church somewhere?"

"We're the church, Mrs. Kilbourn. Soren just goes out in the world and gets the money for us."

"But how does he do it?"

Unexpectedly, she giggled and leaned across the table. "Mark says Soren gets our money by" – and she whispered – "by cuddling up to rich widows."

"The Charlie Appleby Prayer Centre must have taken a lot of cuddling."

"Oh, Mrs. Kilbourn" – she laughed softly – "aren't we awful?" She looked at her watch. "Oh, fudge. I'm late. Thanks for being so understanding. This is my treat."

"Lori, just one thing. Could you and Mark keep an eye on Mrs. Boychuk for me? She's having a hard time." Lori was nodding vigorously again. Grief and adjustment – we were on safe ground. "Please let me know if she gets too sad or . . ." I thought. "If she just isn't herself."

Lori seemed to know what I meant. "A change," she said, nodding gravely. "I should let you know if there's any change in her."

"Yes," I said, "a change. That's the word."

When Soren Eames came out of his office to greet me, he did indeed look like the kind of man rich widows would pay to be cuddled by.

"Black Irish," my grandmother had said the first time I brought Ian to her narrow house on Yorkville Avenue. "Skin like milk, nose like Gregory Peck and broody eyes. You can always spot them. They're passionate men, but often insane." She'd been right, at least in part, about Ian, and Soren Eames had the same dark good looks that my husband had, that my sons have.

I hadn't had a chance to get a good look at Soren Eames until that moment. He was older than I remembered. He was balding; there were hairbreadth lines around his eyes; and he was much too thin. But, romantic as it sounds, you could feel the fire there.

He played on that romantic sense, too. He was all in black again, and he had rolled his sleeves back past the wrist to show off his hands. They were artist's hands, very white, with long, tapered fingers.

He smiled and offered his arm. "Let's walk a little." I would have given odds I was about to go on the widow's tour – the crowded classrooms, the too-small dorms itching for endowment – but he surprised me. We walked away from the college, behind the CAP Centre, over the construction rubble to a hill. As we climbed toward the sun, the air was hot and acrid. It smelled of burning rubber and stubble fires lit by farmers. At the top of the hill was a little windbreak of trees and in front of them a rock, smooth and ancient. Soren Eames gestured me to sit down, and then sat beside me.

Below I could see the whole of Wolf River Bible College. With its neat rows of buildings and lines of yellow aspens, it was, from this distance, as theatrically unreal as the model children who sat in its classrooms and walked across its lawns. Beside me, his profile sharp and oddly youthful in the haze, Soren Eames looked at his vision realized.

It was enough to make me toss my cookies. I had spent too much time around people who cruised from photo opportunity to photo opportunity to tolerate this.

"Very impressive," I said.

"Very impressive, but you're not impressed," Eames said, and I was surprised to hear his voice shake. Normally that vulnerability would have touched me, but not today. There were things I needed to know.

"It's a beautiful setup. Lori Evanson tells me you raised money for most of the new buildings. You must have raised a million dollars."

"More," he said flatly.

"And the Charlie Appleby Prayer Centre," I said. "For the past few months Andy was after me to take twenty minutes to come in off the highway and look at it. He thought it was a really great building."

Eames was silent. I could see his pulse beating in his throat. He swallowed. I wasn't going to be deflected.

"How did you come to know Charlie Appleby?"

"I didn't. It was his wife. She just appeared one day."

"And what happened?"

"Nothing. She came. I told her what we needed. She said, 'Do it, and I'll write the cheque.'"

"Just like that? That's a rather spectacular act of philanthropy, Mr. Eames. A stranger comes in off the street and, with a stroke of her pen, grants your wish. Didn't it seem a little – I don't know – whimsical to you?"

"Widows, especially in those first months after their husbands' deaths, are often a little whimsical, Mrs. Kilbourn. You'll have to accept it on faith as I did. The CAP Centre was a good thing for Lane Appleby. She took quite an interest in it – spent a lot of weekends in Wolf River when it was going

up. She's been a good friend to the college, and I'd rather not
say anything more about her." He sounded ineffably sad.

The silence fell between us again, and I didn't want it to.
I knew there was a missing piece of Andy's life in Wolf
River. I didn't know the shape of the piece I was looking for,
but I did know that I needed to keep Soren Eames talking.

"Anyway, it's an accomplishment," I said lamely.

"But you question the value of that accomplishment," he
said softly.

I turned and looked at him. He was close to forty, and in
the harsh morning sun every mark of living showed. But
there was such vulnerability in his face, and something else
– Fear? Hope?

It struck me suddenly that he was as tired of this aimless
circling as I was. He had, after all, telephoned me. He wanted
something, too. But neither of us would get anywhere till we
cleared the air. I took a deep breath and waded in.

"All right, Mr. Eames –"

"Soren," he corrected gently.

"All right, Soren, I'm mystified. I don't know what I'm
doing here. I'm a widow, but I'm not the kind of widow
you're interested in. I'm not rich. I can't underwrite anything
or give the school an endowment." He winced, but I didn't
stop. "I don't know why I'm getting the tour. What possible
difference can it make to you what I think of all this?"

I looked into his face. It was hard to believe that this was
the Miracle Man of Wolf River. The persona of the confident
charismatic was as remote from this shattered man as the
moon. When he spoke his voice was almost inaudible, but
there was no mistaking his words.

"I wanted you to think well of me, Joanne. I wanted . . ."
His voice broke. "I'm sorry. This isn't working out. I'm sorry.
I just wanted you not to have contempt for me. We can go

back now if you want." As we walked down the hill, the air between us was heavy with things unsaid. Like quarrelling lovers, we walked in silence.

When I pulled up in front of the house on Eastlake Avenue, a woman from a courier service was coming down our walk. I signed a form, took a fat striped envelope from her and went inside. It had been a while since we'd done any housework. The living room was not a disaster, but it wasn't great. The boys had had lunch in front of the television. They had cleared away the dishes, but the coffee table was dusty with sandwich crumbs, and there were rings from their milk glasses. From talk at dinner lately, I knew the World Series was on. Angus had resurrected his baseball cards, and they were in unassailable piles on the sideboard in the dining room. The afternoon sun blazed through the window and turned the crystal vase Rick had given me to fire, but the daisies I had put in it last week were wilting, and the table it stood on was layered with dust.

I had two hours before the boys came home. I could clean house. If I started right away, things would be shining by supper. Or I could make a pot of tea, head for the granny flat, sit in the cool and read through the stuff Rick had sent.

It was the day before my birthday. My last day as a forty-five-year-old. The choice was easy. While I was waiting for the kettle to boil, I dumped the daisies and went into the backyard with a pair of scissors. I cut a generous bunch of giant marigolds, came back inside and filled the vase with fresh water and arranged the flowers. Their smell, sharp and fall-like, filled with room with other autumns, autumns when the kids were little and they'd go off to school with bunches of marigolds wrapped in waxed paper for their teachers. At that moment the mysteries of Andy Boychuk's life seemed just the antidote I needed for the realities of mine. I made a pot of tea, poured a cup and took it and the courier envelope to the granny flat.

The place was beginning to have a comforting order. I had moved the desk in front of the window overlooking the garden. I worked better when I could see the big house and the shadows of the kids passing by the windows every so often. There had been enough rain in September to brighten the asters and the zinnias and the marigolds, so the garden was pretty to look at. But I couldn't smell it. The windows of the granny flat, energy efficient, satisfaction guaranteed, sealed out dust and the smell of late summer garden alike.

I had come up with a filing system that any professional researcher would laugh at, but that I thought would work for me. I had labelled a vertical file for every year of Andy's life, and into each file I was dumping everything that happened in a particular year, not just to Andy but to the people around him: his family, his friends, his colleagues. When I told Rick Spenser about it, there had been silence. For his research he had devised a computer program with a Byzantine system of cross-references. But I liked my files. We don't live in a vacuum, and my vertical files took that into account.

Finding material was easy. The Caucus Office had boxes of stuff and already the files on Andy's political years were bulging. So when I opened the envelope and a fat package marked "Eve Lorscott Boychuk: Family," slid out, I eyed the 1963 file speculatively.

There was a half-inch-thick stack of clippings on Tudor Lorscott. I scanned them quickly. The usual corporate publicity: head shots of Eve's father looking pleased to be appointed to the board of some company or to be heading up a charity drive. There were notices of business acquisitions by Lorscott Limited – some solid, unspectacular stuff, but a

surprising number of gold and nickel mines. Old Tudor was
a high roller. And then – bonanza – a feature article from the
old *Star Weekly*: "The Lorscott Case – The Family Behind
the Headlines." There was not much information beyond
what Howard Dowhanuik had told me that night a thousand
years ago in Saskatoon, but there was a haunting picture
taken, the *Weekly* article noted, greedily licking its chops,
less than a week before the murder attempt. It was a colour
photo, taken in the living room of the family home in Port
Durham – a lovely room, all lemon yellow and ivory, with a
glowing abstract over the fireplace and a graceful bowl of iris
and tulips and yellow anemone on the glass coffee table. In
the forefront of the picture the three Lorscott women sit on
a silk-covered love seat behind the coffee table and the
spring flowers. Madeline Lorscott, as old as Eve is now, a
little heavy in middle age, dark-haired still, worried-looking,
is flanked by her daughters, slim young women in smooth,
sleeveless A-line dresses with matching pumps, Eve's dress
cornflower blue, Nancy's mint green. Their dark hair, like
their mother's, is fluffed into bouffants that flip girlishly at
shoulder level – the Jackie look. Behind them, leaning over
the couch, one heavy-fingered hand resting on (or gripping?)
the shoulder of each of his daughters, is Tudor Lorscott. His
chin just grazes the top of his wife's hair, and his look is
smug, proprietary: "This is mine." Tudor Lorscott, lord of
the manor. A man to be envied.

The final photos are fuzzy grey-and-white reprints of wire-
service pictures. The newspapers' invariable records of crime
and punishment: the crime scene, the arrest, the trial, a
sequence as familiar to us now as photos of Shirley Temple
and Deanna Durbin were to our parents. Except this is Eve
Boychuk's family. The figures on the stretchers being loaded
into the ambulance are Eve's father and mother. The tanned,
lithe figure in a white turtleneck sweater and capri pants,

looking disconcertingly ordinary in the sea of uniforms, is
Eve's sister, Nancy. The girl with the dead eyes, raising her
hand against the camera as if to ward off a blow, is Eve.

The account of the trial was surprisingly circumspect.
Even in a city where a circulation war between the two
evening papers was always on the boil, reporters couldn't
find much juice in an attempted murder trial where no one
would say anything.

But there were pictures and there were captions: a picture
of the alleged weapon – a small hatchet, wooden-handled,
Nancy Lorscott's old Girl Guide hatchet but fitted with a
new steel head with a cutting edge like a razor; a close-up of
a bloody Tudor Lorscott as he was wheeled into the hospital. ("How did he look?" asked the *Examiner*'s reporter. "He
looked," said the reliable source, "as if someone tried to cut
off his head and his private parts.")

There was a brief account of the sentencing: the judge's
decision that Nancy Lorscott should be committed to the
Middlesex Prison for the Criminally Insane (a sentence later
commuted to indefinite treatment in a private sanitarium).
But of the trial itself, not much beyond a dry recital of the
exchange of legalisms between the Crown and the defence,
the expert testimony of the expert witnesses, and a running
account of what the Lorscott women wore to court.

Of course, there were many pictures of Eve – the only
accessible Lorscott during those weeks after the assault. Eve
getting out of her car in front of the handsome Victorian hall
that served as Port Durham's courtroom building; Eve visiting the hospital where her parents were convalescing; Eve
coming out of her dentist's office. And always the same
small smile and the same dead eyes.

Eve Lorscott was twenty years old in 1963. Enough trauma
there to last a lifetime. But this was not Eve's last trauma.

Nor, if one believed the speculations of the psychiatrist called by Nancy's lawyers, was it her first.

Poor Eve. Poor, poor Eve.

I was trying to find the Eve I knew in the tiny grey face in the newspaper photo when the telephone rang. It was Soren Eames, and he sounded awful. Whatever shreds of pride had impelled him to take me down the hill without accomplishing what he had set out to accomplish were gone. There were no courtly preambles this time.

"Joanne, I have to see you."

And then, when I didn't answer immediately, he apologized.

"I'm sorry for what happened at Wolf River. I'm doing a lot to make myself unhappy these days." His voice trailed off and, for a beat, there was silence on the other end of the line. When he spoke again, his voice sounded better – if not strong at least assured and in control. "Joanne, I'm on a really life-denying trajectory now, and I need to talk. I can be at your place in an hour. Tonight or tomorrow – which?"

The jargon and narcissism ate at me – the life-denying trajectory and the string of sentences starting with "I." When I was a kid there was a game we played at birthday parties. Each child was given five beans, and every time we used the word "I" in a conversation we had to forfeit a bean. Soren Eames struck me as a man who would lose his beans pretty quickly.

Whatever the reason, I said no: no to the next hour, no to the next day. After the darkness of the past month, I wanted a birthday that was sunny and uncomplicated, and I told him so. I would see him, but it would have to wait. We agreed to meet at nine o'clock the morning after my birthday at my house. I was not looking forward to it.

CHAPTER

14

The late afternoon sun filtered through the leaves of the cottonwood tree outside the window of the granny flat and made shadow patterns on my desk: a changing play of light and darkness. It occurred to me that before Soren Eames and I had our meeting it would be wise to find out more about the Miracle Man of Wolf River. It was almost 6:00 p.m. in Ottawa. Rick Spenser would be at his house on River Street pouring Beefeaters into a chilled glass. It would be a pleasure to talk to a happy man.

Rick really did sound glad to hear from me. He was buoyant. It had been a good day. The temperature in Ottawa had finally dropped, and the afternoon had been brisk and bright. Even better for a man who hated campaign travel, it looked as if there would be no federal election call. The government polls were down, and just before Rick left his office for the day, a junior minister had phoned to say the government would wait till spring. Rick was celebrating. He'd stopped at the market and he was in the middle of shredding beets for a pot of borscht "in honour of our friend Andy Boychuk," he said, laughing.

But as soon as I mentioned Soren Eames there was a pause, and when I asked if he'd had trouble finding information on Eames, he sounded sullen.

"I didn't see it as being worth the bother. I asked one of our researchers to look into it, and she came up with a one-page summary of a rather dismal life – nothing we didn't know. If you insist, I'll have her look again."

"Yeah, I insist," I said, laughing.

"So be it," he said, sharply.

Whatever ambivalence he felt about Soren Eames the man, Rick's journalistic instincts weren't dulled. When I mentioned Eames's phone call, the line crackled with interest: What had he said? What had I said? What were my impressions? He congratulated me on my decision to put off seeing Soren until after my birthday. "No use wasting your time on a charlatan, Joanne," he said – a typical Rick line, but he hadn't read it well. There was uneasiness in his voice, and I thought I knew why.

Even when I was young I hadn't been good at boy-girl games. Another woman would have been quick to grab hold of this show of vulnerability. I wasn't.

"Rick, listen. The only reason I'm seeing Soren Eames again is because I think he knows something. There's a connection there."

His answer came from far away. "Good night, Joanne. I'll call you tomorrow night before I go to bed, ten o'clock your time, midnight here. They won't have done the daylight savings thing by then." He sounded fretful.

I laughed. "Rick, it doesn't matter. Call when you're near a phone."

"Ten o'clock," he said again. "And, Joanne, I'll get the research person to send what she comes up with on Eames directly to you. Have a splendid day tomorrow. I wish you that."

The first thing I heard on my forty-sixth birthday was the phone ringing, then my daughter's voice laughing, tuneless, singing a crazy birthday song I'd made up for her when she was little. The kids always screamed and yelled when I started to sing it, but it was as much a part of all their birthdays as the ugly plastic tree loaded with jellybeans that was the invariable birthday centrepiece and the mug with parrots singing "Happy bird day to you" that was always at the birthday kid's place on the table. So much a part of their birthdays but never – until that morning – of mine. That Mieka would sing it to me signalled a change in our relationship. When she finished, she was laughing, and I was crying.

"Oh, Mieka, that was beautiful."

"Mum, that was awful."

"Well, yeah, but beautiful that you phoned me up and sang. Does it sound that bad when I do it?"

"Worse, Mum, worse."

"Mieka, it is so wonderful to hear your voice." And then we were away on a lovely, aimless conversation about the boys ("Tell them I miss them and gently remind them the present for you is under the sleeping bag in Angus's cupboard") and her classes ("The woman who teaches my English class is so much like you – that first day I wanted to follow her home like a puppy") and my growing conviction that Rick Spenser was interested in me ("Well, why wouldn't he be? Except for your singing and your worrying, you're practically a perfect person"). Mother-daughter stuff.

Finally I forced myself to look at the clock. "Mieka, I hate for us to stop, but this is costing you a fortune and we can get caught up when we go to Winnipeg for Thanksgiving. It's only a week from today. I can't believe how quickly the fall is going."

There was no response.

"Mieka?"

Her voice was gentle but firm. "Mum, I'm not going to Winnipeg for Thanksgiving." And then, "Greg's parents have a cottage at Emma Lake, and they've invited me to spend the Thanksgiving weekend with them and Gregory. I really want to do this. I've told them yes, Mum."

No room to negotiate. No need to negotiate. She was grown-up. She wanted to spend the weekend with the family of a man she was interested in. Outwardly I was gracious, upbeat, and when I hung up we were both laughing. But inside I was raging. It was, I thought, as I looked at my indisputably forty-six-year-old face in the mirror, one hell of a way to begin a birthday.

It didn't get any better in the next hour. The boys were at each other from the moment they got up. They fought like a pair of six-year-olds over who got to hand me my birthday present, and the truce at breakfast was a fragile one. Peter couldn't find his Latin book, and Angus, for the first time since kindergarten, decided he didn't want to go to school. As I stood on our front porch, shivering in the chill, watching Angus snake up the road toward grade eight, I was not exactly brimming with radiance and peace. When a black Porsche pulled up in front of my house and I saw a slender man in black get out of the driver's seat, I felt like giving up on being forty-six altogether. The man was Soren Eames.

I was still in my robe. I had brushed my teeth, but I hadn't showered. I was in no mood for being on either side of a therapy session. If Soren hadn't already spotted me, I think I would have made it simple and not answered the door, but it was too late. He was coming up the front walk toward me, trying to smile but looking tense. He was carrying a blue box from Birks – the kind you get when you buy a really pricy piece of china or crystal.

He stopped at the bottom of the porch stairs and handed the box to me.

"Many happy returns, Joanne."

I just stood there.

"Aren't you going to open it?"

I started to give the box back.

"No," he said. "Let's go inside. Please. Once you open the box, I think you'll understand some things."

He followed me into the house. I went through to the kitchen, poured us both some coffee and joined him in the living room.

The blue box was on the coffee table between us. Soren leaned over and pushed it toward me.

"Please, Joanne."

I think I knew as soon as I pulled back the tissue paper and saw the little ceramic figure inside. I had seen it before. In fact, one blistering Canada Day weekend I had bought it at a craft fair in the southwest corner of the province. It was the work of a local artist, and it was a lovely, witty piece – a cabbage, perfect in every detail, unfolding its top leaves like a flower. Rising from the heart of the cabbage is a woman with the broad hips and heavy breasts of the Ukraine. She is wearing a brown peasant's dress, and a bright kerchief covers her hair. Her face, with its sweep of Slavic cheekbones and bright blue eyes, is uncannily like Roma Boychuk's. The woman's arms are raised toward heaven, and in her hands, solemn and handsome, is a baby boy. The piece is called "Ukrainian Genesis," and as soon as Andy Boychuk saw it that July day he had to have it.

I did the purchasing. Andy paid me later. When you're in politics and you go to a show where all the work is by local artists, it's prudent not to single one artist out and stiff the rest. Andy had loved that piece. I would have sworn it hadn't left his desk since the day he bought it. Except "Ukrainian

Genesis" had left his desk. Somewhere along the line he had given it to Soren Eames; and now Soren Eames was giving it to me.

"How?" I asked.

"It was a gift, a gift to commemorate a special time for me. It was a wonderful gesture."

I could feel my safe world shifting, and I didn't want it to. I grabbed a handhold. "Andy was full of wonderful gestures. He was a generous man. He gave things to a lot of people."

Soren Eames leaned across the table and looked into my face. His voice was soft, almost diffident, but his gaze was steady. "I loved him, Joanne."

I felt oppressed, as if something were pressing me down. I didn't want to hear this. I didn't want to know.

"A lot of people loved Andy," I said and I turned and looked out the window.

Soren Eames half stood and leaned toward me. His hand touched my cheek and turned my face. "Look at me, Joanne. You're not a simple woman. You know what I'm talking about here. I didn't love Andy like a lot of people. It was more for us – a great deal more. He was my lover, and I was his."

Free fall. The old, safe world gave way. I heard my voice, pleading, stupid. "Who knew? Were you careful?" The political questions. Andy was dead. This man was destroyed by grief, but the political instinct was always alive and kicking. There are a hundred jokes about the referential mania of political people: the husband of a woman running for the House of Commons is killed in a car accident and her opponent bitterly dismisses the new widow's loss as "a great break for her"; a campaign manager tells his workers to make sure all their supporters in the senior citizens' homes vote in the advance poll so that, no matter what, the party won't have lost a vote. And me, right in there with the best or worst of them, treating this fragile man as a political problem, not a suffering human being.

His face was so close to me that I could see the faint blue-black of the beard growing beneath his skin, and I could smell his aftershave, light, woodsy – familiar.

Surprised, I said, "You smell like Andy. Did you always use that cologne? Or . . ."

"I changed after," he said. "Stupid – as if it could change anything." He flinched, and the pain on his face was as sharp as if he had been stabbed.

It all changed for me in that moment. Not Paul on the road to Damascus, exactly, but the shock of recognition was there.

"I did that, too," I said, "after my husband died. At night, before I went to bed, I'd rub his aftershave into my body so that when I woke up in the night . . ."

"You could pretend that he was still there," he finished for me.

"Something like that."

We sat in silence, wrapped in our separate memories. Finally, I wanted to talk.

"I'm sorry," I said.

"For what?"

"I don't know, just . . . Soren, come into the kitchen and let me get some fresh coffee and we'll start again."

He stood up and smiled. "Is being invited into the kitchen a mark of friendship?"

"Yeah, I guess it is."

"Then I accept with pleasure. I need a friend."

We sat at the kitchen table. The sky was threatening. The yard was heavy with leaves from the cottonwood tree, sodden and disintegrating. It was a thoroughly dismal day. Soren Eames was oblivious to the weather. For a long time his eyes didn't shift from the window, but I think he was seeing a different landscape.

He had brought the little baba figure into the kitchen, and as we sat, his fingers traced her lines, like a man playing with worry beads.

Finally, he began to speak. His voice was warm and intimate.

"Joanne, I wish we could stop the movie right here. It's a good frame – the respectable matron and the closet gay reach out to one another over their friend's death. But it's more complex than that. Not long after we met, Andy told me you were one of the few people in his life he trusted. That's going to have to be good enough for me because" – he swallowed hard – "I have to trust somebody."

He was wearing a bomber jacket of buttery, smooth cowhide. As he spoke, he reached into an inside pocket and pulled out an envelope. It was of good quality paper, dove grey. On the front, in elegant and familiar calligraphy, was the name Soren Eames. There was no address. My hands began to shake.

"Hand delivered?" I asked in a bright, artificial voice.

He nodded. "Apparently. It was in my mail slot at the college. It's a fairly public place. Open it."

I turned the envelope to open it. On the back flap were the letters *A* and *E* intertwined the way they are on a wedding invitation, the way they were on the copy of "The Sick Rose" someone had placed in Andy's portfolio the day he was killed. My hands were shaking so badly I could barely pull the enclosure from the envelope.

I recognized it immediately. It was a pre-election brochure of Andy's. I had written the copy. General stuff: a careful biography, a few platitudes and a couple of soaring, meaningless slogans. No one ever reads the words, anyway. But the pictures were extraordinary. They'd been taken by a young man who had wandered into the Caucus Office early in the summer. His name was Colin Grant, and that day he was wearing cheap runners, cut-offs and a Georgia O'Keeffe sweatshirt. He had a Leica slung around his neck.

"What you want," he had said as he struck a match on Dave Micklejohn's no-smoking sign, "is subtext not substance."

We hired him that day, and he hadn't disappointed. His pictures were extraordinary. He could do magic things with light, and the photo on the front of the brochure Soren was holding was one of his best – in part, because it violated all the conventional wisdom about how you show your candidate.

Andy's back was to the camera. Coatless, hands outstretched, he was plunging into the crowd at a rally in Victoria Park. We saw the people from his angle: hands reaching out to him, touching him, faces raised to his.

It was a scene all of us who'd been involved in politics had seen a hundred times. But Colin Grant had played with the light to show what seemed to happen when Andy walked through a crowd. The sun was behind Andy, so that while his shape was dark, the faces in the crowd were illuminated by a light that seemed to come from him. In truth, he could do that to a crowd. It was, I thought, a great photo. But in the brochure Soren Eames handed me, someone had scrawled a word in dark lipstick over Andy's back and head. The word was "Faggot."

"I think we should begin at the beginning," I said, my voice shaking. And he did – with the night he and Andy became lovers. He told his story with such restraint, but every so often his voice would be soft with joy at the simple pleasure of saying his lover's name or remembering a moment of intimacy. His voice was full of wonder when he described the night he and Andy walked at dusk to the prayer centre. "I wasn't his first lover, but he was mine . . . Oh, Joanne, that first time he touched me, I thought, 'This is what it feels like to bloom' – as if I were unfolding under his hands until the dark centre of what I was came into the light. I haven't had a particularly happy life, but that night everything changed for me – for us both. It wasn't a casual intimacy for either of us, Jo. I want you to know that. Andy would want you to know that. There hadn't been anyone before for me, and there had just been one other for him – just one, but he ended that when we fell in love.

"Andy was a person of such honour. That first night we wanted each other so much, but he didn't begin with me until he'd broken off with the other man." He picked up the brochure. "Joanne, this obscenity doesn't make sense because no one knew. We were so careful. For both of us, there were so many other people involved. You, for example – Andy knew how much you'd given to his leadership campaign, and if this had come out . . . Well, you can imagine. Professionally, it would have been the end for me, of course. The good people at Wolf River think my Porsche is kind of flamboyant and daring, but a gay pastor?" He shrugged and smiled sadly. "However, it was Eve we felt we had to protect the most. There hadn't been anything between them for years, but I think Andy would have endured anything rather than cause her to suffer. He said she had suffered enough. She didn't know about us – about me. I'm certain of that. But I always had the sense that she knew the truth about Andy, and I think she knew about the first one."

"Who was he?"

"Andy was a man of honour, you know that, Jo. I never knew the first man's name. I do know they were together for a long time – for years. Andy was terribly shaken about severing their relationship."

Soren looked close to breaking. But I had to press him. "Could it have been him, Soren? Could it have been that first man who killed Andy?"

He didn't answer. He was watching the cold rain falling on the leaves. Finally, he turned to me.

"Jo, what am I going to do about all this?" He tapped the brochure.

"About all this? I don't think you have much choice. I think you have to go to the police. Soren, everything's connected." I pointed to the initials on the envelope. "It's not the first time I've seen that design. It was on a poem someone put in Andy's speech folder the day he was killed."

He looked dazed. I knew how he felt. There had, I thought, been too many shocks.

"Soren, are you all right?"

He held the ceramic cabbage up to the light and turned it gently. "Jo, it's not the first time I've seen those letters, either. I've been trying to remember exactly where I saw them before. I know it was at Andy's house in the city. We were looking through some of his old English texts one day, and I saw those initials drawn together that way a couple of times."

"Did you say anything?"

"I always hated to bring up the subject of Eve."

"So you assumed the *E* and *A* were Eve and Andy?"

"It seemed logical. Who else would it be? And that's one reason I don't want to go to the police. It was always so important to Andy that Eve be protected – I want to do that for him. And, Jo, I don't want people to know about Andy. I don't want anything to hurt him."

His eyes were full of tears. I reached over and touched his hand. "Soren, he wouldn't want anything to hurt you."

He looked up and started to say something. Just then the phone rang. It was Ali Sutherland, breathless, between patients, calling to wish me a happy birthday.

"We are counting the days till Thanksgiving," she said. "Guess what I bought? China with turkeys on it – ten place settings. It's your birthday present but we get to use it first. You'll love it, Jo – a little border of fruits and vegetables and everything – god-awful but right up your alley. There goes my other phone – one of us will meet you at the train – happy birthday!"

When I hung up, Soren was zipping his bomber jacket. "I've taken up too much of your time today. I'll call you in a few days and let you know what I decide about the police." He touched my cheek with his fingertips. "Thanks for listening. It was good just to say his name." He smiled. "And, Joanne, many, many happy returns."

"For you, too," I said. I walked him to the door and watched him go down the front steps.

"Soren, I'm glad Andy had you."

He bounded up the stairs like a boy, kissed me on the cheek and gave me a smile of indescribable sweetness.

"Thank you. Jo, you can't know how much that means to me." He ran down the walk, jumped into the Porsche and took off. Just as he turned the corner the rain turned to snow, huge wet flakes that fell heavily on everything, and I thought, "I'll call him tonight and see if he got home all right." But I never did.

The postman came with a fistful of birthday cards, and a note of thanks from Eve in her curiously schoolgirlish handwriting. There was a Creeds box with a pretty striped silk scarf from Howard Dowhanuik. (A memory – Howard coming to me the Christmas after Marty left. "Jo, what do I get all the women in the office? Booze seems a little crude." And me: "Well, Howard, you can never go wrong with a scarf." Indeed.) There was a first edition James Beard cookbook from my old friend Nina Love, and a handsome book on Frida Kahlo from Nina's daughter, Sally. I looped the silk scarf around my neck, put the James Beard and the Kahlo books on the kitchen table and sat down and looked through my birthday cards.

Then I went upstairs to shower. I stood under the hot water and thought about Soren Eames and Andy.

How could I not have known? That was the thought that kept floating to the top of my consciousness. I shampooed my hair and soaped myself. How could I not have known? I had known Andy for seventeen years. For ten of the years we'd been close, and for two we had been as close as a man and woman working together can be. But it had never crossed my mind. How did I feel about it? Angry. Not angry at it, but angry at Andy for not telling me. Not trusting me – but why would he? Why should he? I turned the cold water down and the shower beat down on me hot and steamy. Why should he tell? Whose life was it anyway?

I went into my room and pulled on jogging pants and a sweatshirt and my old high-tops, went downstairs, put the dogs on their leashes, slipped on a slicker I'd bought Peter to wear to football games and headed for the creek. It was still snowing. In October. "Go for it, prairies," I said as the snow fell steadily, covering the dead leaves. There was no one in the park, so I unhooked the leashes and let the dogs run. Everywhere their feet touched they left a mark.

"A life in translation." That's what a gay friend of mine had called it. His name was Carlyle Wise, and he ran a small art gallery in a heritage house he had restored. He had waited until he was forty to come out, and the only time I heard bitterness in his voice was when he talked about his first forty years. "All that deceit," he had said. "All that energy wasted translating your life into something other people will accept. You're always a foreigner."

The dogs had run down the river bank and were swimming downstream – two sleek golden heads cutting through the grey water.

After he came out, Carlyle Wise had established himself as a kind of informal crisis centre for young men troubled by their homosexuality. Several times a year, one of the hospitals' psychiatric wards would call him, and he would go down and collect a boy who had attempted suicide, bring him home, arrange for counselling, cook for him, get him started in classes or a job and give him a home until he was ready to start life on his own.

"As I hit my dotage I am reduced to being the Queen Mother of the gay community," he would say with a laugh. "But you know, Jo, it's a relief. As Popeye used to say, 'I yam what I yam.'"

Andy had never made it that far. When he died, he was still leading a life in translation, still protecting the secrets of his private world. Somehow that made his death even harder to bear.

The dogs, worried to see me sitting so long on a park bench, came out of the river shaking the wet off, then nuzzled my raincoat. We walked home together through the wet snow. The house was cold and dark. I turned on lights and the furnace, towelled off the dogs and rummaged through the freezer for something good for lunch. I found a container of clam chowder and a loaf of Mieka's sourdough bread, put them both in the oven to warm and took another hot shower. I ate my lunch at the kitchen table wearing an old flannel robe and a pair of fuzzy slippers I'd always loved. At forty-six, you take your comfort where you find it.

After lunch I made myself a cup of tea, opened a new scribbler and wrote two questions: Who knew about Andy and the first man? Who knew about Andy and Soren? I listed the possibilities. (1) Eve. If she knew about the first man, it would explain her outburst at Disciples the day after Andy was killed. (2) Howard Dowhanuik. He had been Andy's teacher and friend and the leader of his party. Would Andy have told him so he could weigh the possibilities of trouble ahead? There was a chance he knew about Soren. Andy was, as Soren said, an honourable man. He might have felt he owed Howard that. (3) Dave Micklejohn. He might know

everything. That would explain his outburst at the Par
Three. In the early days Andy had stayed with him when the
session was on. He was Andy's oldest friend and probably
the closest. (4) Craig Evanson. He and Andy had been in law
school together, then in the legislature together all those
years. Would he have heard rumours? But he would have told
his wife, and Julie Evanson would never have kept quiet
about it when Craig and Andy were contesting the leadership. (5) Mr. X. The first man obviously knew there was a
new man. Did he know it was Soren Eames?

I looked at my list – a good beginning. I picked up James
Beard, went upstairs, curled up with his recipe for honey
squash pie and fell into a sound and dreamless sleep.

When I woke it was three o'clock. I felt better. A man
from the florist came with a dozen creamy long-stemmed
roses from Rick Spenser. My neighbour, Barbara Bryant,
brought over a box wrapped in pink paper. Inside was a
flowered flannelette nightie. Every year for fifteen years we
had given one another a nightie for our birthdays. The first
year mine, I remembered, had been black with a lot of lace;
now it was long-sleeved flannelette with a granny collar.
Milestones.

The boys came home from school cheerful and full of
themselves. They had made dinner reservations at Joe T's, a
favourite restaurant of theirs and mine. Peter quietly suggested that if I wanted a pre-dinner drink, I have it at home.
They had saved enough for either dinner and a drink or
dinner and dessert, and Joe T's cheesecake was famous. I had
my pre-dinner drink at home.

We went to the restaurant, ate a lot and laughed a lot.
When we came home, Dave Micklejohn was waiting on the
porch with a wicked-looking chocolate cake, a bottle of
California champagne and an apology. The kids made a fire
and we sat and watched a ball game, and between innings we

talked about school and ball and politics. Andy's name, of course, came up, and Dave seemed able to talk about him easily and affectionately. The world was starting to piece itself back together, and I was grateful.

A little before 10:00 p.m. the phone rang. On the other end was Rick Spenser. It was good to hear his voice.

"How was your day?" He sounded in high spirits.

"On balance, my day was just fine. Yours must have been wonderful. You sound manic."

"I am exuberant. I'm talking to you. How was your day really, Jo?"

"Really, it was good – very happy. Now let's leave the subject of my birthday." And so we did. We talked about the kids and James Beard's passion for butter, and I told him a crazy story I'd read in a tabloid about how, from beyond the grave, James Beard had written a health-food cookbook. Rick loved that story and matched it with one about the prime minister, and that led to his final wonderful piece of news. He would be free to join us in Winnipeg for Thanksgiving.

I was glowing when I hung up. By the time I said good-night to Dave, let the dogs out one last time, turned out the lights and locked the doors, I felt the fragments of the good old life knitting themselves together again. Maturity, I thought, as I walked up the stairs. Forty-six wasn't going to be so bad after all. When I walked past Mieka's room I opened the bedroom door and said, "Coping," in a declaiming theatrical voice. It was a joke we had when the world fell apart. It was a measure of how good I felt that when I pulled Mieka's door closed, I was smiling.

CHAPTER

15

I had put the dogs on their leashes for their morning run when the phone rang. It was a little before nine o'clock. At first, I thought it was a crank call – for a few long seconds there was background noise, but no one spoke. Then a terrible, unrecognizable voice said:

"Jo, they say I killed him."

"What? Who?" The dogs were going crazy at the front door. Always when their leads were on, it was time to go. I shouted above the racket, "I'm sorry, I can't hear you. Who is this?"

"It's Eve, Jo. Eve Boychuk. Oh, Jo, they say I killed him." Her voice was rising with hysteria.

"Eve, stay calm. Where are you?"

"At the police station in the city. They came and got me this morning. I hadn't even . . . Oh, God, Jo. I can't deal with this." She was almost incoherent.

"Eve, do you know where you are? Ask someone if you're on Smith Street."

I could hear the muffled noise that happens when someone has a hand over the receiver, then she was back on the line. "Yes, Smith Street. Oh, Jo, please."

"I'll be there in ten minutes." When I hung up I noticed how badly I was shaking. Not a good day to drive. I called a cab. Five minutes later, as I slid into the back seat of the taxi, I could hear my dogs barking in the house, still angry.

The new police station was all glass and concrete – "state-of-the-art," as our local paper invariably said. I had been there with Angus's class in the spring, not long after it opened. A nice young constable had shown us around, fingerprinted the kids and talked to them sensibly about drugs and never being afraid of the police and always trusting them when they were in trouble.

Well, I was in trouble now. At the front desk a woman with a round face and granny glasses was waiting for me. Her identification card said "Special Constable Doris Ironstar." She filled out a temporary identification card for me and led me down a corridor and into a small room. There, sitting alone at a square metal table, was Eve. She looked almost catatonic, but as soon as she saw me, she ran across the room and embraced me. She was covered in blood, and the smell was so strong I almost retched. I turned and looked at Constable Ironstar.

"My God, what have you done to her?"

"I'll get the inspector," she said and left.

Eve was sobbing and embracing me. She was a strong woman and it took me a minute to pry myself loose. She was wearing the unbleached cotton dress she had worn the day Andy died, and she was barelegged. Her dress and her legs and hands were caked with blood, but I couldn't see where it was coming from.

"Eve, where are you hurt?"

But the only answer she gave was a low guttural sound. She crooned my name and said the words "no" and "oh" over and over.

Finally my old friend Inspector Millar Millard came in.

"Can't you at least get her a doctor?" I said. "She could be bleeding to death."

The inspector looked at me wearily. "There's a doctor on her way from City Hospital, but the blood isn't coming from Mrs. Boychuk; it came from him."

Now I could feel the hysteria rising in my throat. "Is everyone here crazy? Andy's been dead for a month. How can that be his blood?"

When he bent to calm me, I saw that the good Inspector Millard, the one who gave me tea and biscuits, was back. His voice was weary but kind. "Mrs. Kilbourn, the blood didn't come from Mrs. Boychuk's husband. It seems we have another murder here."

I looked up. Millar Millard was watching me, waiting.

"Mrs. Kilbourn, that blood on your friend came from a man named Soren Eames. Mrs. Boychuk is being held in connection with his murder."

I felt as if I had turned to ice. The inspector continued.

"We had a call this morning from" – he checked the notes on his clipboard – "from a girl named Kelly Evanson . . ."

"Lori Evanson." I corrected automatically.

He smiled and pencilled in the change on his report. "Early this morning Lori Evanson found Soren Eames dead in his office at Wolf River Bible College. Someone had beaten him rather savagely with an axe. We have the weapon. We're checking it out, of course, but it seems to be pretty standard issue, the kind of axe kids use in Boy Scouts. You have children, Mrs. Kilbourn. I'll bet you've had an axe just like it in your house at one time or another. Not that I'm suggesting a connection there," he said, tapping his cigarette package on the corner of the table. He looked again at his notes. "When Lori Evanson walked into the office this morning, Mrs. Boychuk was standing over the body with the axe in her hands."

All on their own, my legs had begun to tremble uncontrollably. I looked down at them. Somewhere in the distance the inspector's voice, patient and gravelly, was talking about physical evidence.

A tiny young woman in a trench coat came in carrying a medical bag. She went not to Eve, but to me. She slid her fingers around my wrist, positioned her face close to mine.

"Shock," she said, still holding my wrist in her hand. Then there was a swab and a pinprick sensation at the crease of my elbow, and I felt warm and weary. "You'll be all right now. You're Joanne Kilbourn, aren't you? Well, Joanne, someone will get you some tea. Plenty of sugar," she said over her shoulder. "Hang in there, Joanne," and then, smooth as silk, she moved along. "Now, Eve, what you need is a hot bath and a chance to get all this muck off. The inspector tells me there is a shower here, and some fresh clothes, but just let me give you a little something to bring you down a bit. There. Now that should keep the bad stuff away for a while." She motioned to Constable Ironstar. "I think it's time we took Eve to the shower; we can sit outside and talk to her as the water runs. Come on, Eve, let's go." She took Eve's hand in hers, and the two of them walked out of the room as coolly as if they were at a pyjama party.

Constable Ironstar picked up the medical bag and followed them. She looked edgy. Tranquillized or not, Eve was an unknown quantity. As soon as Constable Ironstar shut the door behind her, the inspector leaned forward in his seat.

"Are you all right now, Mrs. Kilbourn?"

"Yes, I think so. I'm sorry, it was . . ."

"A shock. I know. It always is – especially the smell. We would have given Eve a chance to clean up if things had worked out. We've had personnel problems here today, a death."

A piece slid in place. A staff sergeant had been killed earlier in the week. I'd read in the paper that the funeral was this morning. "I'm sorry about your colleague, Inspector," I said.

Unexpectedly, he smiled. "Thank you, Mrs. Kilbourn. That's a kind thought. Now." He sighed regretfully. "I guess we have to concentrate on this other matter. Mrs. Boychuk needs a lawyer. Normally, people make the call themselves or give us a name and we make the call for them. But Mrs. Boychuk couldn't seem to get much beyond you this morning. I wonder if you could suggest someone."

"Craig Evanson," I said, then wondered where that suggestion came from.

"Is he in the book?"

"Yes, his office is on Broad Street. Just be sure to tell him what it's about. He'll come."

"Thank you, Mrs. Kilbourn. I'll call him myself." He stood up. "I'll have someone bring you some tea." He closed the door behind him.

In a few minutes Doris Ironstar came with a pot of tea and some cookies on a plate. The cookies looked homemade.

"Police issue?" I said.

"Out of my lunch box," she said. "My boyfriend made them. They're good. You look as if you could use a little nourishment."

I felt tears come to my eyes. "I'm sorry," I said, "I seem to be right on the edge this morning."

"Drink the tea and eat the cookies," said Special Constable Ironstar, and she gave me a small smile as she went out the door.

Then Craig Evanson stuck his head in. "I'll be back. I'm just going to see about Eve," he said, and was gone.

I drank my tea and ate my cookies, gingersnaps with lots of molasses. Constable Ironstar's boyfriend was no slouch. I felt better.

In a few minutes a little party trooped down the hall past my door – the inspector, the doctor from the hospital, Craig Evanson, Eve. When she saw me, Eve started into the room toward me. She was clean and dressed in what appeared to be pyjamas. Her hair was damp but neatly combed and she had a grey army blanket around her shoulders. She had the slightly punchy look of an exhausted child. Craig and the young doctor guided her into the hallway and down the corridor, and Eve gave me a little wave.

The inspector came in and sat down with me. "Mr. Evanson wants to talk to his client privately. We'll be taking her to the correctional centre later. You can leave any time. If you wait a little, I'll have someone drive you." As if on cue, a dozen policemen in dress uniform marched by the door.

"I feel as if I'm in a Fellini movie," I said.

The inspector smiled and said, "I often have that feeling myself. Anyway, you can walk out of this movie whenever you're ready."

I looked at him. I felt as tired and sad as he sounded.

"No, Inspector, I'm afraid you're wrong. I don't think I can walk out of this movie. I think there are some things I have to tell you."

Two hours later, a police car delivered me to the house on Eastlake Avenue. When I went to stand up after my interview with Millar Millard, my legs had turned to rubber. I'd been glad of the ride.

When I walked in the front door, Peter and Angus were home for lunch. They were sitting in front of the TV eating Kraft Dinner. The news of Soren Eames's murder had become public. When I sat on the floor beside them, the television was showing Eve and me walking across the parking lot of the hospital the morning we drove to Wolf River. I hadn't realized the network had filmed us, but there we

were. Eve, tall and elegant, and me, short and matronly.
Mutt and Jeff. There were other pieces of file footage: the
funeral, of course, and the dedication of the Charlie Appleby
Prayer Centre. There was Soren Eames, wired with excitement, talking passionately and sensitively about the design
of the building, then a sweeping shot of the dignitaries
sitting in chairs on the hard-packed dirt in front of the
centre. The premier was there, looking, as always, boyishly
hyperactive (too much sugar, Angus once said knowledge-
ably), and Lane Appleby, sitting not far from Eve and Andy,
then a quick shot of Andy and Soren Eames together at the
microphone: two handsome men in young middle age,
squinting in the pale, cold sun of an April morning. When
everything came out, that shot of Soren and Andy would be
on the front page of every newspaper in Canada.

Then pictures of the body being taken out of the CAP
Centre and loaded into an ambulance. Suddenly, I couldn't
handle it: Soren, blinking in the sunlight, talking about form
and function in architecture, and Soren, an anonymous bulk
under a red blanket, wrapped in darkness forever. My knees
began to tremble again, and I turned off the television, went
to the liquor cabinet and pulled out a bottle of Hennessey's.
I poured myself a generous shot and walked into the kitchen.

As I took the first sip, the phone rang. It was Howard
Dowhanuik calling from Toronto. His news was grim. Already
the Toronto media were having a field day with Soren's
murder. They'd dug up the Lorscott case, and one of the city
TV stations had sent a crew to Port Durham to get Eve's
father's response to the charges against his daughter. The old
man had smashed in the television cameras and chased the
reporters off his property. Apparently, Eve was going to be
spared nothing.

Howard's assessment was brutal: "Thanksgiving came
early for the shitheads of the press this year. They aren't going

to have to scramble for this one. No, this one is going to jump into their word processors all by itself."

It seemed as good a time as any to ask my question. "Howard, there's more here and I think you must know about it."

"What kind of more, Jo?" His voice on the other end of the line was suddenly wary.

"Andy was a homosexual. He and Soren Eames were lovers."

There was a sigh. "Jesus, no. I didn't know that. Not about Andy and Eames."

I pressed him. "But you did know about Andy."

Silence.

"You knew, didn't you? Answer me." I could hear my voice, shrill and demanding.

Then Howard's voice, defeated. "Yeah. I knew, Jo."

"How long? When did you find out?"

"From the beginning, at least from the political beginning. Andy told me the first time I asked him to run for us."

"Damn it, Howard, why didn't you tell me?"

There was anger in his voice. "Because, Jo, there was no goddamn reason in the world for you to know. Because it wasn't any of your goddamn business, any more than it was Andy's business how often you and Ian got it off in bed. Andy did the right thing by telling me, but it was nobody's business but his and mine."

"And Eve's," I said meanly.

"Yes, and Eve's."

"Howard, did you know any of the men?"

There was a beat of hesitation. "No, I didn't – not for sure. There was one I saw just for a second, that first year Andy was elected."

"What was he like?"

"Oh, for God's sake, Jo, it's been almost twenty years . . . Tall and thin, I think. I just saw him for a second and he was . . ."

"He was what, Howard?"

"Naked. He was naked, Joanne. We were in Toronto for a conference. I went to Andy's hotel room early. While we were talking at the door, the other guy came out of the bathroom. I guess he didn't hear me at the door."

"And what happened?"

"I gave Andy hell for not being careful and for balling around, and he said it wasn't like that – that this guy was 'the one and only.' Funny choice of words, but that's what he said . . . Jo, I'm sorry I barked at you. This is a hell of a mess. Look, do you want me to come out there? Does Eve have a lawyer?"

"I suggested they call Craig Evanson. He'll be good with her – gentle. Howard, I'd love for you to come, but really, there's nothing you could do but hold my hand."

"Not the worst fate I can think of."

"The big city's turning you into a smooth talker."

"I mean it, Jo."

"I know you do. You're a good soul, Howard. Look, I'll call you if I need you."

"Don't wait for that – just call."

"Okay. Hey, take care of yourself. Stay away from the painted ladies down there."

"Oh, Jo, I miss you," and then "shit," and he hung up. I sat there for a minute wondering. Then I went into the kitchen and ate some of the boys' leftover Kraft Dinner while I sipped my Hennessey's. It's not a bad combination on a day when the world falls apart.

When the phone rang again, I was in the granny flat sorting through files, looking for places where Andy and Soren might have been together or, more to the point, might have been seen together. The voice on the line was male, young and tentative.

"Mrs. Kilbourn, this is Mark Evanson. The memorial service for Soren Eames will be held on Thursday at the CAP Centre, at ten o'clock in the morning." He hung up.

"Well," I said to the empty room, "I can wear the outfit I wore to Andy's funeral. There'll be a different crowd for this one." And then I repeated Howard's farewell expletive and went back to my files.

I should have been able to predict that Rick would come to Soren Eames's memorial service. The funeral was the climactic coda of the tragedy of the summer, and as his news director said, Rick did have a unique connection with the story. The prospect of his coming was the one small bright spot in the darkness of that day, especially because he was going to stay with us. It made sense. He hated hotels. The granny flat was self-contained, and except for my files and boxes, it was empty. Despite everything, when I hung up after Rick's call, I felt my spirits lifting. It had been a while since I'd had something to look forward to, someone to get ready for.

He was due on the late afternoon flight on Wednesday, and I woke up that morning with the sense of anticipation that a day filled with small and pleasant errands brings. It was a grey and misty day, cool and magic. The snow that had fallen the morning of my birthday was gone, and it really seemed like harvest time. After breakfast I drove down to the valley for late summer vegetables: carrots, Brussels sprouts, squash, potatoes. There was a stand near the highway selling fruit from British Columbia, and I bought a basket of Delicious apples for us, then drove back and bought another basket for Rick. I stopped in Lumsden at the one butcher I know who can cut a perfect crown roast of pork and then, on

impulse, I drove to the correctional centre to leave a note for
Eve. Even with the extra drive to the correctional centre, I
was home well before lunch.

I made a good molassesy Indian pudding, and by the time
Angus came home for lunch the house smelled the way a
house is supposed to smell in the week before Thanksgiving.
Before Angus went back to school, he helped me put sheets
on the hide-a-bed in the granny flat and clean towels in
the bathroom.

"Now what else?" I asked him, looking around.

"Some of those orange things along the fence in that mug
there – a guy would like that." We filled Ian's pewter beer
mug with Chinese lanterns and dried grass. Angus was right,
it did look like the kind of thing a guy would like. When he
went to school, I took the phone off the hook, set the table
with our best cut-work tablecloth and the good silver, prepared the vegetables, made a quick trip to the liquor store for
Rick's brand of gin, and ran up my bill at the florist's by
buying two pots of fat bronze chrysanthemums and a bunch
of creamy cosmos for the Waterford vase Rick had given me.
Peter came home from school, filled the wood box and set a
fire in the fireplace. I showered, dressed in a dark outfit of
clingy silk that made me look glamorous and thin, then
changed into a skirt and sweater that made me feel comfortable and drove to the airport to pick up Rick.

I had forgotten how big he was – tall and heavy. *Maclean's*
said he was the only TV journalist who was larger than life
when you saw him in person. "He doesn't disappoint" –
that's what the article about him said, and it was right. He
certainly didn't disappoint me that afternoon when I saw him
standing by the luggage carousel in our bleak new airport.

He was all in brown, tweed and cashmere and silk. His
dark blond hair was freshly barbered, and when he reached

out to embrace me he smelled of good cologne, Scotch from the plane and something else.

"Deli," he said extending a shiny shopping bag already beginning to darken with grease. "You said you couldn't get good deli here, so there's pastrami and salami, and with my luggage, in a box which, in theory, is insulated, there's a cheesecake from the Red Panzer. Happy Thanksgiving, Joanne."

It was one of the all-time great evenings. The meal was very good, and afterward we had coffee and brandy and went to Taylor Field to Peter's football game. Under the lights of the stadium the players in their crayon-bright uniforms looked theatrical and unreal.

"I feel like I'm in the middle of a Debbie Reynolds–Donald O'Connor musical," Rick said and smiled. His breath was frosty in the fresh, cold air.

"I always feel like that at these things," I said. "I always find myself hoping I'll be homecoming queen and get to go to the harvest dance with the captain of the football team."

"Were you ever homecoming queen?" he asked, looking at me gravely.

"Nope," I said. "Never went out with the captain of the football team, never even went to a harvest dance."

"Thank God." He laughed.

Peter's team won, and we drove some of the kids home. As they climbed into the car they were exuberant. It was good to drive through the moonlit streets and hear their new deep voices cracking with excitement. At home, the boys went to bed, Rick lit the fire and we sat in front of it drinking tea and brandy and talking about everything and nothing: Mieka's classes, Margaret Laurence's novels, why politicians didn't read more, and finally, when the sounds from upstairs died down and I knew the boys were sleeping,

I told Rick about the relationship between Andy and Soren Eames. He was silent for a long while, then he said quietly, "Those things never end happily," and stood up. "Time for bed, my homecoming queen."

I walked out on the deck with him. The sky had cleared, and the night was full of stars, pinpoints of light in the darkness. I had left the lights on in the granny flat, and they glowed warm and inviting across the yard. Rick took both my hands in his and looked down at me.

"Thank you for a perfect night," he said. Then he walked heavily across the yard. I watched him climb the stairs, watched as he tried the door then shrugged and turned toward me. "Key?" he said.

"Damn," I said. "Sorry – in the window box – there's a little plastic bag, taped to the side."

He reached in, then raised his hand in the darkness. "Triumph," he said, and he opened the door and disappeared inside.

I stood for a few minutes in the fresh cool air, watching his huge silhouette moving in the square of light from across the yard. Then I called in my dogs, and because I was at peace with the world when we went upstairs, I let them sleep at the bottom of my bed.

The day of Soren Eames's memorial service was heartbreakingly lovely – a late Indian summer day, all blue skies and hazy autumn light. Rick and I drove to Wolf River right after breakfast. His TV crew was taping some background material when we arrived, and he excused himself and went over and talked to them. I was standing in the sunlight, warm in my white suit, when Inspector Millard tapped me on the shoulder.

"Hello, Mrs. Kilbourn."

"Inspector? I'm surprised to see you here. Did you know Soren Eames?"

He lit a cigarette and shook his head. "No, I'm just kind of looking around."

"But surely when you have Eve in custody . . ." My voice trailed off.

"Well, you never know."

"Never know what?"

He shrugged and started to walk away. "See you in church, Mrs. Kilbourn." But then he turned. "The other day in my office you said you were writing a book about Andy Boychuk – I don't suppose you've changed your mind."

"No, I haven't. In fact, I'm more committed than ever. I don't think Eve Boychuk killed her husband, Inspector, and I don't think she killed Soren Eames." It was the first time I'd said the words aloud, and they sounded right.

He took a drag on his cigarette, threw it on the ground and crushed it with his toe. It was only half smoked.

"Mrs. Kilbourn, do your friends, the police, a favour, would you? Exercise prudence in this research of yours." He pulled a package of Kools out of his breast pocket and took one out. He looked hard at me. "That's a very attractive suit you have on. The perfect thing for this occasion." Then he walked off, leaving me standing in the sunlight, speechless in my perfect suit.

I went over to talk to Rick, but he was taping – or almost. Just as I came up, the cameraman signalled Rick to move. "The way the light hits you where you're standing, it looks like you've got the fucking cross burning on the top of your head."

Rick smiled and shook his head at me, but he moved and started again. As I walked to the entrance of the CAP Centre, I could hear Rick's voice, professionally solemn.

"Six months ago, Soren Eames stood on this spot in triumph. He had personally raised $5.5 million, and the prayer centre behind me had become a reality. He could not have known then that –"

A construction truck went by, blasting its horn. Someone who appeared to be in charge yelled, "Okay, that's it, close it down while we silence our pal with the Tonka over there."

Rick gave me a little wave, and I walked over and leaned against a pile of rocks, carefully arranged by size and colour. There was going to be a rock garden outside the chapel. Soren Eames had told me that the day we walked up the hill.

It really was warm. I could feel the sweat start under my arms.

Rick began again. "Six months ago, Soren Eames stood on this spot in triumph. . . ."

I turned and walked into the cool building.

Soren Eames's memorial service broke my heart. The administration of the college had brought in a grief counsellor to help the students deal with Soren's death. She had suggested that they would recover from their loss more quickly if they had a hand in planning the service. It was a sensible recommendation and a terrible one.

Because they were children who had little experience of death, they hadn't learned the tricks of ceremony and tradition the middle-aged use to mute emotion. After the funeral, Mark Evanson, his young face swollen from crying, told me, "We wanted it to be special for Soren – not something out of a book. We wanted to say good-bye to him in our own voices." The service was full of touches that collapsed the space between us and our grief. The coffin was covered with a flawless piece of white lace that Soren had brought back with him from Dublin the summer before. Placed carefully in the centre was a child's Bible. The president of the student association told us that Soren's grandfather had brought it to the hospital the day Soren was born.

There was a program. The school choir sang a ragged selection of songs that Soren had liked – some solid gospel hymns but also, surprisingly, two show tunes, "Somewhere" from *West Side Story* and a Stephen Sondheim song called "Not While I'm Around."

Between selections, students came forward with memories of special moments, special kindnesses. Finally, there was a tape of Soren's speech at the dedication of the CAP Centre. When his voice, full of music and hope, began, the sobbing in that silent room cut straight to the bone. Beside me, Rick Spenser shuddered.

At the end, Lori Evanson, a small figure in black, stepped to the front and in her sweet, tuneful voice sang "Amazing Grace."

Then her husband came and stood beside her and said very simply, "John 1:5 will help us now. 'The light shines in the darkness and the darkness has not overcome it.'" And it was over.

Rick and I didn't find much to say to one another on the drive to the city. I could feel a knot of tension in my shoulders and the beginning of a headache, so I decided to go to the Lakeshore Club for a swim.

When I told Rick, he smiled. "That seems like an inspired idea."

"Inspired enough for you to join me?"

He looked horrified. "God, no." Then, seeing my face, he added more kindly, "Do you swim often?"

"Every Saturday morning. We all do. Well, we all do something at the Lakeshore Club. It's our one invariable routine."

He smiled. "Routine is comforting, isn't it?"

"Yeah," I said, "it is. Now where would you like to be taken?"

I dropped him off at his network's local studio. Then I drove to the Lakeshore Club. An hour later, damp-haired but relaxed, I decided to drive to the correctional centre to see Eve.

The guard, a tall, pretty redhead whose name, according to her identification tag, was Terry Shaw, told me Eve hadn't talked all day but she seemed "engaged," so they weren't concerned. As we turned the corner to the hospital block, Terry Shaw said, "She's in the craft area doing a little project we got her started on. You can watch her through the glass if you like."

Eve was sitting at a table near the observation window, bent over, drawing the wattles on the head of a construction-paper turkey. The table was littered with turkeys, and they were cleverly done, proud, handsome birds with bright and malevolent eyes. As she worked, Eve's thick grey hair fell forward, blocking her face from my eyes. I stood and watched her for a few minutes. When it was time to leave, I tapped on the glass and waved. She looked up at me distractedly, like a woman called from an important task by something foolish. Then, without acknowledging me, she smiled and went back to her turkeys.

Dinner was a casual and comfortable meal. It was warm enough to eat on the deck, so while Rick went to the store for beer, I put a cloth on the table and set out plates of pastrami and salami and trays of bread and mustards and fat kosher dills. Like the man who brought it, the Red Panzer's cheesecake did not disappoint. It was every bit as good as I remembered.

The train for Winnipeg left early, before 7:00 a.m., so the boys brought our packed suitcases down to the front hall and we made an early night of it. When I was locking up, I looked over to the granny flat. In the square of light in the darkness I could see Rick Spenser on the telephone. After the jagged emotions of the morning it was a comforting sight.

CHAPTER

16

I had worried that Rick Spenser would feel like an outsider, or worse, put a tear in the seamless intimacy that always sprang up when I was with Ali Sutherland and her husband, Morton Lee. But as soon as Rick walked over, hand out-stretched, to greet Ali in the Winnipeg train station, it seemed as if they belonged together. Ali is a big woman, tall, heavy and always brilliantly fashionable. As she and Rick stood under the dome of the old Victorian station, they looked like travellers from a huge and handsome race.

From the moment Rick opened the door of Ali and Mort's brick bungalow in Tuxedo Park, he was at home. The work worlds of Rick and the two doctors might have been dis-parate, but their private lives were fired by the same loves: art, opera and the passionate enjoyment of food.

Two hours after we arrived, Rick Spenser was in the kitchen pressing a square of butter into a rectangle of dough for puff pastry, sipping an icy martini and fighting with Mort about whether the duet from *The Pearl Fishers* was the most perfect piece of music ever written. The evening was full of good talk and easy laughter. Even Peter forgot his shyness and told stories about a boy from school named Gumby who seemed to have achieved mythic stature among the grade elevens. That night as I slid between the soft flannelette sheets in the front guest room, I said aloud, "I'm going to stay here forever," and I fell asleep, smiling.

Saturday morning, Morton Lee pushed himself back from the breakfast table and said, "Here's what Ali and I are going to do this morning. We're going to take Peter and Angus and anyone else who wants to come downtown to the greatest toy store in western Canada." Seeing Peter's polite display of enthusiasm, Mort thumped himself on the head theatrically and said, "Did I say toy store? What I meant, of course, was toys for jocks – a store that has every kind of ball the mind of the jock can conceive of and all the equipment you need to play anything, plus cards: baseball cards, football cards, hockey cards. Everything." Then Peter's enthusiasm was real.

Rick sipped his coffee. "Well, I'm a cook not a jock so I'll make dinner tonight. I have the menu planned and it is, to use Peter's word, dynamite."

As I slid behind the wheel of Ali's Volvo, I knew I had left behind a happy house.

Tuxedo Park Road, where Lane Appleby lived, was just a five-minute drive from Ali and Mort's. It was a street of tall trees, wide, deep lots and houses that glowed with the sheen of money. The Appleby house had the tallest trees, the widest, deepest lot and the most discreet glow. When I lifted the door knocker, I was glad Ali's shiny Volvo was parked out front. Even borrowed glory is better than no glory at all.

Lane Appleby's housekeeper answered the door. She was a square Scot with faded red hair and pale, freckled skin. She was no more welcoming in person than she had been on the telephone. In fact, she made no attempt to disguise the fact that she was not glad to see me. The day was cool, but she didn't invite me in.

"Mrs. Appleby is resting. You'll have to come back at a more convenient time." She turned and began to shut the door.

I edged my purse into the space that was still open. "This is the time we agreed to. I'm certain if you'll just speak with Mrs. Appleby . . ."

"I'm certain" – she pronounced it "sairtin" – "she would prefer another time," she said and began to push the door shut again.

I stuck my head past her into the house and called, "Lane Appleby, this is Joanne Kilbourn here to see you." From inside the house I heard a voice husky and petulant. "Come." I shot the Scot a look of triumph as I flashed past her into the front hall. Ahead was a foyer as big as my living room and a staircase that circled up to the second floor, but we turned left and walked through the dining room into a small room off it that opened onto the garden. I had been on enough tours of houses of this age to know what the room had been – a ladies' sitting room, a place where women could wait out the time until the gentlemen came back from their brandy and cigars.

The room had been restored with taste and intelligence. All the elaborate detail of the woodwork had been left but everything, walls and woodwork, had been painted a soft yellow. There were three flowery love seats, just the right size for female confidences, turned toward one another in front of the window, a pretty grandmother's clock in the corner, and in front of the fireplace, which glowed with warmth on this cold October morning, was a round table, set for coffee. On either side of the table was a wing chair covered in something silky and embroidered with bright, exotic birds. Lane Appleby was sitting in the chair facing the door.

The whole scene was so obviously one of welcome that I

was baffled at the housekeeper's hostility. But when Lane Appleby stood to greet me, I understood. The lady of the house was as drunk as a monkey.

She reached across the table to take my hand and fell, laughing, back into her chair. I would have guessed her age at fifty-five but a great fifty-five: trim, athletic body, good skin, skilful makeup and a terrific haircut. When she smiled, the years melted away and you could see the girl she must have been, flirtatious, with that confidence lovely women often have, that way of saying, without saying, we both know this beauty thing is just silly, but let's enjoy it.

Her voice was husky and pleasant. Next to her was an ashtray, full, and a half-empty pack of Camels. She'd earned the gravel in that voice. She picked up the coffeepot, aimed it at my cup, splashed the tablecloth and laughed.

"Well, maybe you'd better take care of yourself," she said. Then without self-consciousness, she reached beside her to pick up a bottle of brandy and poured a generous slug into her own cup. That time she didn't spill a drop. After she took a sip she sat back and looked at me. Her eyes were as unfocused as a baby's and about as comprehending. She had lost the reason I was there.

"I'm Andy Boychuk's friend, Joanne Kilbourn," I said.

As soon as I mentioned Andy's name, a flash of pain crossed her face. She took another slug of her drink, stood up and said very formally, "Mrs. Kilbourn, I'm not well today. I wonder if you would do me the favour of coming another time," and she moved unsteadily toward the door. The side of the coffee table caught her leg, and she started to fall. I caught her before she hit the grandmother clock. She crumpled against me and leaned her head on my shoulder, like a football player who'd taken a punishing tackle.

"I'd like to go upstairs to bed now," she said. There was nothing to do but take her there.

We walked through the dining room, past a magnificent table that would seat sixteen easily. Somehow, I doubted that Lane Appleby needed to seat sixteen often any more. When we came into the entrance hall, I looked around for the housekeeper.

"Gone," said Lane Appleby, "gone for the turkey," and she leaned even more heavily against me. Ahead, the stairs curved perilously toward the second floor. I adjusted my grip on her and took a deep breath, and we started up. It was a long trip. Lining the wall beside the staircase were pictures of Lane. As we went, she gave me a running commentary. The first one was black and white, a professionally posed picture of her in a figure-skating outfit.

"Nineteen forty-six," she said, "the year I met Charlie. I was in the Ice Capades, but that picture's a fake. I was never a star, just in the chorus . . . Not really good enough but, as you can see, cute as a button."

"You still are," I said, and meant it.

She laughed her throaty laugh. "Well, I think they would have canned me, but I beat them to it . . . Married the boss." We moved up two steps toward the next picture – this one a wedding photo, palely tinted. I'd seen Charlie Appleby's picture in the paper a hundred times, mostly with his hockey team. He was a big, rough-looking man, twenty years older than his pretty bride, but in the photo with Lane on their wedding day, plainly adoring.

That look of adoration never changed. The pictures by the staircase traced a life of rare and singular pleasures. Lane, laughing, struggles under the weight of the Stanley Cup while Charlie, the man who takes care of his wife, reaches to steady it. Lane, fifties-chic in a dark mink coat and a close-fitting feathered hat, smiles up into the face of a very young Lester Pearson while Charlie beams. Lane and Charlie, tanned and vital, drink cool drinks, piled high with fruit, at Montego

Bay; Lane and Charlie, brilliant in their bright ski clothes, stand silhouetted against the blue skies of Stowe, Vermont.

Finally, there is one of Lane by herself. Handsome still, but clearly growing older, she sits alone in the photographer's studio.

"That's the last one I'll get done," she said. "Damn depressing. If I had the nerve, I'd take them all down. Depressing, watching yourself grow old." She turned and made a sweeping gesture with her hand and almost pulled us down the staircase. I strengthened my hold on her and dragged her along the hall to her room.

She didn't put up a struggle. She sat at her dresser while I turned down her bedspread, then she lay on top of her sheets and fell instantly asleep. I was looking for some sort of cover for her when I found the picture – the picture that I had felt all along must exist somewhere. It was in a silver oval frame. A little girl of about six or seven in a white confirmation dress, her hair corkscrew tight in ringlets, stands on the stairs of a church. Beside her, a bishop, paunchy, bulbous-nosed, looks unsmilingly into the camera.

I put a blanket over the woman sleeping on the bed and slipped the picture into my bag.

Then I walked down the stairs, through Lane's life, from the drunken, lonely woman passed out on the bed, to the widow, the wife, the bride, the shining figure skater. Somehow, I thought, as I opened the front door and stepped into the fresh air, Lane Appleby's life seemed better when you looked at it backward.

Barbara Bryant answered on the first ring. "Jo, this is uncharacteristically sentimental of you. Or are you calling to see if the dogs are lonely?"

It was tonic to hear her voice. "No, I trust you to keep them reassured, but I need a favour, Barb. Would you mind going next door to the granny flat and getting a picture that's in a file there and sending it to me here?"

"As that odious toad across the street says, 'No problem.'"

"Great. The key is in the window box."

"Trust you, Jo. Never the obvious."

"Well, you won't have any trouble finding it, anyway. The picture I want is in a vertical file marked 1950. It's Andy's first communion picture. You can't miss it."

"Jo, speaking of the granny flat, there were some guys out there today from –" There was a crash and a howl. Then Barbara's voice again, good-natured and resigned. "Sam just fell off his rocking horse. Have a great Thanksgiving. Sam and I'll drive the picture out to the airport right now. The ride will take his mind off his injuries. The picture should be there by late this afternoon."

"Barbara, thanks, I'll do it for you someday. And happy Thanksgiving."

I drove straight to Lane Appleby's from the airport. I had the two pictures in my purse, and they confirmed what I had felt from the moment Roma Boychuk spit in Lane's face the day Andy died. I knew that if I called Lane would put me off, and I was growing bored with her self-indulgence. Two good men had died, a broken woman I felt was inno-cent was in the correctional centre, and that might not be the end of it. I wasn't sure where this piece fit, but I knew that at this point I couldn't afford to set anything aside out of delicacy.

She answered the door herself. That was the first surprise. She was sober. That was the second surprise.

"Lane, I'm coming in," I said. "I have something to give you."

She must have felt like hell, but she gave me a smile and threw open the door. She led me through the dining room to her little sitting room. There was a fire warm and welcoming in the grate and a fresh bowl of freesias in the centre of the table.

"This time really is drink time," she said. She was pale but she was game. When she alluded to the adventure of the morning she tried another smile. "I think we have almost everything. I'm having tea, if you'd like that?"

"Tea would be fine."

Her hands were shaking when she poured but this time she hit the cup. "Mrs. Kilbourn – Joanne – I'd like to explain about this morning."

"Lane, believe me, that's the least of my concerns. Since Andy's death and then Soren's, things seem to be spinning out of control. I need your help. I can't force you to get involved, but I can tell you that if you know anything about any of this I think you have an obligation to tell someone." I fished into my bag, pulled out the two photos and set them side by side on the table. The frames of both pictures were silver. Hers was oval, chased with a little flowery pattern; his was plain silver, heavier and square. But the church steps in the pictures were the same and the bishop was the same, although clearly younger in Lane's communion picture. Andy had joked once or twice about being the child of his mother's withered loins. Roma must have been much younger when Lane was born.

Lane's reaction surprised me. She took my theft of her picture without comment, but there was a sharp intake of her breath as she saw the picture of Andy. When she picked it up to look at it more closely, the light from the fire warmed the picture's silver frame.

It was, I thought, the right moment to ask my question. "Lane, Andy was your brother, wasn't he?"

She looked up, surprised. The look on her face was the same as the look on Eve's face the day in Disciples when she told me I didn't know the first thing about Andy. Lane leaned toward me. I could smell tobacco and perfume. Her voice was husky.

"I'm afraid you're wrong, Nancy Drew. Andy Boychuk was my son."

It was a familiar story: the pretty young girl and the favourite uncle – Roma's brother. "I thought," said Lane, "that when she found out she'd be on my side, that she would kill him, but it was me she wanted to kill." She raised her voice in an uncanny imitation of her mother's. "'Slut. Whore. It's always the girl's fault, Elena. My brother Sid is a good man. You threw yourself at him. Scum. Streetwalker.'" Lane laughed throatily. "Mother love. She took the baby, of course. 'The innocent baby, may he never know his mother, the whore.' Well, you get the idea."

She lit a Camel and inhaled deeply. "Charlie knew, but not until years after we were married. Oh, God, the guilt. And when I finally told him, he was so sweet. He said, 'Well, Lane, what d'ya want to do?'

"I had this great scheme, straight out of a Bette Davis movie. I was going to go to Andy and tell him he wasn't the son of some little babba out by the railroad tracks. He was Lane and Charlie Appleby's son. The son of rich people who could do anything for him. And, of course, he would fall down on his knees at this amazing news." She laughed. "And my mother would see the error of her ways and repent. Or she'd die. And either way we'd all live happily ever after."

The ash fell off her cigarette onto the perfect carpet. She didn't miss a beat. "But I made the mistake of asking Charlie what he thought I should do." Her eyes grew dreamy. "Do you know what he said? He said, 'Lane, honey, let the guy be and let you be. If you want to do something monetarily, we'll find a way to do it incognito. Enough money to smooth the way without upsetting the apple cart.'" That's what Charlie thought was best and that's what he did – we did. Charlie's lawyer knew Howard Dowhanuik, and he handled it from the time Andy was eighteen. And it was always" – she smiled sadly – "incognito."

"But you saw Andy," I said. "You were at the picnic that day and at the dedication of the prayer centre in Wolf River. I saw you on the tapes."

"After Charlie died I couldn't stay away. I had no one. I have no one. I told Howard Dowhanuik, and he suggested I do something at the Pines where Andy's little boy lives. He said that would give me 'legitimate access' to Andy. I don't know what Howard had in mind, but I was too old to be a candystriper, so I asked Soren Eames what I could do for the college."

"And the CAP Centre was born," I said.

"The Charlie Appleby Prayer Centre was born," she corrected gently. "And that's my involvement." Her cigarette was still burning in the ashtray, but she lit another. "Now," she said, "I have a question for you." Her voice broke. "Who's doing these things? It isn't Eve. I'm as certain of that as I am that I was never Barbara Ann Scott. What kind of monster is loose out there?"

When I pulled up in front of the pretty doorway of the house in Tuxedo Park, Peter and Angus were throwing a football around on the lawn with Morton Lee. Collectively, they were wearing enough equipment to get a CFL team through the season. Mort was a generous shopper.

It was just before dusk, the time in autumn when suddenly the light fades, the temperature dips and I'm glad I have a place to go home to. When I opened the door, the house smelled of roast beef and pies browning. Somewhere

Jussi Björling was singing "O Mimi, tu piu non torni" from *La Bohème*. Rick strode down the hall. He was wearing a huge butcher's apron and he looked agitated.

"Damn. I thought you were Mort," and then realizing what he'd said, "Jo, I'm sorry, it's just that . . ."

"You wanted him to hear the Björling-Merrill duet from *The Pearl Fishers* – I have this record, too. Go get him." And so Mort came in, face flushed with cold and exertion, and we three stood and listened to "Au font du temple Saint," and I thought, Rick was right. It was the most perfect piece of music that's ever been written. Then we drank Bordeaux and ate roast beef and Yorkshire pudding and Mort played Ravel's *Quartet in F* and argued that yes, *The Pearl Fishers* was beautiful, but . . .

In that civilized house it was easy to forget Eve sitting in a prison hospital cutting out turkeys with cruel little eyes, and Lane Appleby running her perfectly manicured finger around the frame of the picture of her dead son. It was even possible to forget for a while the monster who was loose out there just waiting.

Sunday was damp, but Thanksgiving Day was bright and cool.

"Last chance for the zoo," Mort said, "Next week it'll be too cold. Jo, throw that salmon mousse of yours into the oven and let's go. If we're going to eat half the stuff that's cooking around here, we'll need to work off a few calories."

At the zoo, Ali and I trailed behind, talking, while Rick and Mort walked with the boys. I hadn't thought this would be Rick's kind of outing. In fact, I had doubted he would come. But here he was in his heavy Aran Isle sweater, larger than life and as happy as I'd seen him. He was knowledge-able and he was fun. He made connections between the animals and political people: a huge, lugubrious female baboon was our ex-Minister of Energy; a sleepy, moth-eaten old lion who sprang across his cage in a single bound when someone pelted him with a pebble was, Rick said to me solemnly, "Your ex-Premier, Howard Dowhanuik."

"What about them?" Angus asked, pointing to some zebras chasing one another skittishly in an open field.

"Glad you asked," said Rick. "They're the press gallery. In Ottawa, as in the zebra world, young males not mature enough or aggressive enough to claim a group for themselves or lead a herd live in bachelor groups." And then, while we were still laughing, he added seriously, "The lion is their principal enemy."

Dinner was a splendid affair. The table looked like a cover of *Gourmet*. Mort found just the right Moselle to serve with the salmon mousse; the meal from roast turkey to pumpkin pie was as traditional as it was perfect. There was a sense of family at that table, and when Mort drove Rick to the airport to catch the flight to Ottawa, we all felt a sense of loss. It was as if the circle had been broken.

Ali and I went into the kitchen, cleared a place at her oak table, poured coffee and split the last of the pumpkin pie. As we ate, we talked about old times. They hadn't been good old times, especially at the beginning, but with Ali's support and love they had become good times and I was, I thought, a happy woman. And it was me, past and present, Ali talked about as we sat in her handsome kitchen with the light dying outside and the good smells of a holiday dinner still hanging in the air.

Her face was serious as she looked at me. "You know, Jo, I think you've really put it together this time. When I heard about Andy, I worried that maybe you weren't strong enough yet to handle another trauma, but here you sit looking wonderful and full of energy, and with a remarkable man in the picture. As your doctor, I'm proud, and as your friend, I'm delighted." She reached across the table and squeezed my hand. "You're made of good stuff, lady, really good stuff."

I hugged those words to myself all the way to Regina.

CHAPTER

17

The next morning I woke up in my own bed in the house on Eastlake Avenue. The room was full of light, and as I lay there, I could hear in the distance the mournful cries of geese flying south. I got out of bed, opened the window and curled up in the window seat to watch. The air that came into the room was fresh and cold and smelled of the north. I hugged my knees for warmth and looked out. There were no clouds. The sky was a clear, hard blue. It was a flawless October day.

Suddenly the air was black with geese, hundreds, then thousands of them. Their cries filled the room and, like a tuning fork, a part of me that I had forgotten resonated, responding. It was a pure and shining moment – one of the best and one of the last.

That day it all began to fall apart and, for a while, it looked as if all the king's horses and all the king's men wouldn't be able to put it together again.

Nothing seemed wrong at the beginning. When the dogs and I came back from our morning walk, there was a Canada

Messenger truck in front of our house. Two men were unloading boxes. I'd been expecting them. Before we left for Winnipeg, a woman from Supply and Services called and told me there was still a lot of Andy's stuff ("Boychuk-related material," she had called it) in a storeroom at the legislature, and they needed the space. They didn't want to distress Mrs. Boychuk further. (Yes, I thought, the permanently bewildered should be spared something.) Dave Micklejohn had suggested I was working on a book and . . . Here it was. The machinery of government had been kicked into high gear to clean out a storeroom, and I wasn't ready.

I signed the invoice and said I'd pay the driver and his helper if they'd carry the boxes up to my office in the granny flat. I hadn't been in there since I went to Winnipeg, and it was cold. I turned on the heat and paid the men, then I went to the house to warm up. I made a couple of phone calls, so it was after ten by the time I got to the office. I was feeling edgy and frustrated. I hate days that fritter themselves away; this seemed to be shaping up as one of them. And to add to my frustration, there was a fine dusting of pollen over everything: the boxes from the Caucus Office, the desk, windowsills, files. Obviously, the pollen had settled into the heating system all summer long, and when I'd turned on the heat, it had blown out. I tried to ignore the pollen and started to unpack a box of files, but it was getting into everything. I filled a bucket with hot soapy water and washed everything down. By the time I was ready to unpack the government boxes, it was noon, and Angus was home for lunch. As I turned on "The Flintstones" and poured tomato soup into his bowl, I gave myself a little pep talk. "You've learned to handle the big stuff, now don't let the little stuff eat at you."

After Angus went back to school I decided to celebrate my resolve. I unwrapped a basket of dried fruit Craig Evanson had sent for Thanksgiving and took it to the granny flat. An incentive. But I didn't need one. Once I started going through the boxes, the afternoon flew by. There was a huge box of clippings, arranged, of course, by subject, not by year. Getting all the material refiled was too daunting a job for that afternoon, so I opened another box. It was full of gifts, the kinds of things all politicians acquire in the course of a career: a provincial crest made from bits of broken bottles set into a concrete block; a pair of pillowcases with Andy's and Eve's faces drawn on with liquid embroidery; a stack of amateur oil paintings of prairie scenes, garish sunsets and grain elevators that bulged and tilted against turquoise skies; a metal lunch box with Andy's initials. The potash workers at Lanigan had given it to him at the beginning of August so he could "go to work on those bastards in the next election."

Junk, but hard to deal with if you remembered the day the junk was presented and the look on the face of the presenter and how you laughed about it on the way back to the city.

Of course, some of it wasn't junk. I was sitting looking at the weaving in a lovely and intricate Métis belt and eating the last of the sugared figs when the boys came racing up the steps to the granny flat. They looked winsome – always a trouble sign.

Peter began. "Since it's almost dinnertime and since I don't think you've had time to cook . . ."

Angus finished the preamble. "And since we all love pizza and since we have a two-for-one coupon for that new pizza place, why don't we . . . ?"

"Order Chinese food?" I suggested.

"Oh, Mum," said Angus, "you never used to say dumb stuff like that when Mieka was here."

"Sorry," I said. "Pizza it is, but I insist on anchovies."

"On one quarter only?" said Angus.

"Half," I said.

"A third," he said, beaming.

"Fair enough" I said. "But this place better give double cheese."

That night I woke up with a terrible cramping in my stomach. When I turned on the light and sat up to look at the clock, a wave of nausea hit me. I ran to the bathroom and sat on the edge of the tub, shivering and reading an old *Chatelaine*. Finally, I pulled on a robe, went to the kitchen and poured some milk into a saucepan to warm. The dogs were nuzzling me worriedly. In our house, people didn't come downstairs in the middle of the night and sit huddled over the kitchen table. But the warm milk helped, and after a while the dogs and I went upstairs and I slept until morning.

I keep a little daybook by my bed. That morning I wrote in one word – "sick" – but then I got up, showered and felt better. I called the correctional centre to check on Eve, phoned Patterson, New Jersey, to see why the Mets jacket I'd ordered six weeks ago for Peter's birthday hadn't come yet, made a pot of tea, took it to the granny flat and began on the files. At lunch I had some soup with Angus, and by the time Rick called that afternoon, I felt so much better I didn't even mention my bout the night before. The boys weren't sick. I decided it had been the anchovies on my third of the pizza that made me ill. Rick sounded up, buoyed still by Thanksgiving and excited about the stuff the Caucus Office had sent.

"Stick with it, Jo. How I envy you that granny flat. Right now, I'd give six bottles of Beefeater to have the kind of quiet you have there. That's what we need – a place where we can lay out all the material and then just look at it in peace until the answers start to emerge. And they will emerge. Trust me."

The strength of his assurance got me through the rest of the afternoon. I had dinner with the boys, showered, and by

8:30 was in bed with a new unauthorized biography of the PM, good gossipy stuff. I fell asleep still grinning about some of the revelations. No wonder he hadn't called an election at the end of summer. I woke up in the night with another attack, the same thing but worse – nausea, cramping and this time diarrhea. Again I went downstairs and made myself warm milk. This time I took a couple of yogurt pills, which I had bought at a health-food store, to counter the diarrhea. I fell into bed exhausted, but I slept. The next morning in my daybook I wrote the word "sick," followed by the symptoms.

It was a significant moment. I had begun to track this illness, whatever it was. Without realizing it, I had moved across that fine line that separates the world of the well with all its dear and familiar preoccupations to the world of the sick where the only real concern is the sickness itself.

That first week I continued to function, to keep up at least the appearance of business as usual. I went to the correctional centre to visit Eve, who seemed to be sliding away; to Craig Evanson's office to drink tea and talk about Eve's defence; around town to do family errands; to the granny flat to unpack and sort and file. Saturday morning the kids and I even made it to the Lakeshore Club, but I spent most of my time sitting on the edge of the pool shaking. And, last thing at night, every night, I talked to Rick Spenser, whose voice, warm and full of concern, was increasingly becoming my reason for getting through the days. As long as I could keep up the rounds of ordinary domestic routine, nothing was wrong.

By the second week it was becoming harder to pretend. The evidence of my daybook was there every morning in black and white: the word "sick" followed by a growing list of symptoms – diarrhea and cramps and nausea, but also a cold, clammy feeling and, something new, a taste of metal in my mouth that for the first time in my life made eating a chore to be endured.

That second week I played a game with myself – if it's not better tomorrow, I'll call the doctor – but I never did. By the weekend I was frightened and exhausted. I didn't even bother to take my bathing suit to the club. I sat in the coffee shop and watched the boys playing tennis through the glass. The morning seemed endless, and when finally we did get home, I noticed the boys exchanging worried looks. To escape, I told them I had to work. I went to the granny flat, shut the door and collapsed on the couch for most of the afternoon. Peter brought me a tray at suppertime. He was seventeen years old, but he looked close to tears. He remembered the bad time after Ian died, too. I felt so guilty that I followed him to the house like a whipped dog.

"Okay, you guys, if you want to pamper me, go to it," I said and I went upstairs, showered and crawled into bed. In the night the cramps and nausea hit me in waves. I got up and went and sat in the bathroom. But the memory of Peter coming to the granny flat with the tray fired something in me. I heard my voice, frightened but defiant. "I am not going to let this happen again. I am not going to give in." Finally, I went back to bed and slept until morning.

Sunday was cold and sleety. The boys volunteered to stay home from church, and I was too weak to fight them. I stayed in bed most of the day and slept through the night. Monday morning I awoke feeling better – not completely well, but well enough to make some plans.

Hallowe'en was a week away. I decided to treat myself. Andy's old administrative assistant, Rosemary Vickert, had opened a store a couple of weeks before. She'd sent me an announcement. The store was called Seasons, and it sold everything I could want for celebrating a holiday. I dressed with more than usual care, and noticed with a certain grim pleasure that the Black Watch tartan skirt that had been snug around the waist at Thanksgiving was now not just comfortable but loose.

"Today I declare myself not only well but thin," I said as I ran my finger around the waistband.

Rosie's store was in a strip mall, the same strip mall where Ali Sutherland had once had her partnership. I parked as far away as possible from Ali's office. Today I was well. I had no need of doctors.

Seasons was a wonderful store. Rosie was downtown on an errand but her partner was cheerful and unobtrusive and I found some great stuff, a Hallowe'en wreath with orange ribbons and little black cats for Mieka's door, a spooky ghost windsock for our front porch and some cards for friends. I was standing by the cash register when I spotted a pumpkin suit in size two or thereabouts. On impulse I decided to buy it for Clay Evanson, Lori and Mark's little guy. I'd just put the suit on the counter when Rosemary Vickert came in the door. When she saw me, her face lit up, but as quickly as it had come, the joy was gone.

"My God, Jo, what's the matter with you? You look like hell."

"I've had the flu, but I'm better now."

"The hell you are," she said. "How much weight have you lost?" She reached up and felt my forehead. "You feel like you've got a chill."

"I'm better," I repeated numbly.

"Take a look, lady," she said and spun me around so that we were both looking in the mirror over a display case by the door. Suspended from the ceiling were dozens of rubber skeletons. Rosie swept them aside so I could see myself.

It was a shock. Rosemary, pink with wellness, was looking over my shoulder into the mirror. But she wasn't looking at herself. She was looking at a yellow-skinned woman with dry, chapped lips and sunken eyes. She was looking at me.

"What does the doctor say?" asked Rosie, looking over my shoulder at my mirror image.

"I haven't been," I said.

"Well, we're going now," she said. "Do you want to get taken to a doc in a box or do you want to see if someone at Ali's old place can look at you?"

I didn't say anything.

"Jo," she said, "we're not negotiating whether you are going. We're negotiating who you are going to see. Whether is off the table. Now who will it be? Somebody at the Medicentre or someone from Ali's?"

"Ali's," I said numbly, looking at my feet. I knew I'd been defeated.

"There's nothing wrong with you," the slim woman in the medical coat and the impossibly high heels said, smiling as she came into the examining room. "I can't see anything. I've made an appointment with a gastroenterologist just in case, but my guess is you won't need it. No harm in having an appointment, though. Those guys have waiting lists that are yay long." She swung herself up on a stool at the side of the examining table. "Mrs. Kilbourn, I had a quick look at your records. I noticed you had a pretty bad time after your husband died and you know that was only a couple of years ago."

"Three," I said numbly. "It'll be three years in December."

She looked at me kindly. "You've been under an incredible amount of stress, you know. I read the papers, and it seems to me you've been right at the centre of Andy Boychuk's murder – terrible in itself. It must have opened a lot of old wounds for you."

"You're saying this is all in my head."

"I'm saying we can't rule that out, Mrs. Kilbourn. As you

well know, the body often has its own way of coping with stress. Now this is what I think we should do. I'm going to prescribe something to help you over this rough spot – very short term. Sometimes that's all it takes, you know – a tranquillizer to unknot the knots and let your body get in touch with its own wisdom. Why don't we try that, and then if things don't sort themselves out, you can keep the appointment with the gastroenterologist. His name is Dr. Philip Lee. He's a bit brusque, but he's good."

"I know his brother, Mort."

She looked mischievous. "Well, Mort got all the charm in that family, but they're both brilliant." She stood and smoothed her skirt. "I want to see you in a month – even if you're okay."

I walked into the waiting room, clutching my prescription for Valium and the slip of paper with the time and date of my appointment with Dr. Philip Lee. Rosemary Vickert looked up expectantly.

"Nothing wrong with me," I said. "It's all in my head." I tried to laugh, but the sound that came out was jagged and forlorn.

Rosie jumped up and put her arms around my shoulder. "C'mon, Jo, let's go someplace and have a sinful lunch. You can pay – punishment for scaring the . . ." She gave a sidelong glance at the doctor's office. "For scaring the fecal matter out of me."

I took a Valium with lunch, went home and slept through the afternoon. That night I went to Peter's football game, came home, got into bed with the unauthorized biography of the PM and slept through the night.

The next morning in my daybook I wrote a tentative "Better" followed by a string of question marks. I had breakfast with the kids, took the dogs for their run, changed my clothes, grabbed the little pumpkin suit I'd bought for Clay

Evanson and drove to Wolf River. I took a deep breath when I pulled onto the overpass. "So far, so good," I said aloud and then something went wrong in my chest muscles. I couldn't move the air in and out of my lungs. I took a series of gulping breaths. I managed to keep the car on the overpass and get onto the highway. I pulled over onto the shoulder at almost exactly the same spot where Eve and I had stopped six weeks before.

There was a paper bag from a take-out place on the dashboard. I held it over my mouth and nose and breathed deeply. The bag smelled of stale grease and salt, but after a while, my breathing became regular again. I sat by the side of the road for a few minutes, frightened and angry. Then I said loudly, "I'm not giving in to this, you know," put the car in gear and finished the drive to Wolf River.

For once, Lori Evanson was not immaculate. I had stopped in at Disciples for a cup of coffee and was told that Lori was home and ill. When she opened the door of the trailer she and Mark and Clay lived in, she certainly looked ill and, without her careful makeup, very young. She invited me in, turned off the soap opera she was watching, made a futile stab at picking up the toys that were everywhere in the sunny living room, then collapsed on the couch.

Clay's eyes had been drawn by the bright colours of the bag from Seasons, and he grabbed at it.

"Oh, Clay, no." Lori's sweet singsong voice sounded weary.

"It's all right, Lori. It's a present for him."

Like a child, she was off the couch and over to where Clay was, helping him open the bag.

When she saw the pumpkin suit, she began at once to pull it over his little T-shirt and jeans.

"Oh, Clay, you are going to be such a cute little Mr. Pumpkin." She sat back on her heels and looked up at me solemnly. Her eyes were as round and full of wonder as the eyes of her son. "How can I ever thank you?"

"It's just a Hallowe'en costume, Lori. My kids are all grown up now – at least past the pumpkin stage. This was fun for me, and Clay really does look great."

"Then I'll just get up and give you a hug." She was smiling when she reached her arms out to me but something she saw in my face killed the smile. My chest felt tight, as if something were squeezing it. Lori's eyes were filled with concern. "Why, Mrs. Kilbourn, you're sick. You look so very sick. What's wrong with you?"

"Nothing, it's all in my head, Lori. I went to the doctor yesterday and she said it was just stress: Andy's death and then Soren's and then Eve – Mrs. Boychuk – getting arrested. I guess it's just been too much." My chest felt like it was caught in a vise. I tasted metal then my mouth filled with saliva. "It's all in my head," I said again lamely.

Lori looked at me and burst into tears. Clay, who was twirling in front of the window in his pumpkin costume, stopped and ran over to see what was wrong with his mother. Lori was sobbing brokenly, but between her sobs there were odd little fragments of self-accusation. "I've hurt you," "It's all my fault," and "If I hadn't done it, Mrs. Boychuk wouldn't have . . ."

I went to her. When I bent to put my arms around her, the vise tightened on my chest. It felt as if my heart were skipping beats. I broke out in a clammy, cold sweat.

"Lori, why don't you get us some tea, please." I sounded sharp, but she got up and went into the kitchen.

I could hear her filling the kettle, still sniffling, getting down cups.

I sat and said under my breath, "You are not sick. It's in your head, in your head." My hands were shaking but I

managed to pull the bottle of Valium out of my purse and get
a small, pale green pill into my mouth before Lori came back.

It helped – or at least it seemed to. Lori gave Clay some
juice in a plastic glass that had a picture of Big Bird on it, and
she poured our tea into blue and green striped mugs. I put
three teaspoonfuls of sugar into the tea, and when I took a
sip, the metal taste left my mouth. I really did begin to feel
better. I tried to sound kind but firm.

"Now, what's all this about Mrs. Boychuk's problems
being your fault?"

Lori was holding her mug in both hands, and she looked
as if she were about to cry again. I remembered when she'd
asked me to support her father-in-law. ("Mrs. Kilbourn, I'm
not very smart. Sometimes I just have to trust the smart
people to tell me what to do.")

Well, I was smart people. "Lori, what's all this about?
Begin at the beginning and no tears. This is too important."

She took a great hiccuping gulp of air, mopped at her eyes
and began.

"Well, the beginning, I guess was . . ." She hesitated. ". . .
was the phone call I got the morning they found Soren
passed away. But it was before he died. This person told me
to call Mrs. Boychuk to make sure she was at Soren Eames's
office by 7:30 a.m. It was very early but it was important. So
I called Mrs. Boychuk and told her, and she asked, 'Is it about
Carey? Is he all right?' and I said it was something else
altogether, and she said, 'What's it about?' and I said just
what my – the person told me to say, which was 'You'll just
have to trust me, Eve or Mrs. Boychuk.'"

"That's what you said? 'Eve or Mrs. Boychuk'?"

"That's what the person told me to say, Mrs. Kilbourn."
She looked at me confidingly. "And it worked because she
said she would go, and then" – her lower lip began to quiver –

"and then after I got to work, I went over to the CAP Centre like I always do with some coffee and muffins for Soren, for his breakfast, you know, and there he was passed away and Mrs. Boychuk was all bloody and . . ." The scene was playing again in her mind, and she was beginning to hyperventilate.

"Easy, Lori, easy. Take a big breath . . . and another one . . . Better now?"

She nodded.

The vise was squeezing my chest again, but I got the words out. "You've done all the hard part, now I just need to know one other thing."

"Yes?" She was steeling herself for the next question.

My heart was pounding in my chest. "Lori, who told you to phone Eve? Who told you to get her to Soren's office that morning?"

There was silence in the sunny room. I could hear Clay Evanson in the kitchen opening drawers and talking to himself in a low baby voice.

"Lori?" I sounded strong, like the old Jo.

"Yes, Mrs. Kilbourn?"

"I have to know who called you that morning."

She looked at me craftily. "Promise you won't tell?"

"I can't promise that, Lori, you know that. This is too important for games," I said sternly.

She took a breath, licked her lips and out it came. "The person who told me to phone was my mother-in-law, Mrs. Julie Evanson." Then she sat back and looked at me expectantly.

I was stunned. "But why? Did Julie give you any explanation?"

"Just that if Mrs. Boychuk was in Soren's office that morning, he could help her."

"Help her what, Lori?"

"I didn't ask, Mrs. Kilbourn. I didn't ask because Mrs. Evanson scares me. She's never liked me because I was p.g. when Mark married me."

I must have looked puzzled.

"I was p.g. – pregnant," she whispered. "And Mrs. Evanson has, you know, held it against me, so when she asked me to do this . . ." Her face was clouding over again. "She promised me it would be okay, that Soren would help Mrs. Boychuk. But it wasn't okay and then after when I wanted to go to the police she yelled at me and said I was stupid, which I know, and that Mr. Evanson, my father-in-law, would never become leader if this came out and if he didn't it would be my fault. Mrs. Evanson may be a witch, but Mr. Evanson has always been so good to me, and I wouldn't betray him for anything. I knew it was wrong not to tell, but what could I do? And then when I saw you so sick from worrying . . . I hope it was right to tell you."

I felt so tired I didn't think I could move out of the chair. But I stood up and held my arms out to her. She came and laid her head on my shoulder. She was Mieka's size. It felt good to hold her. Her hair smelled like apples.

"You did the right thing, Lori. You didn't betray anybody. Mrs. Evanson was the one who did the betraying. I'll make it all right with Craig – I promise. Now go in there and wash your face and bundle up your little guy and take him for a walk in the leaves. It'll do you both good."

Her lovely face shone with gratitude. Someone had taken the burden away. Someone had taken over. She looked better already.

I drove to the Evanson house on Gardner Crescent. All the way to the city, my chest muscles ached and my heart banged against the hollow of my rib cage. But I wasn't sick.

The doctor had told me. It was all in my head. I pounded on the front door.

"Come on, Julie. Come on out here and deal with your mess."

She was wearing a flowered silk dress, the colour of raspberries, and her hair was a smooth platinum cap.

"I was just going out," she said, and then an honest outburst, "Joanne, you look like . . ."

"I know, I look like hell. Let me in, Julie. You're not going anywhere."

The dining-room table was covered in photographer's contact sheets. I picked one up. Some of Craig, some of both of them.

"Picking the official photo for the new leader?" I asked. "What's your stand on justice, Julie? Are you for it or against it? How about the family? How about the dim and trusting? In favour of giving them full employment doing your dirty work?"

"You'd better leave, Joanne. You're hysterical."

"No, Julie, I'm not. I'm just sick of people dying and people being hurt." A spasm of nausea hit me, and the metal taste came into my mouth, then the saliva. "What's your game, Julie? Why did you set Eve up? Why did you have your daughter-in-law, who is as innocent as she is slow, call Eve and tell her to go to Soren's office the morning he was murdered?"

Julie had gone pale under her makeup. Her hands were clenched into fists.

"That's family business, Joanne."

"That's where you're wrong. It's police business, and I'm going to drive down there now and tell them to pile into a cop car, turn on the sirens and come and get you, Julie. They'll be so interested. Cops are funny that way. They wait and wait, and then finally they look at all the evidence" – I shook the contact sheets in her face – "and they figure, well, what's her connection here? How is the wife of this guy who wants to be premier involved? What the hell is going on? That's what they do, Julie. Take my word for it."

She grabbed me by the wrists and brought her face close to mine. Her breath smelled of coffee.

"Send the police here," she said, "and I'll tell them your beloved Andy Boychuk was a fag."

For a moment, my eyes lost their focus. Julie's face blurred; I blinked, and she became clear again.

"What did you say?" My voice sounded small and frightened.

She pushed her advantage. "You heard me, I said Andy was a faggot. You know, Joanne" – She moved her face so close to mine our noses almost touched – "a pansy, a fruit, a fairy, a ho-mo-sex-u-al." She enunciated each syllable of the word.

"I'll tell them myself," I said and I shook my wrists loose from her grasp and headed for the door. "After I tell them about how you set up Eve Boychuk."

It worked. I'd called her bluff, and she gave in.

"Jo, wait. Hear my side."

I turned the doorknob.

"Not for me, but for Craig. I know you still like him."

I walked into the living room and sank into a chair by the window. Across the road the trees on the creek bank were bronze and gold in the October light. It seemed impossible that there could be such beauty out there, while in here . . .

"All right, Julie, let's hear your side."

Julie's story was weird enough to be credible and unsettling. Early on the morning that Soren Eames's body was discovered, the phone had rung. She'd answered it "in this room here," she said, gesturing to the living room. It was a man's voice on the other end. He identified himself as a supporter of Craig Evanson, and he said he'd come upon some information that could clinch the nomination for Craig. The man was, Julie told me, very knowledgeable about their campaign. His estimate of the number of delegates supporting Craig was just about the same as Julie's. What the man knew and what Julie knew was that Craig didn't have enough votes for a first-ballot win, and it didn't seem likely that he'd be the one who would pick up votes on the next ballots. "You and I know," the man had said, "that it isn't going to work for him unless you can get some of the Boychuk loyalists to support him." Julie looked at me. "He mentioned your name, Joanne, and Dave Micklejohn's, and he said to me, 'You know who the others are' and of course, I did. He said the only way 'to pry you people loose' – that was the phrase he used – was to get someone you trusted to ask you to support Craig, and the person he named was Eve. He said that if I could get Eve into Soren Eames's office within the hour, Eames would give Eve some information that would guarantee she'd do what she was told about the election."

"What did you say?" I asked.

"It was all so bizarre, and it was early, before seven, I think, but I remember I said, 'What's the information?' He didn't say anything for a while, and then he kind of laughed and said, 'Well, there's no reason why you shouldn't know. Soren Eames has information that will prove that Andy Boychuk was involved in a sordid homosexual liaison at the time of his death. Eames has agreed to keep quiet if Eve can get the people around her to support Craig Evanson.'"

"Did that make sense to you, Julie?"

"I told you, it was early in the morning, Jo, and face it, he was saying what I wanted to hear. After I'd called Lori, I thought about it. And it did make sense. Eames could have wanted to help Craig out of loyalty to Mark and Lori. And, you know, some of those fundamentalist churches really hate homosexuals. If Soren had come upon that kind of information, he might have felt he had to use it.

"Anyway, I called Lori. Joanne, you'll have to believe me. I didn't mean to hurt Eve. But . . ." And then the old Julie was back, defiant and shrill. "It's not my fault Eve went crazy and killed him." She looked at me. "Are you going to the police?"

"Not this minute, but I suggest you do." I stood and started for the door. "Julie, do you remember anything at all about the man on the phone? Even a general impression?"

She looked thoughtful. "I don't know. He was agitated, and that 'sordid homosexual liaison' thing seemed overdone."

"Yes," I agreed, "it sounds that way to me, too." My hand was on the doorknob again. "Well, Julie, I'll be seeing you."

"Joanne?" Her voice was small and tentative.

I turned wearily, prepared for a last-ditch appeal that would keep me from exposing her to the police.

"Julie, what is it?"

She looked around then lowered her voice. "It's someone we know, Joanne."

"Who?"

"The man on the phone. He'd muffled his voice, but I still knew it. And he knew so much about our campaign and so much about all of us – about Andy's people. It's someone close to us, Jo. It has to be someone we know."

CHAPTER

18

Where to begin? I sat in the granny flat and thought about what I had to go on. The muffled voice on Julie's telephone; Howard Dowhanuik's voice, exasperated and embarrassed: "For God's sake, Jo, it's been almost twenty years. Andy said it was his one and only." I stared at the vertical files and finally I picked up four and put them on my desk. I chose 1961, 1962, 1963 and 1964 – Andy's high-school years, the years of sexual awakening. It seemed as good a place as any to start.

There wasn't much in the files. Some photos of Andy receiving awards from the Knights of Columbus for essays on chastity and obedience. Roma had given me those. Four years of *Intra Muros*, the yearbook of E.T. Russell High School in Saskatoon. Four years of photos of Andy with his class, with the debating team, with the track team. Four years of end-of-the-year messages. "I'll never forget you," "To a great guy," from girls named Barbara Ann and Gloria and Sharon, and joking insults from people who signed off, "Just kidding, your great!!!" Remembering my own year-book, I shook my head, smiled and started to shut the cover of *Intra Muros*. In the corner, tiny and feathery, was some writing that had been obscured by my thumb. I bent to look at it more closely. "Forever, E." I looked again at the cover: 1964, grade twelve, graduation year. I looked at the signatures in the other years of *Intra Muros*. Nothing. I went back to 1964. There were forty-five people in the graduating class. Counting surnames and given names, in Andy's class alone there were twenty-three people with the initial E. Those had been big years for Elizabeths and Edwards.

There was a group photo of the class. Andy's teacher looked like an original – hair frizzed out to shoulder length, hoop earrings, gypsy scarf, dirndl skirt – but even in the halftones of an old school photo she had an air of great vitality. I looked at the bottom of the page. Of course, Hilda McCourt. The one with the dazzling red hair and the sharp tongue who'd been onstage the day Andy was murdered and who'd been so angry with me when I underestimated her memory at the lunch after the funeral.

She lived, I knew, in Saskatoon. Andy used to take her out for dinner every so often when he was up there. I thought of Saskatoon, and I remembered hugging Lori that morning and the smell of apples in her hair. Then I thought how good it would be to hold my own daughter, and I picked up the phone and dialled information. Five minutes later, I had arranged to meet Hilda McCourt the next day before noon.

When Rick phoned that night, we talked for close to an hour. Like me, he sensed that the pieces were there if only we could see the pattern. I didn't mention my illness. There was no point because it wasn't there. It wasn't real. All in my head.

The next morning, when I went to get dressed, the first two skirts I tried on hung on me. When the waistband of the third skirt gaped, too, I went into Mieka's room, found a wide belt and belted the skirt tight. Sort of like Scotch-taping a drooping hem, but I was starting to simplify.

It was a mild day, but I was freezing. I put on a heavy sweater and then, when that wasn't enough, I went to the basement and dug out my winter coat. The phone rang as I was about to go out the door. It was Dr. Philip Lee's office, and they'd had a cancellation for the next day, late afternoon. Was I interested? If I left Saskatoon after lunch I'd make it easily. As soon as I hung up, I was hit with a knot of abdominal cramps. Just my body's way of saying I had made a good decision, I thought, as I waited till the cramping stopped. I made a few arrangements with the boys, picked up my car keys, slung my purse over my shoulder and went out the door. It wasn't quite 8:30 a.m. With luck, I'd have had my talk with Hilda McCourt and be at Mieka's by noon.

About an hour out of the city, the cramping hit again, and the diarrhea. I was lucky. There was a gas station with a garage – a real garage, the kind where men in coveralls come to watch other men in coveralls peer into the bowels of vehicles. There was a smell of oil and gasoline and something else – an artificial pine smell that must have come from the display of cardboard deodorant pine trees by the cash register.

When I came from the bathroom, the man in the station looked up at me curiously.

"You all right, lady?"

"Fine thanks . . . Just the aftermath of the flu."

"It's going around," he said sagely, and then, surprisingly, "There's coffee, but let me get you some tea. I had that flu and it's a bitch. The tea will settle you, so you can get to . . . I suppose you're going to Saskatoon."

I nodded.

"Two more hours. If you feel as crappy as I did, you'll need something. Put lotsa sugar in it for energy."

The tea got me to Davidson, a little more than halfway. Again, there was the cramping, like a fist tightening in my lower stomach, then I broke out in a cold sweat. I pulled into the parking lot behind a hotel and shook. Then I went into the hotel coffee shop, which was almost empty at this time of morning and still smelled of stale beer from the pub across the hall.

There were cardboard cutouts of pumpkins and skeletons on the mirror behind the counter, and a young albino girl with her back to me was taping orange and black crepe paper around the mirror's edge. On the radio, a woman who said she was a witch was taking calls on a phone-in show. The girl never said a word. She blinked at me incuriously through her white lashes while I gave her my order, set the soup down carefully in front of me, brought a glass of water and a cellophane-wrapped package of crackers and went back to taping her crepe paper. On the radio, the witch was explaining the witch's alphabet.

The soup and the fresh air seemed to do the trick. By the time I got to Hilda McCourt's neat little house on Avenue B, I felt better. When I rang the doorbell, Hilda came around the side of the house from the backyard. The October sunlight was kind to her. She looked her age – eighty, give or take a year – but she looked great. She was wearing lime-green coveralls and a lime-green and cerise cotton shirt. Both had labels from a designer who had dominated the youth market for the past couple of years. She had covered her brilliantly dyed red hair with a scarf, and a slash of lipstick – cerise to match her blouse – was feathered across her lips. Her smile when she greeted me was as open and vital as the smile on her face when she posed with Class 12-A, E.T. Russell H.S. (1964).

"Come around back with me. I'm just about through turning over my garden for the winter. Carpe diem. We may not get many more days like this. I'm going overseas for a short holiday next week, and I want to leave everything shipshape."

"It looks shipshape to me already," I said when we came into the backyard. Orange plastic garbage bags full of leaves were neatly lined up against the garage, shrubs were tied with sacking, rosebushes were covered in dirt, and the flower beds had all been turned over.

"Just this last bit of the vegetable garden to go," she said, "and then we can go in and have a glass of sherry." She picked up her shovel. "Why don't you sit down on one of those lawn chairs and get some sun? You look a little green. What is it, that godawful flu that's going the rounds?"

"Something like that."

Hilda McCourt wasn't a woman who felt she had to amuse a guest. As soon as she saw I was settled, she went back to her digging. She worked with energy and efficiency, and as I watched her, I had a memory of how good it had felt when my body had worked that way, strong and obedient. I wondered if it ever would again, and I shuddered in the warm sunlight.

"That's it," she said finally. "I leave that for the devil," she said, pointing to an unbroken piece about three feet square at the corner of her vegetable garden. "Have you heard of the devil's half-acre? There are a hundred names for it in folklore – all wonderful, all nonsense, of course, but a nice idea still. A little gesture of conciliation to the dark powers. I even have an incantation I use when I sow my seeds: This is for me. This is for my neighbour. This is for the devil. It's American, but before that from Buckinghamshire and before that – who knows? Probably our ancestors were saying it when they were still painting themselves blue. Anyway, it's good to feel connected with what went before." She took off her gardening gloves, undid the scarf and shook her head.

Her hair, improbably orange, fuzzed out around her head. It seemed to have an energy of its own. "Come on." She reached out a hand to help me up. "By the looks of you, you could use a real drink. I have a bottle of Glenlivet an old student brought me at Thanksgiving. The sun must be over the yardarm somewhere."

She sat me down in a little glassed-in porch that over-looked her garden. "Why don't you put your feet up – lie down on that lounge there while I get our drinks."

It was a fine and individual room. Along one wall there was a trestle table filled with blooming plants: hydrangea, azalea and hibiscus. Across from it was an old horsehair chaise longue covered in a bright afghan. At the foot was a television set; at the head, a table with a good reading lamp and a pile of best sellers. The walls were covered with pic-tures of pilots and aviators, dashing young men in bomber jackets or RCAF uniforms or – in the most recent ones – the red coveralls and white silk scarfs of the Snowbirds.

"Heroes," said Hilda McCourt as she came into the room. She was carrying a tray with a bottle of Glenlivet, an ice bucket, glasses and a round of Gouda cheese. With one hand, she pulled out a little nesting table from the corner, and she set the tray on it. "Now, here's our lunch. I don't share the old country passion for drinking whisky neat, but there's no need to dilute good Scotch with water."

She poured us each a stiff drink over ice, then she reached into the back pocket of her overalls, pulled out a Swiss army knife and cut us each a wedge of Gouda. We lifted our glasses.

"To heroes," she said.

"To heroes," I agreed. The Scotch was smooth and warming. I felt the bands that had been enclosing my chest relax a little.

Hilda leaned across the table to look at me. "You look better," she said. "Now, what's all this about?"

"Andy Boychuk," I said.

"Andy was a hero of mine," she said simply.

"Me, too," I said, and I was surprised to feel my eyes fill with tears. I took another sip of Scotch. "Miss McCourt, this isn't going to be easy for either of us, but I have to ask some questions, and I think it's best if I come right out with them."

"That's always the best plan of attack." She took a thin slice of Gouda and peeled the red wax from it. Her army knife gleamed sharp and lethal in the sunlight.

"When Andy was in high school, was there ever any unpleasantness?"

Her clever old eyes looked up at me, alert to a threat to her hero.

I continued. "Anything involving another boy? I don't mean bullying."

"You mean, of course, something sexual," she said, and then, hostile, defending her hero: "What? Has some tabloid got hold of something?"

"It's more serious than that."

She sat back, plunged the knife into the wedge of Gouda and cut again. "Yes, I guess I knew it must be serious for you to come here." She finished her drink and poured another. "To answer the question you pose, Mrs. Kilbourn, yes, there was some unpleasantness, but it was an isolated incident. Over the years, I have decided to disregard it. Teachers see a lot, and that kind of thing happens more than you can know.

"Generally, it doesn't amount to much at that age. The hormones are racing, you know. Sometimes they just boil over. I never worried about Andy. He was always so masculine." She turned and looked out the window, and I knew there was more.

"But you did worry about the other one," I said, "the partner."

"Yes, I did worry about the other one. He was . . ." She turned her hands palms up. "He was different, tall but very delicate and slender, a poetic boy. Now what was his name? It was something unfortunate. A name to plague a boy, but I can't call it to mind now. It'll come to me. Is it important?"

"I think it may be a matter of life and death," I said. "But it'll be in the yearbook."

"I don't think so. He came right at the end of the year." She shook her head with frustration. "I can't remember the boy's name, but I can close my eyes and remember that desk in home room – right in front of me, empty all year, of course, until this poor, sad boy was transferred to Russell. I was furious, too, that that kind of rumour had to attach itself to Andy so close to the end of high school. A blameless record – absolutely blameless."

She looked at my glass. "Damn, you're empty. I'm not much of a hostess, am I? But I can do this for you." She splashed the Glenlivet into my glass. "And one other useful thing: I can go to the board office. They keep records for years. I've looked up students before, for reunions and sometimes just out of idle curiosity. Nothing simpler. Are you planning to drive back to Regina today?"

"No, I'm staying with my daughter tonight. She's going to school here." A spasm hit me in the stomach, and the metal taste came in my mouth.

"I think that's a wise decision, Mrs. Kilbourn. You're looking tired. Does your daughter live far from here? You don't look well at all."

"Not far," I said, standing up. "If I could just use your bathroom."

When I came back, Hilda McCourt was standing by the front door wearing her jacket.

"I'll drive you," she said, holding my coat for me.

"I'll make it," I said sliding my arms into my coat, trying to look capable. "It's not far at all."

"That's a blessing," she said. "Now what's your daughter's number? I'll call you when I get back from the board office. Take care of yourself, Mrs. Kilbourn."

I felt strange when I pulled up in front of Mieka's house on Ninth Street, weak and heavy-limbed. I reached into my purse and pulled out my makeup bag. I rubbed blush across my cheekbones and drew a fresh lipstick mouth over my own. "Putting on my face," as the old ladies always say. I didn't look in the mirror – I was feeling rotten enough already.

I had hoped my visit would be a surprise, and it was. From the length of time it took Mieka and Greg to answer the door and from the way they looked when they finally did, it was apparent that they had been making love.

Mieka opened the door, blinking in the sunlight, looking rosy and happy and vague. Greg was behind her, his arms wrapped protectively around her. She tried to smile.

"Oh, Mummy. I wish you'd called ahead."

I walked past them into the hall. I was trembling. That was a new symptom. "I thought you'd be baking bread or something," I said and kept walking toward the kitchen. There'd be a chair in the kitchen.

"I baked bread this morning," she said, following me. Amazingly, she had – half a dozen loaves of crusty dark bread were sitting on racks.

"Oh, Mieka," I said and slumped into a kitchen chair. The nausea hit like a breaker, and then another spasm, wave after wave. I was crouched in my chair like an animal. My mouth filled with the taste of nails and then saliva. Finally, unforgivably, in the middle of that kitchen that smelled warmly of yeast and fresh baked bread, I vomited.

They were both there at once. She, wrapping her arms around me as the spasms hit and I retched and retched; he, wrapping his arms around her.

"I'm all right, Mieka," I said at last, sitting up.

"I know, Mum, I know," my daughter said in a voice weary, resigned, determined, a voice I remembered from the time after her father died, and I had cracked into a thousand pieces.

"Damn it, Mieka, don't patronize me." I moved to get loose from her grasp. And there in the mirror above the sink I saw it, a tableau. Call it Paradise Lost or Mother Comes to Call: a young dark-haired man, his face still tanned from summer; a girl with ashy blond hair and an oversized university sweatshirt. Handsome people, but looking frightened of the grotesque burden in their arms: a woman with dark ash-blond hair and wild eyes and hectic makeup, circles of colour on her white cheeks and a slash of lipstick smeared across her mouth. Old womanish, clownish – me. The vise tightened around my chest and then, merciful and tender, the blackness came.

I awoke in an unfamiliar room, in a strange bed that still, in its soft flannelette sheets, held the smell of sex. Of course, they wouldn't have had time to change the sheets. And outside the room, voices young and deep and urgent.

"Mieka, I know you love her. I'm going to love her, too, but you could smell the Scotch a mile away. Babe, if that's the problem, we need to help her. I'm not saying we don't. I'm saying face it."

And then my daughter's voice, strong, defending me. "She's not a drunk, Greg. Even at the worst, she didn't go that route. She's been through so much and she wasn't over that horror show about Daddy. Nobody could come through what's happened to her without some sort of reaction. They would have had to peel me off the walls of my rubber room. But she's not a drunk. It has to be something else."

Good old Mieka, defender of embarrassing mothers. I curled up and went to sleep and dreamed strange dreams: Rick Spenser in Mieka's kitchen making bread, pulling points of dough from a long, thin baguette. Soren Eames at the kitchen table with Andy, laughing and saying to Rick, "Now don't forget a seed for you and a seed for me and one for the master," and then the bell on the stove ringing and ringing and then floating up through consciousness to the knowledge that the phone was ringing. I picked it up.

"Joanne Kilbourn speaking."

On the other end, husky-voiced and excited, was Hilda McCourt. "Well, Mrs. Kilbourn, may I call you Joanne? I feel we're into an adventure together, so let's use first names."

"Fine, Hilda. What did you find out?" My voice sounded a hundred years old.

"Nothing, absolutely nothing. Someone sliced through the microfiche."

I felt a prickle of excitement. "Someone did what?"

"Sliced through the microfiche. The board transferred all their school records to microfiche a couple of years ago. Joanne, do you know what microfiche are?"

"Those films that you scoot through a projector and then you see your document on a screen?"

She laughed. "Well, that'll do. Apparently someone scooted the grade twelve records of E.T. Russell High School through the blade of a knife."

"When?"

"The people at the board don't know. Employees are in and out of there all the time. You're supposed to sign in and out, but they're quite lax. These aren't precious documents or even particularly confidential ones. Twenty-five-year-old school records have pretty well done whatever damage they're going to do."

"I suppose you're right," I said. I felt deflated, and I guess I sounded weary.

"Are you all right?" The surprisingly young voice was alert, concerned.

"Well, I'm going to disembowel the next person who asks me that, but, yeah, I think I'm okay, just disappointed. I think that boy's name could help us."

The us I meant was Rick Spenser and me, but Hilda McCourt, my co-adventurer, picked up the reference happily.

"I agree, Joanne, I believe it can help us, but don't despair. I have an excellent memory, and I expect that name will surface. Now give me your Regina number so I can call you as soon as it does."

I gave her the number.

"We'll get to the bottom of this," she said, "never fear, and when we do I still have almost half that bottle of Glenlivet left for our celebration."

I shuddered. "Almost half!" I thanked her, lay back in bed and drifted off to sleep.

When I woke it was dark. I looked at my watch: five o'clock. I listened for street sounds. Almost none; it must, I reasoned, be morning – 5:00 a.m. in the morning, as Lori Evanson would say. I felt weak but purged, and better. My overnight bag was at the foot of the bed. I pulled out clean clothes, tiptoed down the hall and showered and changed. I wrote Mieka and Greg a note, thanking them, explaining I was much better, apologizing without sounding pitiful, and crept downstairs. They were asleep on the living-room floor with their arms curled around one another: the title of a novel, *The Young in One Another's Arms*.

If I could remember the title of a Canadian novel, I must be all right. I looked again into the living room at my daughter's dark blond hair fanned out against the crook of that unnervingly male arm, said a prayer, took a deep breath and walked out the door.

Except for a stop halfway home for take-out coffee and a foil-wrapped Denver, I drove straight through. I was home in time to give the boys lunch and answer Mieka's anxious phone call. Yes, I was better, yes, I had a doctor's appointment that afternoon, yes, it was a specialist, highly recommended, Morton Lee's brother, and yes, I would call as soon as I knew anything.

When I hung up, I didn't even bother going upstairs to get a blanket. I grabbed my coat and, like a transient in a bus station, I covered myself with it and fell asleep where I was.

CHAPTER

19

The gastroenterologist's office was the top floor of a medical building so old it had an elevator operator. The waiting room was oddly comforting although it took me a while to understand why. There were the usual stacks of magazines with cover stories about things that had once seemed important and pages soft with use, and there was the standard office furniture, Naugahyde and steel tubing. But there wasn't that heart-stopping medical feeling, and as the receptionist, a young Chinese woman, exotic as a forties' movie villain, raised a perfectly manicured hand and flicked a lighter into flame, I recognized why. The whole place smelled of cigarette smoke. No signs from the cancer society. No cute cartoons. There were ashtrays, and people were using them. I closed my eyes and that smell, acrid and familiar, mixed with the alien smell of things plunged into sterile baths and ripped from sterile wrappings, carried me back to doctors' waiting rooms when I was young, and to doctors who measured and weighed and made jokes about school and husbands and the future.

When I stood to follow the receptionist into the examining room, I felt my stomach cramp, but safe in the smoky air, I said, "Nothing bad can happen here."

The beautiful Chinese woman raised a perfectly waxed eyebrow and, in the flat accents of small-town Saskatchewan, said, "Well, I wouldn't go that far." Then she turned and glided out of the room on her stiletto heels.

The examining room had a spectacular view of the city, and as I stood and watched the late afternoon traffic, I heard in the next room a man's voice talking on the telephone about some property he had bought. I heard the name "Little Bear Lake" and then, after a while, the word "developer." The conversation was heated. Someone hadn't checked something and now the building couldn't start "till spring if ever," I heard the voice say. Then something muffled and finally, very distinct and loud, "You can tell those rubes I'll drag them into the tall grass on this one." A phone slammed down, then the door to the examining room opened and Dr. Philip Lee walked in.

Physically he was as unlike his brother, Mort, as it was possible to be. Mort was a teddy bear of a man – "A Panda bear," Ali said once, "after all, the man was born in Hong Kong and half the family's still there." But there was nothing cuddly about Dr. Philip Lee. He was tall, balding and scholarly looking. He bowed slightly toward me.

"I apologize, Mrs. Kilbourn, for the delay – a consultation."

"Well," I said, sitting on the examining table, "if the developers fall through, you can always build yourself a cottage. Little Bear Lake is beautiful, especially in the spring."

He looked at me sharply and nodded. "Mrs. Kilbourn, in your estimation, what seems to be the trouble?"

I went through the whole dismal history, starting with the first attack in the middle of the night after the boys and I ordered pizza and ending with my performance at Mieka's the day before. I finished by saying, "I have no opinion – I'm the patient. In the other doctor's opinion, the problem is stress. It's all in my head."

Dr. Philip Lee gave me a wintery smile. "That is, of course, one possibility, but let's eliminate the more interesting possibilities of the body first."

The physical examination he gave me was gruelling, "from mouth to anus" as he told me gravely when he began. After it was over, I dressed and the receptionist led me into the doctor's office.

"I see nothing," he said, lighting a Marlboro and inhaling deeply. "We must, of course, await the test results, but everything appears to be entirely normal."

"So you agree that there's nothing wrong with me."

"At this point, I would agree with my colleague that there appears to be no physical cause for your symptoms."

"It's all in my head, then."

"That possibility cannot be ruled out," he said judiciously. "I'm going to write you a prescription for a little nostrum of my own. You are extremely tense and you appear not to be eating well."

"What's in this little cure of yours?"

"Something to relax you and some vitamins. Since you are not a medical person, the names would mean nothing to you."

I shredded Dr. Philip Lee's prescription into the old brass ashtray in the lobby of the medical building. On the way home I stopped at a strip mall and bought a quart of milk, some dark rum and a dozen eggs. "Just what the doctor ordered," I said, lifting my glass in a kitchen filled with the good smell of rum and eggnog, "something to relax the patient."

The doctor called four days later. I was in the granny flat sorting through some of the early press clippings about Andy. He attempted to be genial, and I had a strong suspicion that

Dr. Philip Lee had talked to his brother in Winnipeg, "the one with the charm." He was certainly trying harder.

The test results were negative.

"Good," I said, "wonderful news."

Had the prescription helped?

"Absolutely," I said.

Then I was feeling better?

"Right as rain," I said, but I had to hang up because a spasm hit and I doubled over with pain.

Pain – that was one of the new constants in my life. The other one was fear. Entry after entry in my daybook began with the single word "sick," and then the symptoms: "cramps, diarrhea, metallic taste in the mouth, have to spit all the time." The last words were underscored in exasperation. And there were the symptoms that couldn't be neatly categorized: the increasingly frequent times when I had problems getting air in and out of my lungs; the sense that there was a band of steel wrapped around my chest; the strange and terrifying tricks my heart was playing, pounding when I was sitting idle at my desk in the granny flat, skipping beats when I did something as simple as walk across the room.

The pretty young woman with the curly hair who was one of the family practitioners in Ali Sutherland's old practice made an appointment for me with a cardiologist. The cardiologist taped disks to me and hooked me up to a machine.

"Good news," she said, smiling, "nothing is wrong. Perhaps a short-term use of tranquillizers?"

Craig Evanson called me one morning to ask me to go to the correctional centre and visit Eve, and I promised I would go soon. He had thrown himself into Eve's case with a passion that surprised me. The floppy man had been superseded by a tense, driven stranger. "The shrink who pops in and out of there is worried about her, Jo. He says she's shutting down. The way he explained it to me was it's like closing off rooms in a house. First you close the public rooms and then the guest rooms, until you box yourself into one little room. The problem is Eve's run out of rooms to shut down."

I knew how Eve felt. I was running out of rooms to shut down, too. Except for the boys, I stopped seeing people. November had settled in grey with misery. The easy, communal times when you stand out on the front lawn and visit with neighbours and people riding by on bikes or pushing babies in strollers were gone till spring. The focus of life had turned indoors, and indoors it was easy to say no to people. Everyone was understanding. The leadership convention was set for December fifth, so there were phone calls soliciting support and phone calls asking me to help write rules for the rules committee or to chair the balloting committee or to buy a ticket to the leader's dance. I told everyone the same thing. I'd been ill, and on doctor's orders I was resting and recuperating and getting back my strength. "And besides" I would add, clinching it, "I'm working on a biography of Andy."

For a few weeks Mieka called every day, but after I'd relayed my passing grades from Philip Lee and the cardiologist, she followed my lead and wrote off the episode in her kitchen as an understandable if unendearing reaction to stress.

I did the best I could with the boys. I sat down for breakfast with them in the morning, had lunch ready at noon, sat around for an hour or so with them at dinner time, took them to the Lakeshore Club on Saturday mornings. But children get used to most things, and the boys simply grew used to my being sick. They were kind always, but they had lives of their own: school and friends and football and hockey.

And, I had to admit, precedent was against me. They had seen this pattern after their father's death. Then as now, I was short-tempered and withdrawn. Then as now, the granny flat had become my refuge.

One windy day I drove out to see Eve. We sat in the pale sunlight of the visiting area in the hospital wing, two women who had been defeated, and played a listless game of double solitaire. The irony of our choice of game struck me on the way home, and I had to pull over because when I laughed, I started the bands tightening in my chest again.

Yes, I understood about shutting down rooms. By the second week in November, I had pretty well shut down all the rooms but one: the big room over the garage where I could close out the world, my clean, well-lighted place. Except keeping it clean had become a burden. Every so often the heating ducts would gather their strength and belch out a fresh dusting of summer pollen, and I would have to fill a bucket with hot sudsy water and scrub everything down.

One day when I was carrying the pail my legs began to twitch uncontrollably, the way an eyelid sometimes twitches spasmodically, for no reason. I had to sit down with my bucket until the twitching stopped. That night in bed the twitching started again. The next morning I added twitching to my list of symptoms.

Twitching and double vision. I had begun to have difficulty reading. The first time it happened I'd been reading some photocopies of old newspapers. The print was small and pale, so when my vision blurred, I wrote it off to eye-strain. I was still doing that, still looking for a reasonable excuse, still searching out a logical explanation for my symptoms, but the careful list of symptoms in my daybook was defining a profile that couldn't be ignored. I was either sick or crazy. I was also terrified.

I said that sickness and fear were the two constants of my life. There was a third – Rick Spenser. Every night, wherever he was, he would call, and we would talk. We had gone beyond the Andy book, he and I. In fact, he rarely mentioned the book any more. He was more interested in me and in my days. What was I doing? Who had I seen? How did I feel? I am not a vain woman but with every call it became increasingly clear that Rick Spenser was as attracted to me as powerfully as I was to him.

Sometimes late in the evening when I sat in front of the television and saw his face, round and clever and knowing, my heart would pound and, sitting in my old jogging pants and sweatshirt, I would feel like a fool: a forty-six-year-old housewife watching her heartthrob, a newsroom groupie, but ten minutes later the phone would ring and it would be him. How was I? What was I up to? Who had I been talking to? And, always, had I seen him on the news? How had he done? Had he been clear, witty, insightful?

This Rick Spenser, the vulnerable man behind the persona, touched something in me. Often when I would hang up the phone, I would feel as intimately connected to him as I would have if we'd made love. And so Rick became the third constant in my life, one of the few fixed stars that lit up the darkness of those early winter weeks. And that was the pattern until Remembrance Day.

The call came early on the morning of November eleventh. It couldn't have been much past six. It was Craig Evanson, sounding strained to the point of breaking. The correctional centre had called him a few minutes before. Somehow in the night Eve had gotten hold of a surgical knife and slashed her wrists. The morning nurse had found her. Crafty Eve had been lying with her blanket pulled up to her chin, innocent as a sleeping child. But the nurse noticed a stain in the middle of the blanket and, when she bent to look at it more closely, she saw that the stain was spreading. She pulled back the blanket, and there was Eve, covered in blood, still clutching the knife and near death. Eve was alive, and she was in the hospital wing of the correctional centre.

That whole morning had a dreamlike, surreal quality. It was still dark, and light snow was falling on the empty streets. The stores and office buildings were lit, but when we pulled onto the Ring Road, there wasn't another car in sight.

"Do you have the feeling we're the last two people left on earth?" Craig asked.

His voice came from a place I didn't ever want to go, and his words made my heart pound. There didn't seem to be much logic left in the universe. I would not have been surprised if I had turned in my seat and found that Craig had vanished, just as I would not have been surprised to go home and see a charred and smoking ruin where twenty minutes before my home and children had been. I didn't answer him. I didn't trust my voice.

The process of being admitted to the correctional centre was, by now, grimly routine. We drove up to the gate and waited as the harsh orange security lights swept the exercise yard and shone into our faces, leaching them of colour, turning them into death masks. The guard, enveloped in a yellow slicker, checked our names against a list, and somewhere somebody activated something that opened the electric gates.

Inside it was the familiar rite of passage: doors unlocking to reveal other locked doors, which opened to reveal still more locked doors. A Chinese puzzle.

The guard took us through double doors at the end of Eve's old ward. As we passed Eve's old bed, I noticed that the mattress was gone, and just the bare frame of the bed was left.

"That'll teach her," I said aloud, and Craig looked at me sharply. Eve was in a small room lit by a powerful overhead light. "Does the light have to shine right into her face that way?" I asked.

The nurse who was standing at the head of Eve's bed stopped writing on his clipboard and gave me a warm and surprisingly human smile. He was wearing a poppy, too.

"It's regulations, but they don't notice it or, if they do, they don't mind. Some of them, afterward, even convert. They remember the light of heaven shining down upon them."

Eve looked past caring. She was hooked to tubes that put things into her and took things out of her, and she was connected to machines that measured the beat of her life. Something out of a sci-fi movie – "The Mechanical Woman – only her face is human."

Human, but not Eve. Not gallant Eve who tried to transcend cruelty and betrayal and death with crystals and colour therapy and a cleansing diet. Poor, poor Eve.

Her wrists were heavily bandaged. I reached down and carefully took her hand and held it between my own, warming it. ("Think of all the hands you have known. Your father's hands . . . your mother's hands . . . Experience my hand. Grasp it tight . . . now release it. The touch is gone, but the imprint will be there forever. Forever and ever in your heart.")

After a while, I felt Craig Evanson touch my shoulder. "I think it's time to go, Joanne." Then he took my hand from Eve's, but he didn't let go.

When the guard came to lead us out of the prison, Craig Evanson and I followed him, hand in hand, like children in a fairy-tale.

CHAPTER

20

"Double solitaire," I said.

Craig turned the key in the ignition and looked at me.

"Double solitaire. The last time Eve and I were together that's what we played." My legs began to tremble. "Oh, God, Craig, when is this going to end?"

He reached over and gave me an awkward hug. "I don't know, Jo. I just don't know."

We sat for a while, isolated, thinking our own thoughts. It began to snow, and the banks of orange security lights turned the snow orange.

Finally, Craig said, "I don't know about you, but I need a drink."

I looked at the clock on the dashboard. "Craig, it's not even nine o'clock yet."

"Fine," he said absently as he backed out of the parking spot, "we'll go to the Dewdney Club. I've belonged to that place for twenty years. If they can't find me a bottle of whisky on a holiday morning, I'll break every window in the place."

I looked at him in amazement. "Whatever you say, Craig."

After the harsh realities of the correctional centre, the elegance of the Dewdney Club seemed like another dimension. There was a fire in the fireplace and in the background, discreetly, Glenn Gould played Bach. Craig led me to a table for two by the fire, took my coat, then disappeared. When he came back he was carrying a bottle of Seagram's, and a waiter was dancing around him trying to intercept him.

"Mr. Evanson, I'm certain I can make you a drink you'll find quite palatable."

"I find this palatable, Tony," said Craig, brandishing the bottle.

The breakfast on the sideboard was the kind you see only in magazines and men's clubs: grapefruit halves sectioned and dusted with brown sugar; silver chafing dishes of sausage and bacon and kippers; hash browns and toast and oatmeal kept warm in warming trays; eggs scrambled fresh in a copper pan.

"Do you want food, Jo?" Craig asked.

"Maybe some coffee to put the rye in."

Craig laughed, but there was no fun in the laughter.

"A lady doesn't drink liquor before noon. That's what" – a flash of pain crossed his face – "that's what the lady in my life always says."

I thought of Julie, guilty of God knows what, but not a lady to drink before noon. I sipped my coffee. The rye was smooth, and it felt good to be by the fire, but I couldn't get warm.

Across from me, Craig had filled his water glass with whisky. He raised it. "To you, Jo. A good person."

I lifted my cup, to return the toast.

"No, don't," he said, holding up his hand to stop my toast. "At the moment, I would welcome a lightning bolt to blast me and mine out of existence."

When I spoke, my voice sounded unused and rusty. "You didn't make the phone call that morning, Craig."

"I might as well have. She did it for me." He drained the glass. His voice broke. "Sweet Christ, she did it for me."

The ambiguity hung in the air. She did what for him? The phone call? Or something unspeakably worse? I felt a spasm in my bowels.

"Craig, I'm sick. I need to go home."

He didn't seem to hear me. "I found out by accident, you know. I found out this morning. When the correctional centre phoned the house, it was Lori who answered. Julie's gone to her mother's for the long weekend – said she was exhausted from everything she was doing for me." He laughed his new hollow laugh. "Everything – that covers a multitude of sins, doesn't it?" He looked at the bottle speculatively, but he didn't touch it.

"Anyway, I thought with Julie away it was a good time for Mark and his family to come home. Lori answered the phone. I was still sleeping. The clerk at the correctional centre didn't ask if the Mrs. Evanson he was talking to was my wife. Lori was hysterical when she heard about Eve. Jo, you know how sweet she is, but she's a very limited girl, and she has that fundamentalist guilt to deal with. She's taking all this on her shoulders. She told me the sequence of events before Soren Eames's body was discovered – including" – he looked at his knees – "including that abysmal phone call from Julie about her anonymous caller. If," he said softly, "there was an anonymous caller."

I felt a cold sweat breaking out on my skin, and my heart began to race. "Craig, could I go home now – please?"

"Right, Jo, of course." He went to the cloakroom and came back with my coat.

We drove up Albert Street in silence. As we came to the bridge across the creek, the air was filled with the sound of gunfire. Terrible, pounding shots that made my head hurt and the marrow in my bones ache. One upon another they came – shots fired across the creek from cannons pulled into position in front of the legislature, shots to mark the eleventh hour of the eleventh day of the eleventh month. Remembrance Day, the day they turned the swords into ploughshares.

Craig walked me to the door of my house. I didn't ask him in. As I started to go, he put his hand on my arm and turned me so he could see my face.

"Joanne, are you okay?"

I looked at him. The tall, floppy man shivering in the thin November snow, his future shadowed, the delicate fabric of his marriage ripped apart, his wife guilty of unknown cruelties and crimes in the name of love.

"Nope. I'm not okay, Craig, and you're not okay. And Eve's not okay, and Julie's not okay. Okay is a concept gone from the universe." I felt hysteria rising in my throat. "I'm sorry, Craig."

As soon as I closed the front door I began to shudder, and my mouth filled with saliva.

In the hall mirror I saw my face, yellow and covered with a sheen of sweat. I could feel my heart beating in my chest. It was the worst attack yet. I bent double and closed my eyes. Worried, the dogs began to nuzzle me and lick my face. I pushed them away. Upstairs, the boys were yelling. I didn't even take my coat off. I walked out the back door and went across the yard to the granny flat.

I had to hold onto the rail to pull myself up the stairs. When I opened the door, the phone was ringing. It was Rick. A report about Eve's suicide attempt had come to the newsroom. When I started to tell him about what had happened that morning, my voice was jagged, shrill.

"Rick, we've got to do something. There are things you don't know. Someone's doing this to her. She's innocent. I know it." Then I broke down completely. I couldn't go on.

Rick's voice was calm, almost professionally reassuring. He sounded like a social worker on the business end of a suicide hot line. "Joanne, where are you now?"

"The granny flat. I couldn't face the boys. I'd rather they think I don't care about them than let them see me like this again."

"Stay where you are. Just curl up on that absurd hide-a-bed thing you stuck me on and spend a weekend in bed, away from the noise of the house and the boys."

"But Rick, we have to save Eve. She's innocent. Someone is doing this to her. Someone has driven her to this."

When he answered me there was a new tone in his voice, something unpleasant and patronizing. "Joanne, listen carefully. There is no 'someone.' Eve drove herself to suicide just as she drove herself to murder. There's a pattern there, a history. You know that yourself. The police have the right person. Now just rest."

"You think I'm crazy." My voice was shrewish, accusing.

He sounded exasperated. "I think you've been through a great deal."

"And cracked under the strain. I have a history, too, don't forget. Well, I'm not crazy. Someone is out to get Eve. I know it."

"No one said you had cracked. The consensus of the doctors seems to be that you're exhausted. Nobody could fault you for that."

"I don't need you telling me I'm crazy. Now listen, Rick." I heard my voice, triumphant, crazy. "I'm pulling the jack for this phone right out of the wall. Now try to get to me." Then I was alone in the empty room, a room so quiet I could hear my heartbeat.

I don't know how long I sat there, shaking and exhausted. A queer phrase kept floating through my mind. "You've got to get your bearings." But bearings had to do with navigation when you were lost, and I wasn't lost. I was safe in my granny flat. "A room of one's own," Virginia Woolf had said. Well, this room was my own. Joanne Kilbourn's room. The walls were lined with pictures of my dead husband and the floor was littered with cartons and files that contained the record in words and pictures of the life of my dead friend, Andy Boychuk. My daughter had crocheted the bright afghan on the bed the summer she'd broken her leg. On the desk, dusty now but still heartbreakingly beautiful, was the crystal pitcher Rick had given me. It was filled with branches of Russian olive I'd cut by the creek. The olive berries were pale in the grey half light of November.

In front of the window, as familiar to me as the lines of my own face, was my desk. On it, next to a picture of Mieka and Peter and Angus, soaked to the skin, laughing, giving the dogs a bath, was that other emblem of motherly pride, the ceramic cabbage I had bought for Andy, which Andy had given to Soren and Soren had given to me – a sequence out of a child's book. The leaves curl back, to reveal the tiny figure inside, her face hard with triumph as she offers up her naked son to the world – Ukrainian genesis.

At the edge of the desk was the phone; its cord, unplugged from the jack, hung lame and useless. Impotent. No one could get at me through that.

My place, a room where I could get my bearings. A room where I could be safe. And then, across the window, the quick shadow of a man and the door opened and the room was filled with fresh, cold air and the dark outline of my son's body.

His voice was deep, a man's voice, but he sounded frightened. "Mum, are you all right? You looked like you had fallen asleep sitting up. Were you sleeping? You look kind of weird."

"I'm fine, Peter, just . . . I don't know. Just working."

He looked at my empty desk and then, quickly, into my face.

"Mum, Mieka just called. She wondered how you'd feel about Angus and me going up there for the weekend. I could have a look at the campus and maybe do a bit of Christmas shopping."

The band was tightening around my chest, and my mouth filled with the taste of metal. The bottom of my feet pricked oddly as if something inside my legs were short-circuiting.

"Mum?" Peter's face had the familiar look of worry.

"Sorry, Pete. It sounds great. How are you going to get there?"

He looked at his feet. "Mieka suggested we come up on the 5:30 bus."

My voice was terrible. Falsely hearty. Mum the pal. "It sounds great, Pete. By all means, you guys take the 5:30."

"You're sure, Mum?"

"I'm sure, Peter . . . But one problem, money. I haven't got any, and today's a holiday."

"Barbara, next door, says she'll lend us some till Monday."

"You went to Barbara before you came to me?"

"Mum, I knew you didn't have any money. You didn't have any last night to pay for the paper. Remember, we talked about it?" His voice trailed away. "I didn't want to make a problem for you."

"No problem, Peter." That terrible voice again. I turned from him and picked up a folder. "You guys come over when you're ready, and I'll drive you to the bus station. Pete, could you make a sandwich or something for both of you? I'm a little shaky today."

The adult look again – worried, tentative. "Mum, we don't have to go – really."

I tried to smile. "Peter, I want you to go – really. Now get out of here so I can get some work done."

I watched him walk across the yard toward the house. The footprints he left in the snow seemed much too big.

I parked the car opposite the bus station and sat there, shaking with cold and something else, until the bus pulled out. As it disappeared up Broad Street, a swirl of snow curled behind it and a picture came into my mind, clear in every detail, of a blinding snowstorm and the bus sliding off the road and bursting into flames. "They'll be killed, and I'll be alone forever," I said to the empty car. It was five minutes before I trusted my hand to put the key in the ignition and five more before I dared to turn it.

The house was cold and dark when I got home. I made myself a hot lemon rum and drank it at the kitchen table, looking into the evening. When it was finished, I made another one, called the dogs and walked across the backyard to the granny flat. I plugged in the phone so I could talk to the boys if they called me from Mieka's house, covered myself with the afghan and fell into a fitful sleep.

I dreamed crazy things. I was looking for my sons on the bus, and it was filled with people I knew. Andy was there, pinning bright poppies to Eve's bandaged wrists. "This is for me. This is for you, and this," he said, driving a third poppy into her vein, "is for the devil." And then his face became Rick Spenser's face, leaning confidentially toward Eve, whose poppies were suddenly pulsing with bright blood. "There's a pattern here, Eve." And then I was Eve. I was the one with the bandaged wrists and the poppies blooming blood.

And then the snow that had swirled around me, blinding me, suddenly cleared, and I could see the front of the bus. Terry Shaw was there with my sons, who were handcuffed together, and the prison security system was ringing and ringing, and when I finally came awake, the telephone was ringing, shrill and insistent.

A woman's voice – reassuring, familiar. "Oh, good – there you are. Well, the boys are safe. I haven't killed them yet."

"Who is this?"

"Mummy, it's Mieka. Did I wake you up? You sound like you're on the planet Org. Did you hear me? I said the boys are here, safe and sound. Angus is in the shower and Peter's building a fire. Greg's making popcorn. It's a regular Disney movie here – a festival of wholesome family fun."

My voice was tight and falsely bright. "Great, good. Have fun." And then, "Thank you, Mieka. I love you. I have to go now." I hung up quickly because I could feel the tears coming. She didn't need them. I reached down and unplugged the phone. Then I changed my mind. Peter was building a fire, Mieka said. The house was old. There could be a crack in the firewall and they could all burn to death, and I wouldn't know. No, I'd have to take my chances on that phone. I plugged it in. The bottoms of my feet began to do their odd new trick – electric pins and needles.

"The world's a rational place, Joanne." That's what Andy had said that September night, nine months after Ian died. "The world's a rational place," I said to the darkness outside. The band around my chest tightened. The darkness outside knew better, and I knew better, too. "Andy, my friend, you were wrong." I poured brandy into a snifter. "The world is not a rational place."

I watched my reflection in the window, lifting the glass, drinking, and I wondered if there'd been enough time for him to find that out before he died.

CHAPTER

21

Sitting in the granny flat, looking into the November night, I knew all my protections were gone. Since we had come up here, my dogs and me, the snow had stopped falling. My backyard was a smooth expanse of white, shining in the light from the house.

Crisp and even, but not deep. I knew how thin that layer of snow was. If you stepped on it, your foot would break through to the leaves, under there, decaying, wet and black, on the cold ground. You weren't safe on that snow.

But you were never safe. Across the yard my house, a place where rational people had once planned their lives, stood in darkness. A spasm hit my bowels, then another. I doubled over, hugged my knees and rocked back and forth, back and forth, making a sound that was sometimes keening and sometimes a growl. Back and forth, back and forth until, sometime toward morning, the sky grew lighter and I slept.

I woke up in the chair, cold and disoriented. The room was full of light. My head was pounding; my mouth was dry; and the telephone was ringing.

The voice on the other end was male and pleasantly accented.

"May I speak with Ian Kilbourn, please?"

I thought, I must be careful here. I must sound sane. I mustn't give anything away.

"My husband's dead."

An intake of breath on the other end of the line and then, "I'm so very sorry, Mrs. Kilbourn. Forgive me for disturbing you at this sad time."

"No, it's . . . He's been dead a long time. I was just surprised to hear you ask for him." My heart was pounding.

"Mrs. Kilbourn, I think, then, that I should speak with you. My name is Helke de Vries, and I've just purchased Homefree Insect Pest Control Service."

"I don't need an exterminator."

"Mrs. Kilbourn, I'm not a salesman, but you're correct about not needing an exterminator, because you already have one – me. Allow me, please, to explain. I spent yesterday going over invoices – familiarizing myself with the business. I'm looking at our records for services rendered to you, and I think there must be some mistake –"

"My mistake?"

"Please, allow me to finish. It is not money. All your bills have been paid promptly – in advance, in point of fact. You have done nothing wrong, but I'm concerned that we have. Are you there, Mrs. Kilbourn?"

"Yes. Please, tell me what you want. I'm not feeling at all well today."

"It's the carpenter ants in your addition. Perhaps if you'd just allow me to read you our instructions."

I was so tired I could barely speak. "Read them, do whatever you want."

"The service is to be provided to a residence at 433 Eastlake Avenue – that is your home?"

"Yes."

"In the backyard, over the garage, there is a self-contained apartment unit, 150 square feet, accessible through a door that opens off a small balcony."

"Yes."

"The key is in a plastic bag taped to the inside of a window box to the left of the door to the unit."

"No . . ." My voice was barely a whisper.

Helke de Vries sounded uncomfortable but determined. "Spraying program for carpenter ants to begin Saturday, October 8, 9:30 a.m. and continue weekly – that is underlined in red, Mrs. Kilbourn – until notice to discontinue. Payment, cash in advance. In the space marked client, there is the name Ian Kilbourn. Then there's something handwritten in red pen – 'Under no circumstances is anyone else in the family to know of the spraying program. The wife and kids are Save the Whales environmentalist types. Trouble.' That last word is in capital letters and underlined."

I felt like Alice after she walked through the looking glass. I picked up a pen and wrote "pest control" on the notepad in front of me.

"Mr. de Vries, could you give me the name of what you've been using?" I was trembling.

"Certainly. We have used an organophosphate spray and a methyl carbonate. In my opinion, we have used them too often, but today is Saturday, time for another treatment, so I thought I would check. Do you wish me to continue, Mrs. Kilbourn? We are paid, in cash, until after Christmas."

"No, Mr. de Vries, I do not wish you to continue."

"Then I should refund your money."

"It isn't my money. Who paid you?"

"The bill was paid in cash, and no receipt was given. The previous owners of the business assumed Mr. Kilbourn was paying."

"Keep the money." I was beginning to see light. "I need to know more. Would any of that stuff, the organophosphate or the methyl whatever it is, leave a residue?"

"The organophosphates would leave a yellow dusting."

"Would it look like pollen?"

"Yes, an excellent description – like pollen."

"Then stop it."

"Your instructions, then, Mrs. Kilbourn, are to discontinue spraying until further notice?"

"No, Mr. de Vries, my instructions are to discontinue spraying until hell freezes over."

There was a long silence, then laughter. "Another excellent description – thank you, Mrs. Kilbourn."

"Oh, thank you, Mr. de Vries. Thank you."

When I hung up, my body was trembling and sweating and pounding and cramping. I felt worse than I'd ever felt in my life, and better. Someone was trying to kill me. I should have been terrified. I should have been hiding under the bed. But all I felt was relief. The darkness wasn't coming from me; it was outside. Out there, where it could be stopped.

I opened the door of the granny flat and stepped onto the porch. It was going to be a cold day. The sky was high and grey, and the sun was pale. I took deep breaths of cold air that knifed at my chest. The dogs ran past me down the steps and chased each other around the yard in the snow.

My stomach was empty, my mouth was dry, and I was trembling with cold and excitement, but I went straight to the phone and called Ali.

"Ali, good news. I'm not crazy. Somebody's trying to kill me."

Her voice was warm and encouraging, but it was her professional voice, guarded, holding back. "Jo, why don't you turn this tape back to the beginning and let me follow along."

I told her about Helke de Vries's phone call, and his revelations. Ali listened without comment. When I finished, her
questions were professional. She asked me to repeat the
names of the insecticides the exterminators used, to tell
her the size of the granny flat in square feet and to describe
the kind of ventilation the room had.

"Jo, I'm going to have to check this out in one of my
college texts. I haven't studied pharmacology for fifteen
years. I'll call you back as soon as I can. Stay where you are.
You're not in the –"

"No, I'm out of there. I left the door open. I'm never going
in there again. Ali . . ." I began to cry. "Oh, Ali, hurry."

She called back in five minutes.

"Well, you have Mort to thank for this. He has the
Oriental passion for order: a place for everything and everything in its place. Anyway, tell me if this sounds familiar.
I'm going to read from the section on insecticides in a
book called *The Pharmacological Basis of Therapeutics*,
Goodmand and Gilman – the G-men, we used to call them
in med school. Here's the clinical profile of exposure to
organophosphates. 'Respiratory effects consist of tightness in
the chest and wheezing respiration due to the combination
of bronchi-constriction and increased bronchial secretion.
Gastrointestinal symptoms occur earliest after ingestion and
include anorexia, nausea and vomiting, abdominal cramps
and diarrhea, localized sweating, fatigability and generalized
weakness, involuntary twitchings.'"

My voice was small and frightened. "I've got all of them,
Ali. Is it too late? Can you do anything?"

"Yes, I can, or my brother-in-law can until I get there.
When was the last time you were in the granny flat?"

"Most of yesterday and all last night."

She swore softly. "Nothing for it but do the best we can. Go
take a hot, soapy shower, wash your hair and your fingernails,

and by the time you're out of there, Phil will be pounding at the front door."

"A house call?" I said.

"It'll do him good," she snapped. "Now into the shower. I'll be there tonight. Mort and I will drive down this afternoon."

I began to cry again. "Oh, Ali, you're so good."

"Jo, don't. Mort bought himself a new BMW last week, and he's been dying to get it on the highway. It's a six-hour drive. We'll be there by ten o'clock. Don't fuss. In fact, it wouldn't be the worst idea in the world if you spent a couple of days in bed. If you want to nap, do it. I still have a key from the last time I was there. Now, go get your shower, do what Phil tells you, and I'll see you later."

I made the shower as hot as I could stand it, soaped my body with some antibacterial soap the kids had for zits and scrubbed at my skin until it hurt.

By the time I was dry and in my robe, Dr. Philip Lee was at the front door, scowling.

"It was good of you to come to the house," I said.

"My sister-in-law is a very persuasive woman," he said. And then he smiled. "Well, what the hell, eh?"

While he examined me, he asked about the granny flat, the same questions Ali had asked. How big was it? How was it ventilated? How often had the extermination people sprayed? What did they use?

"Organophosphates." He repeated my answer as he pressed down on my abdomen with his graceful hands. "Do you know what they used organophosphates for in Germany before the Second World War? They were active ingredients in nerve gases. Your granny flat was a little gas chamber for you, Mrs. Kilbourn. Amazing, eh?"

"Amazing," I agreed weakly.

"Well," he said after I'd pulled the covers over me, "you're going to live. I would put you in a hospital if my brother and

sister-in-law weren't coming. But you need a neurologist
and a psychiatrist and" – he snapped his long, tobacco-stained
fingers – "presto, they appear . . . More house calls." He
grinned. "Ali says you're a nice woman, Mrs. Kilbourn.
You're certainly a lucky one. I'm going to prescribe atropine
sulphate – perhaps you know it by its other name, bella-
donna. You take it orally, every four hours. Set your alarm.
The timing is important. The atropine should relieve your
symptoms. My brother might wish to prescribe something
to reverse the muscular weakness, but I'll leave that to him.
I'll call in your prescription for you, and the drug store will
deliver it."

He started to walk out of the room but turned in the
doorway. He looked at his feet like a bashful boy in a movie,
then shrugged.

"Could I look at it, Mrs. Kilbourn?"

I didn't understand.

"Your gas chamber," he said.

"Absolutely, be my guest. What the hell, eh?" I said and
sank down into the warmth of my bed.

I waited for the prescription, and after it arrived, I took the
phone off the hook, curled up and went to sleep. There were
things I had to do: call the police, call the kids, call Rick. But
the phone calls would have to wait. I needed sleep. I awoke
around five o'clock, made myself a bowl of chicken noodle
soup and ate it with some crackers, then I fell asleep again.

When I woke, it was just before ten. The national news
was coming on.

I turned on the TV in my bedroom and put the phone on
the hook. Sometimes Rick called as soon as his report was
over, and suddenly I wanted very much to talk to him. I
wasn't crazy. I was a woman with a future again, a woman a
man could think about loving, a woman who could think
about having a man as part of her future.

And not just any man. I lay back on the pillows piled against the headboard of my bed and remembered. I remembered how his smile started in one corner of his mouth and spread, slow and knowing, until his face was transformed. And I remembered how his hair, dark blond like mine, fell forward when he bent his head to look down at me, and how he had sat on the bleachers with me in the twilight, and cooked with me and laughed with me and worked with me. And I remembered how he'd fit so smoothly into all our lives at Thanksgiving, and I thought, when Ali and Mort come, I'll invite them for the holidays here with us, with my children and me, with Rick.

The phone rang and at just that minute his face filled the television screen. I picked up the receiver, but my eyes never left Rick's image. He was still wearing his poppy. He must have rushed to the studio and grabbed yesterday's jacket, with its poppy and its day-old creases, from the dressing room before going on the air.

I strained to listen to the television, but in my ear there was a woman's voice, familiar and old: "And I thought, well, I'll put all these books I brought back from overseas away until after Christmas when I can have a really good look at them. So it was while I was trying to find some space in that little garage of mine that . . ."

Rick was saying something about a group in the prime minister's party meeting at a cottage in the Eastern Townships to talk about challenging the PM's leadership before the next election.

The voice went on in my ear: "And that's when I found the box. I can't imagine why it didn't surface before."

Rick was taking a hard line against those who were plotting against the prime minister. "It is a question not just of party solidarity but of fundamental decency," he said. "Decency has been a commodity in short supply during the life of this government, but in the dying days perhaps it is not too much to hope . . ."

"At any rate, our little mystery is solved," said the woman's voice.

"Hilda McCourt," I said, suddenly making the connection.

"Yes, Joanne, it's Hilda. I'm sorry, I should have identified myself. Egotism seems to be as much a part of getting old as creaks and flatulence. Anyway, it is I, and the box I unearthed in the garage contained all my old grade books from E.T. Russell. It was the easiest thing in the world. I looked up grade twelve and found Boychuk, Andrue Peter – that's Andrue with a *ue*, as I'm sure you know." Angus had left an old spelling test on my night table. I picked up my pen and wrote, "Boychuk, Andrue Peter" in a clear space at the top of the paper.

"The boy with the unfortunate name, as I had remembered, came late in the year. His name is added at the bottom of the roll. The name is Primrose. Eric Spenser Primrose."

I wrote the name beneath Andy's and circled the initials of their given names, Andrue and Eric.

"You see it, don't you, Joanne?" Hilda McCourt was saying. "That delicate boy, Eric Spenser Primrose, grew up to be Rick Spenser. Isn't that a shocker? When I saw him after Andy's funeral I knew there was something in Rick Spenser's face that I recognized, but of course, I was upset. I remember you offering the explanation that I was just responding to the familiarity of celebrity. I didn't care for that explanation, Joanne, and I was right not to. They can get grey or bald or even fat but I always remember my students' faces. Still" – she laughed – "Eric Primrose being Rick Spenser strained even my powers. The last place one would think to look for a thin boy is in a fat man. Anyway, there's our mystery solved."

On the TV screen, Rick's face dissolved and was replaced

by a commercial for camera film. A handsome family was getting ready for Christmas. Words came on the screen: "For the times of your life."

Hilda's voice sounded in my ear. "And you can't blame him for dropping the 'Primrose.' The jokes would have plagued him forever, and he suffered so with them. Memories are coming back to me now. Our grade twelve curriculum, for example. We used to do William Blake's 'The Sick Rose.' Do you know it, Joanne?"

I said the lines mechanically in a voice that sounded like Lori Evanson's.

> O rose, thou art sick.
> The invisible worm
> That flies in the night,
> In the howling storm,
>
> Has found out thy bed
> Of crimson joy,
> And his dark secret love
> Does thy life destroy.

"You must have had a good teacher," Hilda McCourt said admiringly. "Well, you can imagine what high-school children did with that poem and an effeminate boy named Primrose."

On the screen, the president of the United States boarded Air Force One and went somewhere.

"Yes," I said, "I can imagine."

"Joanne, this has been a shock for you, hasn't it? But no harm done. I assure you, Eric behaved very handsomely when I confronted him with it, if 'confronted' isn't too strong a word. He said he was upset that day, but he always finds it difficult to be reminded of those times. That's understandable, I think. Adolescence must have been a painful time for him."

"When did you talk to Rick?"

"Early this afternoon. I called him just before lunch."

On the television, there were pictures of a benefit production of a Broadway musical. The choreographer had died of AIDS the week before. "One more reminder," said the announcer. The prime minister and his family, bundled into handsome fall sportswear, were going to Harrington Lake for the long weekend. Everybody was on the move. I reached over and turned them all off, vanquished them.

"Joanne, are you all right?"

"Yes, I'm all right, Hilda – just assimilating," I said and wondered at my choice of words.

"Good. Eric suggested that I shouldn't tell you. He said you'd been under a great deal of stress."

"Yes," I repeated dully, "a great deal of stress. Hilda, I'm grateful for your help – truly. I have to go. I have things to do."

I didn't give her a chance to respond. I hung up the receiver and sat staring at the television set as if I could conjure up his face, make him materialize from the hidden electronic dots.

"You bastard," I said to the empty screen. Despite the atropine, my heart was pounding. "You murderous son of a bitch." I stood up and grabbed my robe. There was something I had to see.

At the bottom of the stairs, Peter's snow boots lay abandoned. I shoved my bare feet into them and grabbed a ski jacket from a coat hook in the entranceway. It was an old one of Mieka's, ripped under the arms and heavy with buttons and pins from rock groups that, by now, had disbanded and gone their separate ways. I put the ski jacket on over my nightgown and walked out the back door and across the yard to the garage.

The door to the granny flat was still open. It had been open all day. My legs were trembling, but I climbed the stairs. I knew what I wanted.

It was in the vertical files for the current year, in a box marked "August 28." No other reference was necessary. I slipped it out of its box, checked the label and slid it into the VCR. My hands were trembling. I had had the tape for weeks. A woman I knew in the newsroom at CNRC-TV had given it to me when she heard about the book I was writing, but until that moment, I hadn't been able to face looking at it.

I hit the play button and it was August again. There were crowd shots. I recognized a few people, sweating and happy, and with a start, I saw the man from the poultry association brushing barbecue sauce on chicken halves that were just beginning to sputter and smoke.

I hit the fast-forward button. There was the makeshift stage, empty still. There was Dave Micklejohn, bringing Roma on stage. And there was Eve, looking the way she always did in public, strained and anxious, ready to bolt. Then Dave leaned toward her and whispered something, and she smiled.

In that moment, Eve Boychuk's face was transformed. She was both carefree and lovely. There couldn't have been more than a handful of such times in her life, and now her face was waxy white as she lay beneath stiff hospital sheets, her wrists blooming blood. "Eric Primrose, you bastard, you'll pay for this, you'll pay for doing this to her," I said, and my breath made little clouds in the cold air of the granny flat.

On the television, the big woman who would hand Andy the black Thermos of water appeared at the top of the portable staircase at the back of the truck, and in the cold, dead room, I stopped breathing. She picked her way carefully through the snakes of wires from the sound system and finally, safely across the stage, she put the leather speech folder on the podium.

He always did that, handed the speech to someone who'd be onstage before him, so he could bound on boyish, spontaneous. There she was, putting the folder down so carefully, right where we had told her. Inside was the sheet of paper, grey as a dove's breast, and on it the Blake poem, and at the top of the page, two letters, *A* and *E*, curled together like the initials of a husband and wife on a Victorian headstone. *A* and *E*, Andy and Eric. But Andy hadn't seen that – not yet.

My teeth were chattering. In the yard, my dogs were barking, but I was transfixed. Craig Evanson was on the screen, introducing Andy. Another victim, but I didn't want to see him. I pushed the fast-forward button. There was a blur then Andy was there, suntanned, so slight in his blue jeans and cotton shirt as he walked across the stage to his death. He was laughing. Then he took off his baseball cap and waved it. Graceful, doomed, he was, in that moment, the last of the boys of summer. In the cold moonlight in the yard, my dogs were barking frantically, but I was lost in the eternal summer of Andy's last picnic.

Then he turned from the podium and the woman in the flowered dress handed him the tray and on the tray were the black Thermos and the glass. I couldn't watch it. I closed my eyes, and when I opened them again I saw myself on the TV screen kneeling by Andy, twenty pounds heavier, and so strong and capable. I had forgotten I was like that. I pulled the hem of my nightgown around my knees for warmth. Rick Spenser was on the screen, his back to the podium, shakily raising the glass to his lips. Then there was a blur. In the next shot, I was wrapped around his knees, and he was coming down hard.

In the yard the dogs were frenzied, yelping and growling. On the tape, Andy and Rick were lying on a metal truck bed under the August sun. Then Rick was talking, but not on television. He was in the doorway of the granny flat, his bulk blocking out the moonlight. I could smell fear, but he didn't sound afraid. He sounded like he knew he was going to win.

"I have always detested ad hockery, Joanne."

"What?" My voice was barely audible.

"You had an excellent education. You know the meaning of the term 'ad hoc,' and this whole affair has reeked of it. Everything cobbled together on the spot. You know, I'm not a monster. It's never been a question of calibrating the attacks against you. I've just had to do the best I could. Improvising, although I've always shrunk from improvising."

He moved closer, and I could see his face in the moonlight. He didn't look like a maniac, but he was saying terrible things.

"It's working, though, Joanne, and that, of course, is the test, isn't it. There are no loose ends. Certainly there's nothing to connect me with this place tonight. I've discovered there's an advantage to dealing with women. There's always such a miasma of hysteria around them that you can get away" – he smiled a little sadly – "well, with almost anything. You're not quite as dramatic as Eve, but still, no one would be surprised if you walked down the stairs and into the garage. I think it would be a very logical way for a despondent woman to die, asleep in her own car with the motor running.

"I talked to Mieka yesterday. I told her I feared you were heading for another breakdown. Do you know what she said? She said, 'That would just kill her. She's such a good mother. I think she'd rather die than let us see her like that again.' Your own daughter, Joanne." He shrugged and gave me his professional smile, amused at the vagaries of the world. "Look at yourself. You've even dressed for the part – a crazy woman in a nightgown, a ripped ski jacket, a man's snow boots and bare legs," he said, bending closer and shaking his head.

"You were wearing a poppy," I said.

"What?" I had thrown him the wrong line, and he was at a loss. "What did you say?"

Underneath my nightgown I could feel my knees knocking together, but my voice sounded okay. "Half an hour ago on your special report on the news, three million people saw you wearing a poppy on the day after Remembrance Day. A man as fastidious as you . . . Someone's sure to put it together. Some smart young cop or some assistant producer you've been snotty with. Maybe even some hick out here in the prairies. Most of us know about the magic of video-taping by now."

I had no plan. I watched his face in the flickering light from the VCR. There seemed to be something tentative in his smile.

Ad hockery. "It's just a matter of time now, Eric," I said. He flinched from the name as if it were a blow. I'd scored a hit. "They're going to catch you, Eric, and then everyone will know. Not just that you're a murderer – that still has a certain Nietzschean appeal." I was shaking uncontrollably. "Or even that you're gay." My voice quavered. "That still has a certain cachet. But they'll find those old pictures, you know." In the silvery light, I could see a fine line of saliva between his lips. It was now or never. "Little Eric Primrose, the fairy boy. They'll find those old pictures, and they'll have a field day. Rick Spenser, the erudite friend of people who matter, is really little Eric Primrose. Little Eric, the delicate fairy boy who dreamed of weddings and lace and who connected his initial to his beloved's with little curlicues and flowers. Just like a girl. O rose thou art sick. Blake will be in the headlines, Eric."

As I talked, I stood and walked toward him, and he backed

away as if I were exerting some kind of physical force. I had a vague idea that I might back him out the door and knock him over the balcony, like in the movies, but I was too sick and too terrified to focus on any plan.

Ad hockery. I had to keep talking. His chest was heaving, and there was an animal smell in the room. I didn't know whether it was coming from him or me. He seemed mesmerized. The crueller the cut, the more intent he became.

"Poor Andy, having you in his life. But, you know, he did find real love with Soren Eames. He and Soren were equals. Soren told me once that when Andy touched him for the first time, he knew what it felt like to bloom. To bloom, Eric. It must have been so good for them both."

He was going to break.

"I don't blame Andy for falling out of love with you. Not just because you're fat, but because you're a fake."

He braced himself against the desk. His fingertips touched the base of the crystal pitcher he had given me. His hand curled around the handle, then he raised it like a club above his head. Moonlight streamed through the open door and caught the curve of the pitcher. He looked as if he were holding a club of pale fire.

My eyes lost their focus. I blinked, then I blinked again. Standing on the balcony, just behind Rick, was Ali Sutherland.

She was a shade less than six feet tall, and heavy. She seemed like a match for him. She was looking straight at me. It was hard to read her expression in the half light, but she nodded her head slightly, and I took that as a sign of agreement and encouragement. I took a deep breath.

"Are you going to kill me with that? That would bring the total to three, wouldn't it? Four, if you want to count Eve, who's as good as dead, lying on her back, counting the cracks in the ceiling. Five, if you want to count her son – that beautiful bright boy who's a vegetable now, his sister dead." Then

suddenly I knew. "Because that day, before Eve got behind
the wheel of the car, you made sure she knew, didn't you?
Didn't you?"

He nodded, raised the pitcher higher and took a step
toward me.

I moved toward him and I put my face so close to his I
could smell his breath. And then very low, I said, "Why
didn't you just kill yourself, Eric?"

He spit his answer at me. "Because, bitch, I wasn't the one
who deserved to die."

Behind Rick's shoulder Ali Sutherland looked at me
levelly, then I saw the slightest nod of her head, almost
imperceptible. I thought, she's going to make her move.

Ali's voice and her hand came at the same time. "You
must be so tired of all this, Rick," she said, and she reached
from behind him and took the crystal pitcher. And then,
very calm and unhurried, she led Rick out the door, put the
vase in the window box, took Rick's arm and, murmuring
reassurances, led him carefully down the stairs. I stood on
the little balcony and watched them cross the yard and go
into my house, two large and handsome people, silvery in
the moonlight, visitors from another country, going home.

I went into the granny flat, called the police and turned off
the television. Then I went to the balcony, took the pitcher
out of the cold dirt in the window box, sat on the top step
and waited until I heard the sirens. The crystal vase was safe.
I used the hem of my nightgown to rub the dirt from the
deep lines of its pattern. I rubbed until I thought they'd have
enough time to take him. I rubbed until it was safe again.

When I went in the house, Ali was making tea. Beside her
was a tumbler of Scotch – neat.

"The tea's for you," she said. "There must be quite a
chemical soup in you at the moment. I don't think alcohol
would be a smart move." She turned her back to me,

swirled boiling water in the teapot. "Mort went to the police station with Rick. Mort really liked him, you know. I guess we all did." She poured out the water and carefully measured tea into the pot. Suddenly, the kitchen smelled of oranges and spices.

"Does any of this make sense to you?" I asked.

Ali looked into my face. "Rick talked to me while we were waiting for the police. He wanted me to understand, I think. He and Andy were lovers for over twenty-five years. Then in the spring Andy suddenly left him. Rick hated Soren Eames for taking Andy away from him, but he hated Andy even more for leaving him. And so, he contrived to kill them."

"His dark secret love/Does thy life destroy," I said.

Ali looked concerned. "Perhaps you're not ready to deal with this, Jo."

"Maybe not," I said, "but one more thing. Why would Rick drink the water from Andy's glass if he didn't want to die?"

"Subterfuge?" said Ali. "You were a lucky break for him, but if you hadn't happened along, he could simply have pretended to drink. You told me there were five thousand people in the park that day. There would have been one credulous soul prepared to swear that Rick was innocent because he'd lifted that glass."

"Smoke and mirrors," I said.

"Time for tea." Ali put her drink, the teapot and a cup on a little tray and walked into the living room. I followed her. When she sat on the couch, I curled up against her warm bulk and cried like a baby. She held me in her arms and rocked me until I fell asleep.

CHAPTER

22

Writing this account was Ali's idea. "Get it out," she said, sitting on my bed one morning before she drove back to Winnipeg. "Give it shape then move along. You don't need an analyst any more; you just need rest and a little time to evaluate. Besides," she said, brightening, "a journal will give you something to do while you're cooling your heels in all those specialists' waiting rooms." After the initial rounds, I ended up with just one specialist, a neurologist, a gentle man with a crewcut who explained in terms a lay person would understand what had happened to me. The pesticides had blocked the enzyme that governs the transmission of nerve impulses, so my nervous system was in a constant state of stimulation. That, directly or indirectly, caused all my symptoms.

"So what do I do now?" I had asked him.

"Well, stay away from organophosphates for a start," he said seriously, then smiled. "Sorry, that was stupid. From what Ali tells me, I gather you didn't exactly bring this upon yourself. Anyway, I'm not planning anything heroic here – some B-12 shots, a prescription for oral B complex, some good food, lots of rest and an exercise regime. The CFL season's over, and there's a guy I know who's a trainer for the Riders. He can help you with the exercising – muscle-strengthening stuff, some leg raising with weights, hamstring lifts. He'll turn you into a jock, Mrs. Kilbourn. The only thing wrong with him is that he's a Barry Manilow fan. He plays one tape after another."

And that's my life: vitamin shots, eating, resting, jock stuff and writing this. Ali says I should give myself over to invalidism for a while. And introspection. "But don't let it go on too long," she said. "Watch out for the Magic Mountain syndrome – taking your pulse every thirty minutes and checking out your BMs. New Year's Eve seems a nice symbolic time to move along, but until then let the world dance without you."

And so I do. The leadership convention came and went without me. The party elected a radical young farmer from the southwest of the province. He won't win the election for us, but in the long run he may be what we needed all along. Craig Evanson nominated him. Julie was not there.

Christmas is two weeks away, and although I have a nice stack of invitations for holiday parties, I am not taking part in what Ian used to grimly call "the mulled wine and salmonella season." Mieka and Greg will be home next week, and Ali and Mort will arrive on Christmas Eve. Mort made reservations for Christmas dinner at a splendid old hotel downtown. This will be the first year since I was married that I haven't cooked a turkey. Somehow that seems significant.

Peter and Angus are doing most of the cooking around here, so we've been through the take-out list a couple of times. For the first week or so after the "incident in the granny flat," as my friend Millar Millard calls it, the boys were unnervingly solicitous, but we're back in our familiar grooves now. They come, singly or together, and throw themselves on the bed to pass along the news or gripe about each other, and I ask them why they can't get along better and complain about no one recognizing my need for peace and quiet. We're all relieved to pick up the old roles and the old lines.

I find it odd to be an outsider. Everything I know about other people comes from Christmas cards. In the normal course of things, I'd pick them out of the mailbox, rip them open and glance at the signatures, but this year I'm reading the cards carefully, looking not just for news but for subtext.

There are some beside me now that I keep coming back to. There is a lithograph of Osgoode Hall in Toronto from Howard Dowhanuik. The card came tucked inside a silk scarf. He is staying in Toronto for the holidays but will be back early in the new year. Not a word about Marty.

Terry Shaw from the correctional centre writes a note of thanks for a small gift I sent and says that she is "not hopeful about Eve's chances of psychological recovery but after all this is the season for miracles."

Hilda McCourt's card is hand-done, a brass rubbing from the tomb of the Venerable Bede ("Something I did for some special friends when I was overseas"). With her card, she encloses a letter in which she details the contributions "gays" (her word, carefully chosen) have made to the arts and asking me not to be embittered by "one tortured boy."

Lori and Mark Evanson's card is a conventional and pretty nativity scene. Inside, behind a cutout oval, is a picture of Mark and Lori and their son, Clay. Mark stands behind a chair with his hand on his wife's shoulder. Clay is on his mother's knee with his face turned toward her. As she looks down into her son's face, Lori Evanson's look, dim, radiant and trusting, seems to me eerily like that of the Madonna on the front of her card.

There is one final card, a large and handsome one on which a grey dove with an olive branch flies against a pale grey sky. Inside in raised letters is a printed message:

Peace on Earth. Goodwill to All.

A Holiday wish from
Homefree Insect Pest Control Services
The Name Says It All.

If you enjoyed

DEADLY
APPEARANCES

treat yourself to all of the
Joanne Kilbourn mysteries,
now available in stunning new
trade paperback editions
and as eBooks

McCLELLAND & STEWART

www.mcclelland.com
www.mysterybooks.ca

DEADLY APPEARANCES

When Andy Boychuk drops dead at a political picnic, the evidence points to his wife. Joanne takes her first "case" as Canada's favourite amateur sleuth as she seeks to clear Eve Boychuk, discovering along the way a Bible college that isn't all it seems . . .

"A compelling novel infused with a subtext that's both inventive and diabolical." – Montreal *Gazette*

Trade Paperback 978-0-7710-1324-9   Ebook 978-0-7710-1322-5

MURDER AT THE MENDEL

Joanne's childhood friend, Sally Love, is an artist who courts controversy. When Sally's former partner turns up dead, Joanne discovers the past they shared was much more complicated, sordid, and deadly than she ever guessed.

"Classic. . . . Enough twists to qualify as a page turner. . . . Bowen and her genteel sleuth are here to stay."
– Saskatoon *StarPhoenix*

Trade Paperback 978-0-7710-1321-8   Ebook 978-0-7710-1320-1

THE WANDERING SOUL MURDERS

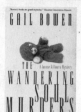

Joanne's peace is destroyed when her daughter finds a young woman's body near her shop. The next day, her son's girlfriend drowns, an apparent suicide. When it is discovered that the two young women had at least one thing in common, Joanne is drawn into a twilight world where money can buy anything.

"With her rare talent for plumbing emotional pain, Bowen makes you feel the shock of murder."
– *Kirkus Reviews*

Trade Paperback 978-0-7710-1319-5   Ebook 978-0-7710-1318-8

A COLDER KIND OF DEATH

When the man convicted of murdering her husband six years earlier is himself shot, Joanne is forced to relive the most horrible time of her life. But it soon gets much worse when the prisoner's menacing wife is found dead a few nights later, strangled with Joanne's own silk scarf . . .

"A terrific story with a slick twist at the end."
– *Globe and Mail*

Trade Paperback 978-0-7710-1317-1   Ebook 978-0-7710-1316-4

A KILLING SPRING

The head of the School of Journalism at Joanne's university is found in a seedy rooming house wearing only women's lingerie and an electrical cord around his neck. When other events indicate that it was not a case of accidental suicide, Joanne finds herself deep in a world of fear, deceit, and danger.

"A compelling novel as well as a gripping mystery."
– *Publishers Weekly*

Trade Paperback 978-0-7710-1315-7   Ebook 978-1-5519-9613-4

VERDICT IN BLOOD

The corpse of the respected – and feared – Judge Justine Blackwell is found in a Regina park. Joanne tries to help a good friend involved in a struggle over which of Blackwell's wills is valid, and those who stand to lose the inheritance may well be murderers willing to strike again.

"An entirely satisfying example of why Gail Bowen has become one of the best mystery writers in the country."
– *London Free Press*

Trade Paperback 978-0-7710-1311-9   Ebook 978-1-5519-9614-1

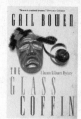

THE ENDLESS KNOT

After journalist Kathryn Morrissey publishes a tell-all book on the adult children of Canadian celebrities, one of the parents angrily confronts her and as a result is charged with attempted murder. When the parent hires Zack Shreve, the new love in Joanne's life, to defend him, her own understanding of the knot that binds parent and child becomes both personal and very urgent.

"A late-night page turner. . . . A rich and satisfying read." – *Edmonton Journal*

Trade Paperback 978-0-7710-1347-8   Ebook 978-1-5519-9246-4

THE BRUTAL HEART

A local call girl is dead, and her impressive client list includes the name of Joanne's new husband. Shaken that Zack saw the woman regularly before they met, Joanne throws herself into her work and is soon embroiled in a bitter and increasingly strange custody battle of a local MP, who is simultaneously trying to win an election.

"Elegant. . . . Joanne rules the narrative. [*The Brutal Heart*] slips along with grace and style." – *Toronto Star*

Trade Paperback 978-0-7710-0994-5   Ebook 978-1-5519-9233-4

THE NESTING DOLLS

Just before she is murdered, a young woman hands her baby to a perfect stranger and disappears. The stranger is the daughter of lawyer Delia Wainberg, and soon a secret from Delia's youth comes out. Not only is a killer on the loose, but the dead woman's partner is demanding custody of the child, and the battle threatens to tear apart Joanne's own family.

"The underlying human drama of love and good intentions gone very, very bad make the novel a compelling read." – *Vancouver Sun*

Trade Paperback 978-0-7710-1276-1   Ebook 978-0-7710-1277-8

Edward Willet

GAIL BOWEN's first Joanne Kilbourn mystery, *Deadly Appearances* (1990), was nominated for the W.H. Smith/ Books in Canada Best First Novel Award. It was followed by *Murder at the Mendel* (1991), *The Wandering Soul Murders* (1992), *A Colder Kind of Death* (1994) (which won an Arthur Ellis Award for best crime novel), *A Killing Spring* (1996), *Verdict in Blood* (1998), *Burying Ariel* (2000), *The Glass Coffin* (2002), *The Last Good Day* (2004), *The Endless Knot* (2006), *The Brutal Heart* (2008), and *The Nesting Dolls* (2010). In 2008 *Reader's Digest* named Bowen Canada's Best Mystery Novelist; in 2009 she received the Derrick Murdoch Award from the Crime Writers of Canada. Bowen has also written plays that have been produced across Canada and on CBC Radio. Now retired from teaching at First Nations University of Canada, Gail Bowen lives in Regina. Please visit the author at www.gailbowen.com.